Sabina Spencer has spent many years travelling the Universe to help children of all ages believe in themselves and free their creative spirits. Inspired by her personal experience, she believes that by trusting our deeper knowing we can connect to an unlimited source of imagination. Through her writing and speaking Sabina helps us discover worlds for ourselves that are full of mysterious adventures, laced with a touch of magic!

Dedication

To all those, who have ever questioned if they were good enough, smart enough, strong enough, and every kind of enough you can think of.

This story is for you…

Sabina Spencer

THE FANG AND THE FEATHER

Legend of the InfiniKey
Book One

AUSTIN MACAULEY PUBLISHERS[tm]

London • Cambridge • New York • Sharjah

Ordering Information:
Quantity sales: special discounts are available on quantity purchases by corporations, associations, and others. For details, contact the publisher at the address below.

Publisher's Cataloging-in-Publication data
Spencer, Sabina.
The Fang and the Feather: Legend of the InfiniKey Book One

ISBN 9781641821667 (Paperback)
ISBN 9781641821650 (Hardback)
ISBN 9781641821643 (E-Book)

The main category of the book — Fiction / Action & Adventure

www.austinmacauley.com

Second Edition Published (2018)
Austin Macauley Publishers Ltd ™
40 Wall Street, 28th Floor
New York, NY 10005
USA

First Published 2016
Cosmic and Wild Publishing
ISBN – 13:978-1-944546-90-8

mail-usa@austinmacauley.com
+1 (646) 5125767

Acknowledgments

My gratitude to the amazing team, who helped shape this project and take *The Nuffs* out into the world. Your unique contributions have been invaluable. With special thanks to Richard Bazley, Stan Berkowitz, David Bushaway, Andy and Maria Cle Dawson, Christoph Ferstad, Michel Gagné, Simon Gardner, and Gary Kurtz.

The Mythology

Long before time began, all was one. There was no near and far, no yesterday and tomorrow, no good and bad. Peace and love were valued by all beings, throughout the Universe and energy flowed freely, without limitation. Then suddenly, without warning, something happened in one of the many galaxies that peppers the vast expanse of all that is. This single event impacted the entire Cosmos and until this day it remains known, amongst alchemists, as *The Split*.

Some say it occurred far from the Milky Way, though others think it was in our own backyard. In truth, no being really knows. Story has it that two things happened simultaneously, which changed the way of all worlds. It is said that a giant golden bird swooped down from the skies and stole a silver kitten-cub from its mother's lair, carrying it off in its massive claws, never to be seen again. At exactly the same moment, a magnificent silver panther crept stealthily through the undergrowth, snatched a golden-feathered fledgling from its mother's nest, and disappeared into the void.

The consequence of these happenings was instantaneous. Every being in the entire Universe felt something rising within them that none had ever known before; something that had never existed in any world. For the very first time, and from that moment on, the connection was broken, one from the other. All felt afraid and confused and nothing made sense anymore, in the ways that had existed before. Time and space were born out of the oneness, and each being saw the other as separate. The experience of Universal peace became a memory of what once was and...a dream of what might be again.

The golden bird came from a cosmic clan known as the Auriandrons who represent the energies of the sun. The silver panther was an Agapanterran, whose cosmic clan represents the energies of the Moon. Until *The Split,* they had always lived in harmony alongside one another, and no being had ever imagined it would be different. Since that moment, both tribes have remained in a constant state of alertness believing each to be at fault. They fight at every opportunity manipulating others, by fair means or foul, to help their cause.

The Auriandrons rule the day and the Agapanterrans rule the night, but neither has ever gained supremacy. Now, as this trilogy begins, Aigledor is the Sovereign Ruler of the Auriandrons, and his given destiny is to use his power to heal *The Split*. Sylvameena is Queen of the Agapanterrans and has a different desire. She still carries her clan's hunger for revenge after the loss of the kitten-cub at the beginning of time. No longer satisfied with simply destroying the Auriandrons, her drive is to possess the InfiniKey, a sacred amulet that controls universal forces, granting the bearer dominion over all the elements, including the power to determine day and night.

Chapter One

The afternoon sun was shining through the forest canopy as the silver panther-like cub jumped out from his lair, fashioned out of a tree hollow, where his mother was still sleeping. He couldn't wait for his next adventure. Playtime at the start of the day, with his brothers, had been brilliant he thought to himself. He skipped happily through the darkening forest, making his way around the gnarled trunks of odd pine-like trees with their bright-colored and quite deadly vines. Lush fruit hung low, tempting him to jump up on his hind legs but he knew better—he'd learnt from his mother—they were poisonous.

Moving away from a small clearing and distancing himself ever further from the safety of the lair, the cub pulled each of his legs into a magnificent stretch that made him seem twice as long as usual. Shivering with excitement, he gave a big yawn, holding the pose for several seconds and revealing to the world miniature fangs that one-day would be lethal. Quickly gaining confidence, he began running through the brush, dodging fallen twigs and stones, loose vines and bunches of tall wildflowers, which littered his path.

He stopped by the edge of a still water pond and gazed admiringly at his reflection. Yes, an ear was gone, the left one, from this morning's scuffles. It would grow back by tomorrow. It always had done before. He was fairly certain that the cub responsible for his loss, was nursing at the very least, a lacerated liver, so justice had been done.

He was quite a handsome little Agapanterran, he decided—even with the temporary absence of an ear—sleek and muscular, with liquid platinum-silver skin. There were also some growing nubs of dinosaur-like bony ridges pushing up from his long, straight spine all the way to his powerful tail. He'd be quite a catch for a female feline when he was older…If he lived long enough.

A quick movement, seen out of the corner of his eye, gave the cub pause; he instinctively froze in place as he caught sight of another creature's reflection in the water. Something above him. Coming near. Coming fast. Something bad. Suddenly, a terrifying shape hovered overhead with a gigantic wingspan, and a curved glinting beak, big enough to tear into any animal that dared to stay in its line of sight. It was a giant golden bird and it was diving down, to the exact spot where the cub now stood, ice cold with fear.

Seconds later, coming to his senses he realized there was no choice. He started running in mindless panic as fast as his little legs could move, careering through the forest ignorant of the myriad of other dangers. An ear grows back he thought to himself, but a life lost to the death-that-comes-from-the-sky, is forever forfeit.

His fearsome predator reached the spot where the cub had been just milliseconds before, its claws still going through the motion of clutching for its prey, only to close around a clump of grass instead. Swooping back up the eagle-like creature gave a blood-curdling screech, realising that it had missed its target.

The footfalls of the running cub and the distinct sound of this powerful creature, with its wings cutting through the air, awakened another forest dweller— a small cat equally silver-skinned—but with the sharp amber eyes of a huntress, instantly alert.

The Agapanterran cub sprinted heedlessly past the smaller feline, scattering dust and fallen conifer bits in its wake. Sylvameena, for this was the cat's name, instantly knew what the situation was and what to do about it. It didn't matter that the huge golden bird, which was diving again at the cub, with razor-sharp talons and hungering beak, was perhaps 20 times her size. It didn't matter to Sylvameena one little bit because she was an Agapanterran too.

Without a moment of hesitation, Sylvameena transformed herself, shape-shifting from a small cat into a very large and extremely fierce adult feline, with fully formed back ridges and fangs the size of butcher's knives—only sharper.

She leapt after the others, accelerating in a silver blur.

A second screech tore through the air—and the cub knew the bird would dive again and this time, this time, it could all be over. Terror seized him once more, as he looked behind to see that the massive winged creature was making its descent to snatch him from the ground. It seemed inevitable—there was nowhere to run, it was moving too fast and the little cub was getting tired.

But as he looked back again, hope filled him and he saw something else—the hulking form of an adult of his kind. As their eyes met, a deafening roar echoed through the forest and Sylvameena launched herself into a powerful sprint towards the struggling cub. The bird was bearing down with great speed, and just as it was reaching the ground, in another clearing the cub, distracted, slipped on a small pebble perched on a rock and tumbled sideways. The bird's talons scraped against the rock a hair's breadth away from his face. He'd missed his target, this time, but he would strike again.

The fully-grown Agapanterran was catching up but the giant winged creature was now gearing up for what would be its final pass. The cub was hundreds of yards deeper into the forest, now running as fast as his young legs could carry him, still trying to use the wing-breaking branches of the trees above to deter his pursuer. It had worked out pretty well so far, he'd beaten it twice and the bird was forced to duck, dive and sideslip. Had the cub been a bit older and wiser, he would have known one thing.

Forests end.

As did this forest. Right here at the edge of a cliff. The cub had just an instant to admire the quite stunning view; then with his heart beating wildly he closed his eyes and bowed to the inevitable. "At least, it won't get both my..."

Before the words could materialize in the cub's head, the bird grabbed him by the neck in his massive talons. Not wasting an instant on the ground, he jerked the cub's body into the air, wings flapping hard, two feet up, four feet up, ten...

Then the bird screeched in pain as Sylvameena's outstretched claws ripped through his tail feathers, scattering several of them in the wind. But even her immense strength could not force her leap to be high enough to do the damage the bird so richly deserved.

The giant winged creature rose safely into the sky, the cub limp in his claws. He turned to look down to see what had almost pulled him to the ground.

"One of them!"

As he flew upward, he watched with some satisfaction as Sylvameena fell back, hitting the top of the cliff with stunning impact. Her momentum carried her over the side and her body ricocheted off a protruding ledge, falling, falling...

"One less of them." He continued rising!

The wind howled past her as she plunged into the maws of the chasm below. NO! She told herself. No! This was not the end; this was not how it would finish. From a glint in her deep amber eyes, a silver shimmer moved its way down to the tip of her tail and the ends of her claws, all over her dark body until it enveloped her.

Below, outside the bird's view, the silvery flash that was a large falling feline morphed in midair. What can change from a cat into a fully formed Agapanterran, can change again. In one graceful movement, as she floated through the air, her body began to shift its shape once more. Her front legs stretching out into thin but muscular arms as Sylvameena left the quadruped world. She chose, for good reason, a human-like form with the distinct advantage of less mass and more hands; hands that clutched and grabbed at the vines draping the cliff rock, snapping one after the other until finally one was equal to the task of supporting her shuddering body.

Swinging towards the side of the mountain, her torso shifted with the lengthening of her spine and her back legs grew outwards to make contact, knees bending to brace for the impact as she slowed her fall. She lay finally, safely arrested against the rough-but-welcome stone, hanging 200 feet above what would have been quite a messy place to die. Her eyes, still the eyes of a cat glowing with amber fire, narrowed in blazing intensity and focused on the horizon where a vast pair of wings was swallowed up by the setting sun. She made her way to the ground and joined with others of her kind.

"Aigledor and the Auriandrons!" She spat and hissed. "They take our young again and again, as hard as we try, we cannot defeat them."

Roars of indignation came from the gathered Agapanterrans.

Sylvameena continued, "We will find their nests and smash their eggs."

A voice spoke out from the crowd, "But we've tried that before and it didn't work."

"I know," said Sylvameena, "but this time it's going to be different!" Her voice was cool and calculating as the light in her amber eyes intensified. "Forces are at work to bring me the Sacred Key that legends speak of. Once we possess it...and we will possess it, then we will have the power to destroy the Auriandrons once and for all."

An astonished silence fell over the crowd, as she felt a steely chill of determination run down her spine.

Chapter Two

"Wake up, Zak," Zara whispered as she jabbed her friend in the ribcage with her elbow.

"What...er...what's happening? Did I miss something?"

Seemingly oblivious to Zak, and still deep in storytelling mode, Grandma Elizabeth continued...

Sylvameena hissed and spat as she transformed back into her feline form knowing that once she had the Sacred Key to the Wellspring of Everlasting Energy, she would...

"Grandma," Zara said as politely as she could, given that she was interrupting, "Zak has to go and do his homework now. So maybe, we can finish the story later in the week?"

"But don't you want to know about the Nuffs and the secret of the InfiniKey?"

Zara's eyes opened wide. "What kind of secret?"

Zak gave her a dirty look.

Zara caught it. "Oh, no...er...it's okay, maybe on Friday Grandma."

Elizabeth smiled knowingly. "Zak, don't you like my stories?"

"Yeah, sure I do; it's just that I don't get who the good guys are?"

"That's because there really aren't any." She paused. "And there aren't any bad guys either!"

Zak found this hard to take. "C'mon, every story has to have good guys and bad guys otherwise you wouldn't know whose side to take, and the good guys wouldn't get to win and kill all the bad guys."

"You think killing bad guys is good?" Zara jumped into the conversation. "Zak, you can't just divide people into good and bad. It's not about taking sides. Think about it; is day good and night bad? If you were an owl, what would your answer be? You can't have light without dark, they don't exist without each other."

Zara was on a roll while Zak was feeling like he'd been ganged up against. "They are there because of each other, silly. Anyhow it's not about winning or losing, right or wrong, it's about harmony."

Grandma Elizabeth smiled at her granddaughter, pleased by Zara's reply. She had obviously been listening to some of her stories.

Zak didn't get it. "Alright then, so tell me, how can you be in harmony with bad guys, huh?"

Zara rolled her eyes at him as her grandmother brought the conversation to a close.

"Oh yes, it must be time for my swim," Grandma Elizabeth announced as she stood up from her old leather winged back chair. She never read from a book, the stories just seemed to be a part of her soul and nobody ever questioned where they came from. People just put it down to her colorful imagination.

"Let's go, Zak, Grandma needs to get changed, and we need to do our homework."

"Oh yeah, good idea!" he said as he yawned and shook off the remains of his snooze.

It was a lovely sunny Sunday afternoon, the kind that people talk about in England because there just aren't enough of them. Elizabeth, Zara's grandmother, had been feeding Zak and her granddaughter, a steady diet of wild tales about adventures in other galaxies, for as long as they could remember. Now Zara was thinking that maybe they were getting a bit old for this, but knew how much it meant to her grandma.

The two of them had been best friends from the beginning, and neither one of them had any brothers or sisters. Zak was two months younger than Zara and they had grown up together in the little Devon village of Hope Cove. They had always been very close and really enjoyed being with each other.

Jake, Grandma Elizabeth's dog, was lying on the other side of the room basking in a patch of sunlight, which made his silky golden coat shimmer and shine. He'd been part of their lives for ten years now and as he looked across the den, he seemed to be winking at them through his half-open eyes. Jake loved to think of himself as Zak and Zara's protector and was never far from their sides. Zara looked back at him and smiled, knowing it wouldn't be too much longer before he would be hiding under the old oak roll-top desk to escape from the heat. Such was a dog's life on a summer's day!

"Enjoy your swim and see ya Friday at the latest," Zara said, giving her grandma a hug.

"Learn lots and have fun, remember life doesn't wait for you to work everything out in your head." It was a hint for Zak not to get too lost in trying to find a logical explanation for everything.

As they were saying their goodbyes, Zara was sure she saw something move, out of the corner of her eye, over by the fireplace. It looked like the tail of a silver cat disappearing into the other room. *But that's not possible; Jake wouldn't be sitting still if there was a cat in here!* She thought to herself and dismissed it.

She gazed for a moment at the giant amethyst geode that almost filled the fireplace just to the right of where they'd been sitting. It must have been over five foot high. It was round at the top and looked like a purple cave with hundreds of crystals lining the inside. When she was smaller, she remembered sitting inside it. It made her feel better whenever she was a little low. Zara always knew it was magical; it just seemed to give off this wonderful glow.

"Are you coming, Zara?" Zak said with a little frustration.

"Yeah, it's just that I thought I saw something moving over here…er…but it doesn't matter, it's nothing, let's go!"

They headed down the path to the little gate of the small thatched cottage that Elizabeth had moved to, twenty-two years ago, after her husband had been killed in a car accident. Inside, it was full of colored crystals and geodes—some were as large as the amethyst in the fireplace, but others looked more like chunks of rock. There were Buddhas of all different shapes and sizes, stuffed in corners and sitting on bookshelves. Assorted tapestries from around the world, hung on the walls, intermingled with shields made of fur, feathers, and arrowheads, all of which Elizabeth had collected on her travels.

Zara's grandmother, after all, was an old hippie. When she first moved to the village, the locals weren't sure what to make of her. Some even thought she might be a witch or a sorceress. It didn't take long for them to warm to her, and although she was a bit of an eccentric, Elizabeth had become part of village life. Everyone could count on her to draw the crowds at the summer fete with her *crystal planet readings*, and they admired how she had raised Zara's mother and uncle, as a single parent.

Now, somewhere in her sixties, this feisty blonde with sparkling eyes and a mischievous air about her was feeling free of such responsibilities. All that was left was to ensure that her granddaughter was ready for the adventures that lay ahead. Elizabeth felt confident that she had given Zara almost everything she needed, and on Friday, she would tell her the secret of *The Nuffs and the InfiniKey.*

The two of them sat for a moment on the low wall, with their backs to the cottage, looking out over the cliffs and the ocean. Zak, whose mother was of Asian descent and whose father was English, had short dark hair and brown eyes in contrast to Zara's fair hair and blue eyes. He was a couple of inches taller than her and liked to remind her of that from time to time. They were opposite in other ways too. He liked things to be safe and predictable, she, on the other hand, was a wild free spirit who loved to go adventuring. She always saw the bright side of every situation, while he was more realistic. He was practical and down to earth and liked to discover how stuff worked. He'd spend hours taking things apart just to put all the pieces back together again.

Zara was a real explorer and often took risks that made her friend cringe. She had got them in and out of trouble more times than he cared to remember. Zak secretly envied her pioneering spirit and hoped that some of it would rub off on him. In turn, Zara liked how responsible he was and felt it gave her permission to be even wilder. They rarely fought, and, if they did, it didn't last for long.

"I think your grandma is getting weirder every day. And by the way, thanks for getting me out of there," Zak said as he dropped his skateboard onto the pavement.

"That's okay!"

"Hey, I'm being sarcastic you were about to stay for at least another six chapters!"

"We really should have let her finish the story, Zak."

"Why? It's only *make-believe.*"

"And your video games aren't, huh?"

"At least, I can shut them off when I want to!"

"Zak, she's a lonely old lady living all by herself, if we don't listen to her who will? Anyway, I want to know the secret of the Key, don't you?" Zara stuck her elbow into his ribs again.

"Ouch. It's just a story. Besides, we are getting too old for all this. It's time to grow up." And with that, Zak jumped onto his skateboard and glided down the pathway.

They were both unaware that Grandma Elizabeth had heard every word they were saying as she thumbed through her drawer to find her swimsuit. There was no sign of sadness or hurt, just a faint smile, or maybe it was a knowing grin. She quickly undressed and although the black number was a tight fit, she decided it was perfect.

Zara looked back at the cottage and began walking down the cliff path that ran parallel to the road. She loved living by the sea. Every day was different. She never knew what color the water would be when she woke up. Sometimes it was grey, other days blue and green. Occasionally at sunset, Zara remembered it turned an eerie purple-pink color and she pretended she was living on another planet.

She gazed up at the big sky, as the sun appeared to move closer to the Earth. Earlier in the day, she and Zak had been shrimping in the rock pools left behind when the tide went out and had chased the crabs as they scuttled sideways over the rocks. The most they ever got in one day was 11. They always put them back otherwise there might not be enough to catch the next day.

The two of them had done almost everything together since they were small, which made both sets of parents very happy hoping that they would keep each other out of trouble. When they were seven, they made a pact. They promised that whatever happened, they would always be best friends, even if they ended up living in different galaxies millions of miles apart.

As Zara walked on, something caught her attention. Once again, she thought she saw the tail of a silver cat, only this time it was disappearing under the hedge. At the same moment, an unhappy golden bird, with its chest puffed out, was squawking uncontrollably in the apple tree just behind her.

Zara got down on her hands and knees to see if she could find the elusive creature beneath the bushes. The grass was dry and the ground was dusty. Some convolvulus had twisted itself around the rugged roots of the hawthorn hedgerow. There were nettles in there too, and she didn't really want to get stung. It always itched so much.

She was about to get up when she heard a rustling sound coming from further in. As she blinked to adjust to the darkness under the hedgerow, she saw the intense amber eyes of a silver cat. Trapped in its razor-sharp teeth, she could just make out the limp feathered form of a golden baby bird. Zara stretched her arm out fully, wincing as she scratched it against the thorns. She tried as hard as she could to reach it but it was too far away, and the feline predator had tight hold of its prey. She felt helpless; there was nothing she could do.

For one long moment, as the two of them stared at each other, Zara was certain she heard a revenge-filled voice echoing loudly in her head. *One less of them!* The slanting amber eyes of the cat held a look of menacing victory before it turned away, slithering deeper into the long grass that lay on the other side of the hedge.

That was in Grandma's story, Zara thought to herself, *how weird is that. Maybe I'm losing it, or maybe...no, it couldn't be.* She dismissed the thought as she pulled her arm out and stood up. She looked down at the scratches. They were surface only with just a little blood, nothing deep. Zara was a tomboy, after all and it took more than a superficial graze to faze her. She wiped the dust from her hands onto the side of her jeans, and then looked over her shoulder. The frantic little bird, in the apple tree, was now sitting silently with its head hung to one side.

Zara looked up at it. "I'm so, so sorry I didn't get here sooner—it was too late to save your little one."

The goldfinch looked back at her as if to say thank you, then quickly took one more glance at the hedge, before flying off in the direction of Grandma Elizabeth's cottage. Zara turned the other way and headed down the cliff path to find Zak. She loved mystery and adventure. *Hmm in Grandma's story, it was the other way around—the big golden bird killed the silver cub.* Her imagination was running wild.

Meanwhile, Elizabeth was ready for her swim. She picked up a towel and her large, somewhat eccentric, blue sunglasses before heading to the small cove, which was seven minutes away by foot. Taking a swim was her end of the day ritual, and although in the last ten years she had stopped going in the wintertime, she still swam for nine months of the year.

As she walked towards the little gate, she smiled when the wind chimes caught the late afternoon sea breeze. The garden was full of assorted statues and sculptures. Some had rusted, while others were overgrown with wildflowers. There was a pair of dolphins that had once been a water feature; a large collection of cherubs and fairies; and several totem poles. The wind chimes hung to the right of the porch, and a shield showing half a sun entwined with a crescent moon was nailed to the panel above the front door. Red wellington boots and some old trainers were shoved under a small bench on the left-hand side.

The cottage had been her home for a lot of years and when she reached the cliff pathway, she stopped for a moment and turned to look at it. She smiled again, shut the white gate, and climbed down the 32.5 steps that led to the beach. The one at the bottom often disappeared under the sand after a spring tide, but today it was visible with a tiny gap between the wood and the beach.

She looked ahead and saw a man walking towards her. "Hi Harry, what's it like in there today?" Elizabeth asked.

He had a broad Devonshire accent. "Water's not baaad at all, a little chilly at first, ah but yur'll get used to it."

Harry and Elizabeth were about the same age and had been friends for a while. As he got closer to where she was, he admired her choice of swimsuit.

"Ah, would ya loike to haave dinner with me tonoight?" he asked in a more intimate tone.

"I can't, I'm starting a diet…"

He was disappointed.

But Elizabeth continued, "Why don't you come over to my cottage around eight and we can have a beer?"

Harry was both a little surprised and delighted by the invitation. "Sure, sure enough, oi'll see ya then. Enjoy yur swim." He had never before been to her home after dark.

A short distance from the small breaking waves, Elizabeth placed her towel on the sand with her sunglasses on top so they wouldn't get scratched. The breeze was soft, nothing strong enough to create any disturbance to the sea. All was calm as she put her foot in to test the water. It was a little cold for a moment, and then as she stepped further in and passed the shudder point where standing up makes no sense anymore, she dived into the salty water and began to swim.

Chapter Three

Zara called in on Zak on her way home to tell him about the silver cat and the golden bird. He had tried to look interested and said, *yeah, yeah,* in all the right places, but she knew he thought it was all too fluffy to be important. Nowadays, he only went to Grandma Elizabeth's cottage to hang out with Zara. The stories he'd given up believing in when he was nine.

It was about 8:30 that same evening, and Zara had just finished the last of her homework back at her parent's house when she heard the sirens. There seemed to be a lot of them, and in this quiet little seaside village, after the summer holidays were over, there wasn't usually much drama. She went to the window and saw the reflection of blue and red flashing lights in the night sky. They seemed to be coming from the beach. She sent Zak a quick text to see if he knew what was going on.

wot's up at the beach.

He replied,

no idea—hmwrk done c u you in 5 at lfbt hse.

Zara promised her parents she'd be back by nine and headed down to the Lifeboat House to meet up with Zak.

He was already there when she arrived.

"Hey, d'you think they're filming a movie and no-one told us?"

Zara didn't answer. She was starting to feel very funny inside. She looked through the little window at the back of the grey-brick, red-roofed building that housed the blue and orange rescue vessel. The moment she heard herself saying, "Zak, the lifeboat's gone!" her whole body started trembling with fear.

"Grandma, Grandma, where's Grandma?" she yelled out and started running down the beach, towards the centre of the activity, with her friend following right behind her.

There must have been five or six police cars, an ambulance, and a fire engine. Zak counted four men in wetsuits. Someone had skillfully rigged up spotlights in the sand that now lit up the whole beach. They flashed across the water to reveal a collection of small craft, including the missing lifeboat.

The wind had picked up and was clipping the top of the waves. The sea was much rougher than it had been earlier. Some of the rubber-clad men, with their oxygen tanks and black webbed feet, were diving into the surf. They looked weird. A search and rescue helicopter circled over the water a little way out dropping a couple more divers into the lumpy sea on the other side of a concrete breakwater. Its searchlight was helping the desperate rescuers to find the missing swimmer, but it was so dark and so vast that it was a hopeless task.

Locals had begun crowding the beach and as Zak and Zara broke through to the edge of the water, Zara saw her grandmother's purple towel lying in the sand with the blue sunglasses on top. She bent down and picked up the unusual-shaped shades, then started playing with them nervously.

Silent tears were running down her face as the local policeman came over and gently told her that her parents would be arriving any minute. Zak stood beside her but she barely glanced around at him, she just stared at the breaking waves too numb to say anything. He opened his mouth but no words came out. Slowly, cautiously he reached over to put his arm around Zara's shoulders. As he did, she turned towards him and burying her face in his chest, she began sobbing, dropping the sunglasses onto the sand.

Harry had raised the alarm after going around to Elizabeth's cottage for their tryst. He found it immediately strange because there were no lights shining out of any windows. He knocked on the wooden door and went inside. Elizabeth never bothered to lock it. Jake was barking loudly, so after quieting the dog, and getting no reply to his calling out, he did a quick search of the open living area and the three bedrooms upstairs. As he rounded the corner at the top of the crooked staircase, he yelped as his shin connected with a Buddha that was sitting on the landing, and he tripped over. He'd never been up there before and got quite a surprise.

After failing to find any sign of Elizabeth, he left Jake and hurried to the cove where he had last seen her, only to discover her things still lying on the beach where she had put them. He called the police who came as quickly as they could. Following a few minutes of explanation, they launched the lifeboat and begun searching for her immediately.

Around midnight, the decision was made to stop the search. There was really no point in continuing until first light, which was around 04:30 at this time of year.

"Don't make me leave, let me stay here," Zara pleaded with her parents. "What if Grandma comes back and can't find her towel in the dark?"

Her father convinced her that she needed to go home and, in the end, she was just too tired to fight.

"Zak, meet me at the breakwater in the morning as soon as you can, promise."

"But what about school?"

"I'm not going to school until we find Grandma!" she said defiantly, and then, holding her father's hand, walked up the beach to the safety of her home.

After some hot chocolate and a lot more tears, she went to her room. She was exhausted. *How could this happen, Grandma is such a strong swimmer, there's no way she would have drowned.* Thoughts just kept running around her head until finally, she fell asleep.

Zara always had vivid dreams. It wasn't unusual for her to wake up convinced she was in a parallel reality, only to find that she was still in her own bed. Grandma Elizabeth was great at listening to her talk about all the details of what happened and helped her to understand what the dreams meant. The bond between them was very strong and as she fell into a deeper sleep on this troubled night, she had a dream.

In it, she saw her grandma in a strange place that was quite dark. She wasn't alone but Zara couldn't see who else was there. She knew it was a man but he had his back to her and his head was a weird shape as if it was covered with something. They were talking in a language she didn't understand. The person who looked like Elizabeth was dressed in strange clothes with a cloak over her shoulders. It was kind of funky.

Zara tried to get her attention. "Grandma, I'm here. Can you see me?"

There was no reply and the two characters in the dream continued their conversation.

"Grandma, it's me, Zara, can you hear me?" But there was still no response.

Then Zara shouted as loud as she could, "Grandma, is this just a dream?"

She shouted so loudly that she woke herself up feeling very confused. She was shivering and crying but didn't want to wake her parents. Zara just lay there wondering if it really was just a dream.

It seemed like forever before the light started to come through the bedroom window. She pulled on her jeans and her favorite hoody, the one her grandmother had given her last birthday and went downstairs. Jake was on his snoof in the kitchen. Her father had gone around to Elizabeth's cottage after Zara was in bed, and brought him home so he wouldn't be left alone.

She wrote a note to her parents. She'd always been very feisty and a bit of a rebel but she was considerate of others. Reaching for the bread and the butter, she quickly made some marmite sandwiches. After grabbing Jake's lead, she closed the door quietly and headed for the rocks.

There were two breakwaters in the cove, a big one and a smaller one. They were both massive structures made out of reinforced concrete and they stood about 20 feet high. Sometimes, when the sea was rough, Zak, Zara and the other kids would play a game of dare to see who could run across without getting wet. If they timed it right, it was okay. If not, they got drenched as the waves crashed against the wall and splashed as high as ten to 15 feet above the breakwater. The two of them often got to Grandma Elizabeth's cottage dripping wet, and she would tell them stories while their clothes dried.

Zara and Jake scrambled over the rocks and up the steps onto the big breakwater. Zak hadn't arrived yet but there were already people gathering on the beach. As she looked out to sea, she could see the lifeboat and some fishing boats searching the water. There were seagulls squawking and circling around the mini-armada.

She was old enough to know that her grandma could not have survived a night in the water, and so the search must be for her body. But that thought was too hard to take, so she let it go and had another one. *Maybe she climbed onto the rocks and someone is taking care of her. We wouldn't know until at least nine o'clock because she'd probably stay for breakfast.* Then she remembered the dream. *Of course, she's not dead at all, she's been kidnapped and is being held captive by that guy I saw. The dream was her way of telling me she's okay.*

Zak arrived just as she finished her thought.

"Did you sleep?" he asked.

"Nope, not really, did you?"

"A bit—as soon as I lay down, I was gone."

"Did you dream?" She was curious.

"C'mon, Zara, you know I never dream, and if I do I forget it instantly."

"I did, Zak, I had a dream, and Grandma is still alive. I think she's been kidnapped!"

Hearing herself talk about it, somehow made it all the more real. "In fact, she's being held against her will somewhere that's quite dark."

"Ookaaaay," Zak said, trying to disguise the scepticism in his voice.

He knew he needed to get it just right. "So where do you think she is?"

"I don't know I tried to talk with her but she couldn't hear me."

She moved a little closer to him as the tears started to well up in her eyes again. Then the two of them just sat there looking at the boats and the divers. For Zara, it felt so good to have a friend at a time like this, especially one who'd been there forever.

Life was fun in Hope Cove. They had always been free to play on the beaches and in the fields. Sometimes when they were younger they used to pretend they were shepherds and tried herding the sheep up on the cliffs. That was when they weren't down on the beach, playing pirates amongst the seaweed-covered craggy rocks, or out on the boats with the fishermen. They both liked surfing and boogie boarding and were good swimmers. There was always so much to see and do, and with Grandma Elizabeth's storytelling, Zara never remembered being bored.

"D'you think if we'd stayed to hear about the Nuffs and the secret of the Key, things might be different?" She was starting to feel guilty.

"Zara, all it would have meant is that she'd have gone swimming ten minutes later."

"D'you think that silver cat had anything to do with it?"

"Doubt it, there are lots of cats around here."

"Yes, but this one caught a golden bird. D'you think it was a sign?"

Zak was trying his best not to be too logical, but Zara's questions were pushing him to his limits.

"It's just a coincidence that's all. You saw a cat doing what cats do, the rest is…"

He was about to say something he might have regretted, but luckily, she interrupted him.

"You know Grandma used to say that there was no such thing as a coincidence and I believe her," she said with force.

He got the message and decided to say nothing more.

A few minutes later, Zara broke the silence, "Like a marmite sandwich?"

"Sure!" She handed it to him, but not before Jake took a quick sniff.

"Don't you think her stories are soooo amazing?"

Zara didn't need an answer. Anyhow, Zak's mouth was stuffed full of bread.

"Do you remember the one she told us when she was visiting the planet Tussto and had joined their tribe? Then one day, something that looked like a white giraffe with six legs chased her. She found her way back to the portal with only seconds to spare."

"That was wicked," Zak replied, this time enthusiastically, remembering how much he'd actually enjoyed that story because it was full of monsters. It reminded him of one of his video games where he got the highest score.

"Just think how cool it must be, to visit all those other worlds. Some people think she's a bit weird but I don't think she could have made all that stuff up. Do you?"

Zak wasn't sure and so he took another bite of his sandwich and made a grunting sound that could have meant either yes or no depending on what you wanted to hear.

They had both spent a lot of time with Zara's grandmother growing up and thought she was very special. She told them stories about intergalactic travel and about planets other than Earth. She talked about strange creatures and worlds very different from this one. Grandma Elizabeth always described what she called her adventures, in great detail, sometimes drawing little pictures of the beings she'd met on her journeys to other galaxies. She'd been there with her stories and home-baked cookies, all of their lives.

The two of them sat on the edge of the breakwater, with Jake; gazing out to sea and knowing that life would never be the same again.

"I can't let it in that she's gone, Zak. Something must have happened."

"Yeah, Zara, maybe." It was all he could think of to say.

Zara was sitting there, praying as hard as she could that they wouldn't find any trace of her beloved grandma. Her prayers were answered.

Chapter Four

It had been a week since Grandma Elizabeth's disappearance. The search had gone on for only a little while longer but was called off when no body was found.

Zara's dreams had continued, although some nights she just slept so deeply that she couldn't remember anything in the morning. Without any evidence to the contrary, she was absolutely convinced that her grandma was still alive and in another world. She was even more certain after hearing that there had been a possible break-in at the cottage.

The day after Elizabeth went missing the police sealed off the property as a matter of course. They wanted everything to stay exactly the way it was on the Sunday evening before she left for her swim. Three days later, when Zara's parents asked to secure any valuables, they discovered a number of things lying around on the floor.

A shield made of animal skin and eagle feathers that hung on the wall above the fireplace, had been torn up and the feathers scattered all over the room. In addition, a statue of an Egyptian winged Goddess, which sat on the bookcase, was smashed into pieces. Some of the papers that were in Grandma Elizabeth's roll-top desk were on the floor, and a drawer was left partially open. The leather chair she sat in to tell her stories, was torn at the back and some of the stuffing had been pulled out.

The police were baffled because no windows had been broken and the doors were still sealed. There really was no other way to enter the cottage except through a small cat flap, in the back door, that hadn't been removed after Elizabeth's cat died five years ago. But even this had been partially blocked by the rubbish bin. Anyway, no cat could have jumped high enough to take the fixture from the wall, or open a drawer in the desk.

When Zara first heard about the break-in, she insisted on taking a look; after all, she and Zak were the last ones there and they would be able to say exactly what things had been moved. She sent a text to tell him what had happened and arranged to meet him at the cottage with her parents and the police.

"Zak, something is going on I just know it," Zara said in a quiet but animated whisper.

"Uh-huh." He wanted to stay open minded but knew what Zara was trying to prove.

"Look how could that statue have fallen off the bookcase when there was a stone in front of it?" she said, pointing to a large jasper sphere that was still where it had always been.

"And this slash in the back of her chair, we would have seen that, wouldn't we?"

Zak wasn't convinced but he did find it a little strange that the shield had come off the wall and the feathers had been ripped out.

"Er…maybe a cat did get in," he said, walking over to the back door.

Zara followed, but much to her disappointment, because of the bin, the flap could only open a tiny bit. It wasn't even enough for a kitten to crawl through, let alone a fully-grown cat.

"Nah, see, Zara—not possible."

He turned and went back into the living room.

Zara was about to follow when the sun came out from behind a cloud and she saw something glistening on the tiled floor. It looked like a silvery slime trail leading from the cat flap to the middle of the kitchen.

"Zak, quickly come here, look at this," she said excitedly.

By the time he got there, the sun had disappeared again and he couldn't see anything. She grabbed a torch from one of the drawers to try to make it reappear. In the end, she gave up, but not before she heard a voice in her head. *What can change from a cat into a fully formed Agapanterran, can change again.*

"It's Sylvameena, she came through the cat flap as a snake and shape-shifted. I know it."

"Zara, those were make-believe stories, there is no Sylvameena."

"Then how do you explain what happened here. Huh?" She stood there with her hands on her hips and stared at him.

"Er…um…don't know what to say—it doesn't really make sense, but there has to be a logical explanation."

Zara was getting angry. "Okay, so when you can give me your *logical explanation* then I might change my mind. Until then, I'm sticking with my theory."

72 hours went by and Zak still didn't find an answer. The two of them had seen each other at school but Zara was very much inside herself, and Zak found it hard to connect. All was cool though; they'd been in this place before and always hooked up again.

Ten days after the break-in, the cottage had been tidied up ready for the wake. Zara's mother and uncle had decided to hold a service for Elizabeth to bring closure to the days of wondering, and to celebrate her life. It was clear to everyone, except Zara, that she had most likely drowned and her body had been taken away by the strong riptides.

The service was held in a grassy area outside an ancient church, which sat on the cliff top overlooking the sea. It was a small 15th century building, with white stonewalls that had eroded over the years due to the salty air. The short spire sported a weather vane and a clock that hadn't worked for a long time but was right twice a day at 9:25. A row of seagulls sat along the roofline watching the people arrive on this late September afternoon, where the air was a little chilly, but the sky was bright.

Grandma Elizabeth would have described herself as someone who was spiritual rather than religious. In her lifetime, she had visited Temples, Synagogues, Churches, Cathedrals, Sweat Lodges and everything in between, so the ceremony was far from orthodox. Harry had taken the lead in putting it together and Zara's mother was more than happy to let Elizabeth's friends take charge. It had been a difficult time and she agreed to prepare the food while others planned the service.

It felt a little strange not having a coffin, so instead, Harry had arranged a small table covered in assorted geodes with cedar chips and sage. There were a couple of family pictures, an American Indian peace pipe, and a large Shiva Lingam from India. The glow from several different candles made some of the quartz crystals sparkle, and with the afternoon breeze, they looked like they were made of liquid light.

A crowd of bikers rode in on their Harley Davidson's. The roar of the pipes could be heard as they came through the village to the church. It was a different kind of music to the normal funeral march. With their arms covered in some colorful tattoos, the bikers stood over on the far side of the gathering. One of them, with a bronzed face and a glint in his eye, had an image of Elizabeth on the back of his black leather jacket with *Love All, Serve All*, written underneath. He was most likely the same one who knew the location of her tattoo, a souvenir from her days as a biker babe.

The sound of 'Ommmmmmmmmmmmmmmmmmmmmm' was carried by the wind and echoed over the cliff tops, not once or twice, but three times. Zak, who had almost choked from holding his breath too long during the second one, was sitting with Zara in the back row. As he coughed and spluttered, she gave him an annoyed look and told him to be quiet.

"Hey, it's not my fault," he said in a loud whisper.

"Then whose fault is it?" Zara scowled.

She didn't like this ceremony one little bit and wanted to be as far away as possible. In her opinion, none of this was necessary because she knew her grandmother was still alive. After the third Om, Zara started growing increasingly uncomfortable she didn't want to listen. As much as she loved her grandma, it was getting too hard to take. *Why are they talking about her as if she isn't here anymore?* She got up and slipped away hoping that nobody noticed and not caring if they did. She just didn't want to be there. So she walked around to the back of the church and stopped at a low fence, a safe distance from the old building.

Looking into a strange little forest made up of equal numbers of trees and gravestones, she could feel herself starting to crumble, but she didn't want to give in. The trees were all leaning in the same direction and the tops were flattened from the relentless breeze that blew off the sea every afternoon. Their gnarled and twisted trunks were in contrast to the smooth stones of the different monuments, many of which were no longer standing. Grass had grown up over those that had fallen, and the last remains of some plastic flowers, left behind to grace the final resting place of someone's loved one, were scattered across several plots, adding a splash of color to the grey-green landscape. It was a lonely place.

She fought with her feelings; there was something sad and mysterious about it all. Then as Zara looked down to see the name carved on a newly appointed grave, she felt the tears start to rise. *What if Grandma is dead and we never find her body, there would be...*

Her thoughts were interrupted by a sound coming from the right where twin six-foot headstones still stood upright, guardians to the corpses that lay at their feet. She looked across and saw nothing, but was suddenly aware of someone standing behind her.

"Why d'you leave?" Zak asked.

She jumped.

"Don't sneak up on me like that, not here, not today," she said a little nervously.

"Sorry, didn't mean to scare you."

"Zak, she's not dead I just know it."

"Whatever…"

"I know you don't believe me but I wouldn't feel this way if she'd died." She looked him straight in the eyes.

"Zar, all these people think she's gone and…"

"So…that doesn't mean they're right. She wasn't their grandma, so they can't know what I know. Anyway, they never found her body. Not even a trace."

"That doesn't mean…"

"She's still alive. I…I can feel it."

Zak sighed and shook his head before turning to walk back to join the others. Zara just stayed standing there, staring into the ghostly forest.

Suddenly, all the birds that had been sitting in the trees took flight and darted into the sky. There must have been 50 of them, starlings most likely. Before she had time to wonder what had startled them, she heard an awful screeching sound coming from behind two other tombstones. They were large and modern and looked like concrete misfits in amongst the old-fashioned stone and marble.

Seconds later, the original noise was followed by a strange growling sound with hissing and spitting. Then, in the distance, she saw two monstrous creatures, locked in battle. At first, they looked like they were made of jelly and their outlines were blurry, but as they rose and fell behind the stones she saw them quite clearly. One was a big silver panther-like animal with ridges on its back, and the other was a giant golden bird. Zara stood mesmerized, she felt butterflies in her stomach, but she wasn't too scared.

She watched as a massive wing started to flap. The bird was trying to rise up, but some long cat claws scraped the air and locked into the fluttering feathers. Next, a hooked golden beak flashed for a moment before bearing down on the large gnarly back of the silver feline, which turned and pounced again, with force, on top of the bird. The sound of gnashing and roaring, coupled with that blood-curdling screech, made her want to cover her ears but she didn't want to miss a thing.

The fight was reaching its climax as Zara stared at the outline of these great creatures silhouetted against the sky. She tried hard to get a better view, just to be sure, but there really was no doubt in her mind. Grandma Elizabeth had described this kind of scene many times before in her stories, and with eyes wide open she called out.

"Zak, come back."

She yelled again, only this time even louder, "Hurry!"

He started towards her but she couldn't wait for him, so she leapt over the low fence in the direction of the fight. He wasn't too keen to follow at first but then jumped over it too, stumbling on a root and nearly falling face first into the shrubbery.

Zara rushed to the gravestones through the long dry grass, until she was only a few feet away. Standing very still she listened hard, but the only sound she could hear was the sound of her heart beating, fast. Even the wind had stopped blowing. Gingerly, at first almost tiptoeing, she peered behind the vertical concrete slabs to see if the creatures were still there, but they were gone.

Zak had caught up and was staring at her. He was wearing a confused expression, trying to understand what she was up to.

"They were here. I saw them," she said excitedly.

"Who was here?"

"Aigledor and Sylvameena. They were fighting and making horrible noises."

"I was only over there and I didn't hear nothing." Zak was beginning to think Zara was losing it.

"You didn't hear anything." She was correcting his use of English but he thought she was asking him a question.

"Nothing, nada, zilch!"

Zara was scouring the ground to see if she could find any evidence that would prove she was right, not only to Zak but, to herself. *Could it have simply been my imagination?*

Seconds later, she saw something lying near a broken gravestone. She stared down into the grass and then bent over to pick it up. It was a giant golden feather. She gazed at it for a moment—it must have been almost four feet long. Instinctively, she looked up into the sky with her mouth hanging open.

"Zak, look," she said, pointing upwards.

But he was too busy searching through the grass, not far from where Zara had found the feather.

She shouted at him, "Look up, Zak. Now!"

There in the sky far above their heads was an enormous bird spiraling round and round, higher and higher until finally, it disappeared into a cloud.

"So, did you see it?"

"See what?" Zak asked, staring up at an empty sky, except for a few passing clouds.

"The big golden bird that lost this feather."

Zara sighed as Zak shrugged and stared at the feather.

Okay, she thought, *so he hadn't seen the bird but he can't deny this feather.*

"Zak, we don't have golden eagles in England do we?"

"Nope. There are some in Scotland and others in Ireland but that feather is huge, bigger than anything I've ever seen or read about." Zak studied hard and knew a lot. Zara liked that about him because she wasn't good at remembering facts. "Their normal wingspan is only six and a half feet and they have two thousand feathers on average, although, I guess this one only has 1,999."

"C'mon, this couldn't have come from a normal bird, could it?"

Zak didn't know what to say because the feather was almost as big as Zara. Before he had time to answer, something caught his eye, something glistening in the newly trampled grass. Bending down he cleared away some dead leaves to discover a massive silver fang that must have come from the mouth of some kind of large animal. As he held it up, Zara moved closer to look. Zak was blown away and didn't know what to say because none of it made any logical sense.

"What do you s'pose that came from?" Zara asked.

"Whatever it was, it was big. This has to be two foot long, and look at the diameter!"

"See, they were here!" She was convinced. "Now do you believe that there's something going on?"

"Dunno; it is kinda weird-like. Don't know what to make of it." Then wanting to get back to something ordinary, he said, "Let's see if they've finished the ceremony yet."

Zara wanted to find out more, but even she was feeling a bit shaken up. So she decided this was proof enough for now and happily followed Zak around the side of the Church. She stuck the feather up the back of her dress so the tip of it was showing just above her head. He stuffed the fang under the belt of his trousers.

Luckily, the gathering had broken up and people were heading down the cliff towards Grandma Elizabeth's cottage for the wake.

"Zak, I'm telling you, it's right out of one of her stories: the big golden bird and the silver panther creature."

Sarcastically, he replied, "Could be a giant seagull and a feral cat."

Zara grabbed the fang from his trousers with one hand, and pulled out the feather with the other, right in Zak's face.

"I saw what I saw, Zak. And now I'm sure she's still alive."

"So even if you did see what you thought you saw, how would that prove that she's still alive?"

"I already told you."

"Oh yeah, because you can feel it. Well, tell me this, if she's not dead why hasn't anyone heard from her?"

"Maybe she hit her head and got amnesia, or the kidnappers have taken her somewhere."

"Kidnappers? Why would anyone want to kidnap an old lady?" It sounded so illogical to Zak.

"Grandma wasn't always old you know," she said sharply.

They walked in silence for a few minutes then Zara suggested that they take the fang and the feather back to his house for safekeeping. They had to pass it on the way to Elizabeth's cottage, so it was easy to do.

"Yeah, yeah, good idea," Zak said, although he was feeling so confused he would have agreed to anything just so he could get back inside his own head and sort stuff out.

They didn't want to be late, so they quickly put their findings in a safe place in his bedroom, which looked more like a workshop with a bed in it. It was full of different rocks, shells, and stones that he collected whenever he could. Almost half the room was covered with old computers, and bits and pieces of metal and plastic. He liked taking things apart to see how they worked, although there were always pieces left over when he put them back together again. It didn't seem to worry him, as long as whatever it was, worked.

As they closed Zak's front door and walked towards the cottage, Zara couldn't help wondering what was going to happen next. She hadn't noticed that something had been stalking them ever since they left the graveyard. Neither of them had seen the small silver cat with amber eyes, slinking in and out of the bushes as they made their way to Zak's place, and then to Grandma Elizabeth's cottage. They didn't hear her hiss or see her snarl at a passing dog, revealing the gap where the missing incisor belonged. They weren't aware of her presence at all. This feline was, among other things, a mistress of deception. The success of her mission depended on it.

Chapter Five

As soon as she walked into the cottage, Zara cringed. There was so many people in her grandmother's house. They were eating, drinking, and making small talk with each other; the temptation to run back down the garden path was huge. Almost everyone there was a grown-up except for a couple of younger kids who were playing with some toys near the fireplace. It just looked so surreal.

The dining room table was covered in plates of cakes and cookies, plus the traditional Devon cream tea fixings of scones, clotted cream, and strawberry jam. Elizabeth's collection of teapots were visible on different tables around the open spaced living area. One was shaped like a thatched cottage, another like the sun, yet another in the form of a black cat, and still one more that was a bright red old-fashioned phone box with a handle and a spout on it. Much to her relief Zara's favorite, the dolphin teapot was still in the glass-fronted corner cupboard, on the right of the fireplace. Her Grandma kept it for show purposes only and would have hated to see it chipped or, even worse, broken.

Zak followed Zara through the chatting mourners towards the stairs. Before they got that far, she stopped abruptly and darted into a nook under the staircase with him close behind. Her father was putting a long piece of tape across the stairs, from the bannister rail to the wall, to prevent the guests wandering up to the bedrooms.

"'fraid we're going to steal sumthin', Bill?" Harry asked.

Bill chuckled. "Hardly, it's only junk up there, but we haven't cleared it yet, and I don't want anyone tripping over a stray crystal."

It was Harry's turn to laugh as he finished a sip of his drink. "Oi knows just what yur mean, oi fell over a Buddha when oi came lookin' for Elizabeth the noight she went missin'. What's yur going to do now? Given it any thought?"

"Oh yeah lots, we're moving to London."

Zara couldn't believe what she was hearing her father say. Her mouth fell open in surprise as Zak turned to look at her.

"I've had a standing offer from my company for the last 18 months, but the wife didn't want to leave Elizabeth down here alone."

"'ow's our Zara takin' it?"

"We haven't told her yet, what with Elizabeth's disappearance. They were very close."

"Yes, oi knows."

Zara was listening hard to everything her father was saying and had a shocked expression on her face. Zak was watching her closely; he couldn't believe it either. Her father continued, "It will be good for her. Frankly, I was getting a little worried."

"What d'yur mean, Bill?"

"Well, it was hard enough having one member of the family who lived in *la-la land*. I want Zara to see what the <u>real</u> world looks like."

Harry took a step back, after all, he had been wooed by Elizabeth's ways.

"Hmm, London, the real world, aaah? Don't yur think there's such a thing as too real?"

"Maybe, but when I get tired of it I'll let you know, Harry. My hunch is it will probably be another 20 or 30 years. Anyway, we'll keep the cottage pretty much as it is, as we'll come back here for school holidays."

Zara felt a small sense of relief but was scowling at her father as he walked across the room towards the kitchen. He was unaware she'd heard every word and that he would have to face her later.

The kids glanced around to check no one was looking and crawled under the tape and up the stairs as quickly and as quietly as possible. Her father was right, there was so much stuff on the landing. The two of them stepped gingerly into her bedroom. There were crystals and stones everywhere; rose quartz, purple amethyst, blue lapis lazuli, rutilated quartz, and golden calcite. It was like an Aladdin's cave full of so many different treasures. There was a very large piece of quartz sitting on the floor that Zara remembered her grandmother calling a cosmic computer. Apparently, it held lots of information about the wisdom of the Ancients Ones and was supposed to be very powerful.

On the bed, lay a teal-colored swimming towel. *She must have chosen the purple one instead that evening*, Zara thought to herself, *I wonder why?* Sitting between the pillows was a little teddy bear holding a big red heart. His name was Valentino. Zara went over and picked him up. She had given it to her grandma two years ago on Valentine's Day. Now, as she hugged it tightly, she wished so hard that she could rewind time.

Above the bed hung one of the biggest dream catchers ever. It was handmade with a willow hoop and what looked like a spider's web woven across it in a random pattern. Several of the threads passed through some colored beads and turquoise nuggets, and three feathers hung from the bottom.

"She always had very big dreams," Zara said wistfully.

"Huh?"

"That's why she needed such a huge dream catcher. The web traps the bad dreams so they can't hurt you. The good ones move through it, pass down the feathers and fall on the dreamer, so you get to keep them."

Zak was miles away. "What are you talking about, Zar?"

"The dream-catcher."

"Oh, that thing...b...but haven't you got anything to say about London." Hearing her father talk about them moving away had freaked Zak out.

Zara had dismissed it for now. "I went to London once. All I remember is the weird food and the even weirder public loos. When you go out and close the door behind you, the whole room thingy flushes—the walls the floor everything is washed down with disinfectant. Can you imagine what it would be like to get stuck in there while it does its thing?"

Zak wasn't interested. "When do you think you'll be leaving?"

"Don't know. Why?"

"Just because..." he paused, "Well...er...nothing really." He decided to change the subject and went over to a small plastic bag that looked like it was filled with dried green tea or oregano.

"What's this?"

"Herbs, probably," Zara said, taking a closer look and opening the bag to sniff it. "Pooh, it's stinky!"

Zak smirked. "If it's herbs, then why isn't it in the kitchen?"

Zara shrugged her shoulders and put it on the bed. "It's probably a sleeping potion."

She was way more interested in the letter with a golden seal, sitting on the bedside table. She picked it up and took the yellow paper out of the envelope. She felt a little uncomfortable reading it but thought it might give them a clue about her grandmother's kidnappers.

"What's that?" Zak asked.

"A letter…a…love letter."

"Lemme see it."

He reached for it but Zara held it to her chest.

"C'mon…I really want to read it!"

"It's personal!"

"I know, bet it's from Harry."

"No, it's not, it's signed…er…er…Aigledor." She was stunned. "How can a big bird-like thing write a love letter?"

Zak thought for a moment. "So now you see, she uses the names of people she knows in her stories, that's all. Why not, it makes sense. After all, they were only stories." He was starting to feel some relief—this to him was a decent explanation. He couldn't buy into all that fantasy stuff without feeling like a bit of a dork.

"What kind of name is Aigledor anyway?" he asked sarcastically.

"It's got to be a name from another galaxy." Zara wondered if Aigledor was also a shape-shifter, then he'd be able to write, even if he was a giant bird.

"No, it's not, it's hippie…Huh, I bet it's one of those bikers."

She didn't reply.

Zak started exploring the other end of the room, with its lovely old beamed ceiling, when he looked up and saw a trapdoor with a chain dangling down above his head. "What's that door thingy doing there?"

Zara followed his gaze. "I don't know. I never saw it before. The only place it can go is to the roof."

"But why would there be one in here and not in the hall?" Zak was curious.

Zara knew the answer. "To fix the TV aerial."

"The what…"

"You know, they had aerials before there were satellite dishes." Zara continued reading the letter hoping to find a clue, while Zak dragged a chair over to where the chain hung down. He stood on it and reaching up started pulling. Nothing moved.

"I can't budge it, give me a hand, will ya?"

Zara was a little irritated but decided to go over and help him. "I'm telling you it's nothing. Look, I'll show you."

As she jumped up from the bed, a pendant she was wearing popped out from under the hooded sweatshirt she'd changed into at Zak's house. It was now visible and dangling from the chain around her neck. She treasured it and hadn't taken it off since her grandma had given it to her. It was an amulet shaped in the letter $\mathcal{E}$, for Elizabeth.

Zara climbed onto the chair with Zak, and the two of them pulled on the chain together, but it still didn't budge. She spun around to try it from another angle and

31

in doing so the light from the bedside lamp caught her pendant. It generated a bright flash that reflected onto the metal chain and sent a bolt of lightning upward, illuminating the trap door.

"Did you see that?" Zara asked surprised by what had just happened.

"See what?"

Before she could answer, the square-shaped trap door in the ceiling began to creak and groan. As it slowly opened upwards, it released an ornate metal staircase that came down so quickly, that Zak and Zara had to jump off the chair to get out of the way of being crushed. They were both sitting on the floor watching, wide-eyed, as the stairway came down to meet them. It was quite out of place in this 18th-century cottage, art deco in style with beautifully polished chrome and brass rails and rods.

"Whoa, what's happening?" Zak asked with a hint of fear in his voice.

"I don't know, let's find out," Zara said excitedly as she got to her feet

A purple light, faint at first, was glowing brighter and brighter above them. Zara thought she could hear the sound of some kind of music as she started up the staircase.

"Wait a minute, wh-what are you doing? Wh-Where are you going?" Zak stuttered.

"Going to see what's up there, you dork. Hey, the rails are warm."

They felt nice as if there was some kind of energy running through them.

"But there's not s'posed to be anything up there, you said so yourself."

"I know, but that was then, and things are different now. You're scared, aren't you?"

He gulped. "Who? Me?"

Zara shook her head in exasperation and climbed a few more steps until the upper half of her torso disappeared above the line of the ceiling. She could now see into the roof space, but it wasn't at all what she expected.

"Zaaaaaak, oh Zaaak…" Her voice was that of a temptress.

"Nah-uh. NO!" He was resolute as he watched her disappear through the opening.

"Oh Zaaaak, there are computers up here…" Her voice was alluring.

"Computers! You can't be serious, you'll have to do better than that."

"Lots and lots of them. It's hi-tech heaven."

He wasn't sure, but then curiosity got the better of him for once, and he headed up the staircase after her. As he arrived at the top, he was overawed. This was no ordinary loft it was stuffed full of the most up to date computer paraphernalia. The space was much bigger than it should have been under the little thatched roof, and all the screens were giving off a purple glow that filled it with a lavender hue. The walls that weren't covered with equipment had 3D pictures of galaxies, planets, and exploding nebulae; they were spectacular. Hanging in the middle of the loft above their heads, was a holographic image of a solar system quite different to the one they knew.

There were many more crystals, only bigger than those in the bedroom below. Several tall quartz generator geodes that looked like mini monuments, stood in the middle of the room around a central console. Zara was ecstatic it was like all her dreams had come true in an instant. Her Grandma wasn't crazy after all, and the stories she'd been telling all these years, were absolutely from her adventures.

"I knew it," she said with certainty.

"Knew what?"

"It was all real."

"Yeah, maybe, but how come she had all this cool stuff and never told me about it?" Zak was feeling a little wounded.

Zara took sympathy for a moment and tried to make him feel better, "Er…maybe it's not hers, maybe she didn't know it was here."

Then changing her mind she added, "Alright, maybe she just wasn't ready to tell us or she didn't want you messing with it…remember she's seen inside your bedroom!"

Zak wasn't listening, he'd made his way across to where there were two massive amethyst geodes that looked like curved backed, hooded thrones. Inside each of them were hundreds of deep purple crystals. They were giant-size versions of the one in the fireplace downstairs and must have stood, at least, eight feet high. He sat inside the one on the left and looked down at a transparent keyboard that was built into the console in front of him. It was like a touch screen and so he started stroking the letters. As he did, an image appeared on a mammoth flat screen at the end of the attic. To his surprise, it was an enlarged version of Zara's pendant, the same stylized letter $\mathcal{E}$.

"See, she did know this stuff was here, it's even got her own personalized logo on it. She knew about it all this time and didn't tell me!" Zak was indignant.

Zara joined him and sat in the other geode chair alongside his.

"Get over it, Zak. Maybe if you'd listened to her stories she might have told you about all this. Anyway, we've found it now and maybe it will help us get her back, wherever she is."

For a moment, Zara felt a little downhearted, *the universe is so huge that she could be anywhere.* She didn't want to share her thought with Zak, she was happy that he was now starting to believe that there might be something going on.

Meanwhile, he picked up two pairs of goggle-like headpieces with earphones attached and put one of them on.

"Whoa, this is so cool." Wearing the headpiece transformed the attic even more. He was still seeing everything, but it was more brightly colored and it looked larger than life-like. It was a total 4D experience.

The sound was amplified too, and the equipment seemed to be giving off an eerie kind of melody that was quite haunting. At the same time, a lavender aroma wafted around them.

"What is it, Zak, what can you see?"

"It's virtual reality…I think…here, wear the other one."

He handed it to her. As she put it on, she gasped in amazement.

On the screen in front of them, hanging in space, the word *password* flashed before their eyes.

Zak was disappointed. "Oh crap. What do you think it is?"

He typed in Elizabeth.

Rejected.

Zara snapped at him. "C'mon, she'd be much more creative than that."

Zak typed in another word, and again *rejected* appeared on the screen.

"We could be here forevvvvver." Zak sighed wanting to get on with the game. "I know; what about 'Zara'?" He typed it in.

Rejected.

"Zak, I know what it is, try Aigledor. A-I-G-L-E-D-O-R."

As Zara spelt it out, Zak typed it in. It worked.

The word, *enter* then floated in front of them.

"Yes." He punched the air.

The headpieces prevented them from noticing that the geode chairs had started to glow a deeper shade of purple. Then the roof of the cottage began to open like the lens of a camera, revealing a vast star-studded sky.

Zak reached for the mouse to click in the password. "Er…maybe we shouldn't be doing this, not without her knowing." He was starting to get back to his normal cautious self.

"I want to know everything. And I want to know where she is. We have to find her, Zak," Zara said passionately as she stretched over and, without any hesitation, clicked the mouse.

Chapter Six

The geode chairs started to vibrate gently at first but then more vigorously.

"That's it, I should never have let youuuuuuuuuu…"

Zak's last word was stretched beyond anything anyone would have heard before as the two of them were pulled, head first, by some huge energetic force, into the starlit sky and beyond. Their bodies also stretched out and elongated like soft treacle toffee, before they started spinning out of control, screaming their lungs out, as planets, nebulae, and super novas passed by them at increasing speed.

Staying as close as they could to each other, they didn't realize that their headpieces had fallen off the moment that their bodies had snapped back into a normal shape. Everything was crazy. One minute they were surrounded by color, then black and white, then back to color again. All sorts of strange symbols were passing before their eyes in tune with an odd whooshing sound, which seemed to go on forever.

They stopped screaming abruptly when, ahead of them, they saw a giant whirlpool of millions of swirling stars being sucked into a vast cosmic drain…or maybe it was simply a black hole. They tried fighting and flailing against the extraordinary force drawing them further in, but they couldn't save themselves. After accepting what was inevitable, Zak and Zara started screaming again.

In the centre of the hole, everything was calm, like the eye of a hurricane, and they were suspended in a dark yet peaceful empty space.

It only lasted for a nanosecond before things speeded up once more, only this time it was different. Zak looked across at Zara and saw she was getting older and older, in no time at all. He was freaked by the transformation as he watched her age so fast in front of his eyes. What he didn't realize was that the same thing was happening to him too.

He decided to look ahead, and in the midst of the blackness, he saw a point of light. It was distinctly purple and the same color that they had seen on the screen in Grandma Elizabeth's attic. It was coming closer and as they were catapulted out of the other side of the hole, everything started to slow right down. They were getting younger again, returning to their thirteen year old bodies.

The blackness gradually faded away and was replaced by the purple color that was starting to fill the space. It was clear that they were being pulled towards a planet.

As they got closer, they could see that it was covered in a half-light. It was neither day nor night; the planet was engulfed in a purple haze. Then just as they were finding some kind of equilibrium, everything speeded up again and they hurtled towards the land mass convinced they would be smashed into zillion pieces.

Luckily, for Zak and Zara things slowed down as they floated closer to the purple planet's surface, gliding on the thermals, and feeling a wonderful sense of bird-like freedom. Before they knew it, they had landed gently in a sort of field and were lying on a bed of lavender-colored grass surrounded by a strange-looking landscape. The two of them were so relieved; they just stayed there side by side trying to catch their breath while mentally scanning their bodies to check everything was still in one piece. After a few moments, their hearts ceased beating so fast, and their hands stopped shaking. The adrenalin rush began to slow down.

"Best game EV-VERR!" Zak said once he'd got his breath back.

"Game? Did you say game? Are you crazy?" Zara couldn't believe he was being serious. "Look, are you still wearing your headpiece? Well, look, are you?"

He put his hand up to his head. "Well, no. But…"

"But what?"

Before he could answer, the two of them looked up and saw they were surrounded by some bizarre-looking beings. There were four of them and although they stood upright like humans, that was where the similarity ended.

The creatures were a mixture between a cat and a bear, with a sprinkle of a fox. Each one of them had different colored fur. At first glance, they seemed to be friendly. Zak studied them in detail. They had cat-like ears; bear-shaped muzzles and lavender eyes. He noticed that they had three long digits and a thumb, all of which were a bit pointed, with the index finger a lot longer than the other two. Their furry heads, instead of being round at the top, were sort of triangular, and their ears weren't that easy to see, it depended on the length of their fur. Each of them had a strange colored light, shaped like the ace of diamonds, beaming out of the middle of their foreheads.

All of them were dressed in weird-looking outfits and carried what could have been hoes. They stared at Zara and Zak who were now sitting up to get their bearings. The creatures started talking with each other but the noises they were making were unintelligible to the two visitors from Planet Earth.

Zara leant across and whispered in Zak's ear, "I think they might be scared of us."

"How d'you know?" Zak asked a little uneasily.

"I just get that feeling…"

"Huh, I hope your feelings are right."

She stood up, followed quickly by Zak. The suddenness of her movement caused the creatures to take a step backwards with their hoes raised up in front of them

"Hi, I'm Zara and this is Zak."

The local residents just stared at them studying their forms with a curious expression. Zara took a step forward holding out her hand and tried again, only a little louder this time.

Pointing at her friend, she said, "He's Zaaaaaak," and then at herself, "and I'm Zaaaraaa."

One of the creatures reacted by poking her with a hoe.

Quite out of character, Zak responded and moved further forward to protect her. "Hey, what do you think you're doing?"

Zara was a little surprised and tried to calm him down.

"It's okay, Zak." She turned to the creatures and said in a softer voice, "It's okay you don't need to be afraid of us we don't have any weapons."

She held open both her hands.

"We're not going to hurt you, see?"

The same creature poked her again and she grimaced. Zak wasn't having any of it and leapt to her defense. He grabbed the end of the hoe-like object and pushing it sharply downwards used the creature's own weight to flip him over onto his back. The fallen hoe-holder looked angry and surprised, but not half as surprised as Zak at his own strength.

Zara was blown away. "Where did thaaaat come from?"

"My mum made me take martial arts classes for self-defense." He was a little embarrassed.

"Why didn't I know that?"

They looked at each other just as one of the aliens made a strange howling sound to alert others, who started appearing out of nowhere from different parts of the vast field.

"Okay, c'mon, let's leg it, we're outnumbered," Zara said with conviction.

She realized that being nice wasn't going to work, especially after Zak's quick display of force.

On the count of three, they ran across the purple heather-like field dodging some of the creatures that were coming towards them from all directions. Zak and Zara were both fast, darting in and out of strange-looking haystacks that were scattered across the terrain. After a few minutes, they ducked down behind a heap of the cropped heather to catch their breath but saw the creatures gaining on them with hoes held high.

Without any idea of where they were going, the two of them leapt up and sprinted at high speed, to put distance between themselves and their pursuers. Puffed and safely out of harm's way, at least for a moment, they took shelter behind another of the piles of dried heather to think about what to do next.

"You didn't have to grab his stick and toss him over, he didn't really hurt me."

"Maybe, but he was poking you."

"I'm sure I was just getting through to them and we could have talked them around."

"Okay perhaps, but I wasn't going to let him mess with you, I wanted them to know who was in charge."

Zak was showing a different side of himself than Zara had seen before.

"You didn't protect me from Mark Watts."

Zak looked at her. "That's pretty random, what's Watts got to do with all of this?"

"He bullied me for a whole year, and you did nothing."

"Oh yeah, but that was a long time ago and…"

Zara interrupted him, "You're squirming…"

"No, I'm not."

"Yes, you are."

Suddenly, a worried look crossed both their faces as the heather haystack came to life and started lifting them into the air. Looking down they saw that they were sitting on a bed of red and yellow feathers on the back of a huge bird that had been sleeping under the heather. It was massive.

They started screaming, clinging on as best they could as the bird climbed higher into the purple sky heading towards some distant mountains. As it turned, Zak lost his hold and started slipping off its back.

"Zara, Zara, don't let me go. I'm going under."

"I've got you, don't worry, hold on and stop wriggling."

Zara had hold of his sleeve and quickly tried to grab another part of his body, but he was sliding under the belly of the bird.

"I can't, I'm losing my grip…don't drop me." He was panicking.

"Hold on, it'll be okay, just relax."

"Reeeeeelaaaaaax?"

Just as he said it, Zara started to slip too. She was holding onto a clump of feathers with one hand and Zak with the other. They were quite a way off the ground and she couldn't let him fall.

As she was trying to decide what to do next, the bird miraculously turned the other way as if to correct the imbalance. With Zara's help, Zak slid onto its back again. Desperately trying to calm himself down, he stared right at her.

"Relax, you told me to reeelax when I'm hanging by a sleeve, hundreds of feet above the ground, on the back of a huge red and yellow bird on an alien planet that…"

"Zak, it worked! As soon as you yelled reeeeeelaaaaaax, the bird turned the other way and now we're safe."

"Oh, okay. Thanks for saving me anyway." He was really grateful because he was thinking about how many points he would have lost if he'd fallen off.

They both held on much more tightly hoping that the creature wouldn't do any more aerobatics with them on board. Fortunately, their four-winged rescuer continued to stabilize and Zak and Zara realized they were secure, at least for now. So, the two of them did relax—a little. They looked back and in the distance, saw that their pursuers were now clustered together staring up into the sky.

Zara was feeling pumped. "This is kinda cool. I always wondered what it would feel like to really fly like a bird. I do it in my dreams all the time."

Zak agreed. "It is, isn't it?"

They were high above a strange patchwork of fields, but it didn't look like much of anything was growing, everything looked very dry. In the distance, were some odd-looking windmill-like things and some low-lying hills. They couldn't make out if it was dawn or dusk because the sun was just hanging above the horizon. The half-light was making everything look purple.

Directly ahead of them, Zara noticed a cluster of dome-shaped buildings.

"Zak, I know where we are now," she said with confidence. "This is Quomos. Grandma was always talking about it. Remember?"

"Oh yeah, you're right, the purple place. It's starting to make sense."

"Reeeeally? I wouldn't go that far." Zara was surprised he was so clear and calm.

"Well, I can see now that the stories we thought she was making-up, came from the game."

"Huh, what game are you talking about?"

"This game. The one we're in now!"

"C'mon, Zaaak, you don't honestly still think this is a game, do you?"

"It better be…"

The bird made a sudden dive swooping close to the ground, destabilizing Zak and Zara and causing them to lose their grip seconds before they fell off. They rolled onto the spongy earth and quickly picked themselves up—unhurt.

"Wow, that was quite a ride," Zara said, brushing the dust and heather stuff off her jeans, while she got her bearings. "And you still think this is only a game? Then tell me what happens next?"

Zak didn't know what to say, he just surveyed what appeared to be city streets, but not like any he'd ever seen before. Some of the buildings were short and domed shape; others were taller and looked like giant pickles. They were all made of something organic, not bricks and cement. Some were completely round, sitting upon webs of vine-like plants. Each was different although there were some similarities, and all of them seemed like they could be members of the fungi family.

The two of them suddenly realized they were standing on the roadway of a city where the streets were lined with buildings made from weird varieties of, what could best be described as, assorted mushrooms and other vegetables. Most of them had been hollowed out and had openings, like windows and doors, in the main part of the structure. They had different rambling plants climbing up the outside as if they were holding them in place.

There were all sorts of unusual trees along the streets and in between the buildings, and although they only had a few leaves, they added some texture to the cityscape. Some water canals ran parallel to the road and were obviously irrigation channels, but they weren't very full.

The strange windmill-like things that they had seen while they were flying, were dotted along the sides of the canals. It was clear now that they were actually a type of rotating tree. A few of them were going round and round, while others stayed still in the light breeze.

Zak and Zara stood there staring.

"What is this place?" Zak asked gazing at the organic structures.

"I guess it must be their main city."

Zara was adjusting to all the different sights, sounds, and smells that were bombarding her senses. She wasn't sure exactly where they were, but one thing she knew beyond a shadow of a doubt, was that Grandma Elizabeth was still alive, and they were here to find her.

For a moment longer, the two of them scanned their surroundings until one of the local residents caught sight of the uninvited visitors. Then with the same strange sound that Zak and Zara had heard in the fields, it raised the alarm. They knew exactly what that meant, so without hesitation, started running in the direction of the main canal, which was lined with windmill trees. The pathway ended abruptly so they turned around to see what was chasing them. Only a few feet away, running in their direction, was a larger version of the creatures they had met in the fields only this time instead of a hoe it was carrying a big net.

Okay so stay calm. Zara heard a familiar voice in her head. *You know exactly what to do.*

"Zak, standstill and wait for my signal."

"You've got to be kidding me."

The creature was almost on top of them.

"Zak, take a step back." She pointed to one of the spinning trees.

He did what she said.

"Now watch."

The creature took a step forward and was just about to throw the net over the two of them when one of the rotating branches caught hold of its cloak and threw the alien for a loop. He hit the ground with a thud and the net fell over his own furry body. He was trapped!

"Wow, that was pretty slick, Zar, but now what?"

"Follow me. My mum didn't make me study martial arts but she taught me how to stand my ground and, how to swim."

She jumped up and grabbed hold of one of the lower branches. As it rotated out over the canal, she let go and fell into the water.

Zak wasn't sure about Zara's strategy but saw a whole load more of the same creatures heading towards him. So, he grabbed another passing branch and waited until it was over the water before letting go.

With his head above the water, he called out to Zara, "Hey, this reminds me of that tree branch that hangs out over the estuary where we tied the rope and swung from the river bank. Maybe we can go there later when your grandma's wake is over."

Zara didn't reply because the flow of water had speeded up and they were heading towards an edge beyond which she couldn't see. The current was very strong and although capable swimmers, it didn't matter how hard they tried to fight it, there was nothing they could do. Suddenly, a whirlpool of swirling waters came to swallow them up.

"Hold your breath," Zara yelled just before she dived into the mass of bubbling liquid.

She didn't hear Zak say, "I'm planning to." He took a last gasp of air and disappeared.

The water crashed down into a lower reservoir as Zara popped back up again and taking a deep breath, glanced around at where she'd arrived. A little further along, she noticed another rotating tree with some low hanging branches and swam towards them. Grabbing hold of one of the limbs she was lifted out of the water on to the bank. She thought Zak was right behind her, but then she couldn't see him anywhere.

"Zak, Zak, where are you?"

She waited a moment longer but he didn't appear.

"Zak, Zak, you have to come up." There was panic in her voice. "I can't lose you too, not here and not now."

She stood there not knowing what to do. It was the longest minute she had ever known. Just as she was about to dive into the water again to search for her best friend, she turned around and saw him swimming towards her from the other direction. He'd been carried further downstream. Zara pointed to one of the branches. As it came closer, he jumped up and grabbed it, landing beside her. He was pooped, and for a moment, lay there coughing and spluttering. As she knelt over him, he started laughing insanely. Instead of being worried, Zara was now curious.

"What's so funny?"

"All of this, I know what it is." Zak was rolling around.

"What are you talking about?"

"This…all of this…it's a dream."

"Oh Zak, I thought you were being serious!"

"I am."

"Come on, how could it be a dream if I'm having it too?" Zara was finding it hard to accept his logic.

"You're not, I'm dreaming you just said that, watch."

With that, Zak stood up and walked around the other side of the tree into the open. Then, much to Zara's amazement, he called out to some of the creatures that were obviously searching for them.

"Hey, we're over here…here."

"What are you doing?" She couldn't believe what she was seeing.

"Just watch me, it's only a dream so I won't get hurt."

"And if you do?"

"Then we're in deep…"

He didn't finish the sentence because the large creature, which had earlier trapped itself in his own net, slammed into Zak and knocked him out cold.

Chapter Seven

The two of them were taken by their captors to one of the dome-shaped buildings not far from where they'd been caught. Zak was laid flat on a low bed-like thing inside a room that was all white. It was a little bit shabby, but it was clean. Zara was sitting on the floor talking to him and waiting for her friend to come around. She'd learnt that carrying on a conversation was the best thing to do when someone was unconscious because part of them could still hear. Inside herself, she had been flipping between feeling worried and feeling angry.

She had explored the room and found that there was no way out except through a door, which was blocked by a guard. Zara had tried to talk with him but there was absolutely no way she could get through. She resigned herself to sitting there hoping Zak wouldn't be *out of it* for too much longer.

Her wait was soon over as he groaned and sat up rubbing his head.

"Hmmm! Maybe I'm wrong and this isn't a dream after all. I'm such an idiot."

"Zak, a person wouldn't have to be an idiot to think this was just a dream. He'd have to have an IQ of, at least, 35."

He covered his face with his hands as Zara realized that she had reacted a little too harshly. She sat on the edge of the bed and put her hand on his.

"I'm sorry."

"No, you're right but…but what are we going to do like now that we know it's not a game? It kinda changes things a bit. I mean a whole lot. How do we get back?"

Zara didn't know what to say, she just sat staring at him wishing she had an answer.

The door opened and a creature, looking a little more human-like, walked in; he was still pretty weird. His skin texture and coloring was like pale red sand as if he had tiny little pimples all over his face. It gave him a rather coarse appearance. He had active eyes and a big nose that was fatter than it should have been on a face like his. Zara got an uncomfortable feeling as she looked across at him—she couldn't say why, but there was something definitely not right. She turned to Zak to explain that he and his kind were the ones who had brought them here and, taken care of him.

The red-faced *man* walked towards them palm upwards and held out his hand. At first, they were a little nervous but when they saw two little purple beans with a small curly twisted wire root, they relaxed. He picked one up and made a gesture to show how they were to be placed in their ears. So, Zara reached out and took them both. She handed one to Zak who watched as she fitted hers. He then did the same.

"…cn yu stand e?"

It was garbled at first.

"Do you understand me now?" he said in a raspy voice.

The two of them nodded, as the guard warned him not to get too close to the strangers. He took a step back and looking at Zara, asked, "Who are you and what are you doing here?"

Stuttering a bit at first, Zara replied, "We're...uh...not from around here. We were using my...er...Grandma Elizabeth's computer, and Zak—that's Zak there, and I'm Zara...and...uh...we were..."

The guard at the door spoke next, "Did you say Elizabeth?"

Zara's eyes opened wide. She was surprised. "Do you know her?"

Zak wasn't buying it. "Zara, they wouldn't. How could..."

He was cut short as the guard replied, "Of course, I know her. Well...er...I know of her. Every being on the planet knows her."

"See? They do know her. I told you her stories were real." Zara gave him a bit of a smug smile because she thought that at last, Zak might start to believe her.

The guard was the one that continued, "Are you...er...saying that you are...er...Elizabeth's granddaughter?"

"Yes, I am and this is my best friend Zak and we..."

"What if she's lying, Yorazz?" The guard whispered loud enough that they could overhear. Then he caught himself. "I know just the Nuff who'll be able to tell us."

He opened the door and went off leaving the two of them with the strange, round-looking being with pale red skin.

"Did he say Nuff?" Zara asked.

"Yes, that's the name of their race. They came to join us on Quomos deca-decazytags ago when their home planet got hit by an asteroid."

His raspy voice grated on Zara a bit.

"Hey, Zar, that was one of the stories your grandma told us." Zak was starting to get it. He turned to the odd-looking character and asked, "So who are you?"

"I'm Yorazz, leader of the Yobuns. We were here before the Nuffs but we did our best to make them welcome."

Zara didn't really believe him, she had always been very intuitive and couldn't say why, but there was something definitely not right. She could feel it inside. Suddenly, the door flew open and in walked a mature version of the furry creatures they'd seen in the fields. Yorazz introduced him, "This is WiseyNuff, he is a great sage and seer."

His fur was fox-brown with a few grey edges to his whiskers, and the light in the middle of his forehead shone very brightly. He wore a purple and gold cloak that covered part of his chest and flowed down his back. An ornate quartz crystal pin held it together. If Zara had been paying attention, she would have seen that it was a familiar shape.

It took a moment for him to fix his eyes on the visitors. Then as they focused on her, his nose twitched and he tugged on his left ear. He walked right up to Zara causing the youngster to jump back a bit.

Unfazed, he stepped again into her personal space to examine her even more closely, for what was a very long moment. Then, as he backed away, he said quite conclusively, "It's her...it is definitely her, she looks exactly the same as Elizabeth did at this age when she first came to Quomos."

Zara couldn't help herself, and turning to Zak said in a whisper, "See, I told you it was Quomos."

Yorazz and the guard just gawped, stunned by WiseyNuff's announcement. They stepped to one side, becoming very deferential, and moved to open the door. As the elder Nuff ushered Zara and Zak out of the domad and into the fresh air, Zak spoke quietly to Zara, "You know what this means, don't you?"

"That everything she was telling us is true."

"Nope, it means that you are going to look just like your grandma when you get old!"

Zara elbowed him but this time he protected his ribs and got it in the arm instead. It didn't hurt and he smiled at her, happy they were safe and together.

"Did Elizabeth ever mention me?" Wisey asked as they stepped out onto the spongy street. His voice was deep and gentle and he sounded younger than his fur suggested.

It was Zak who answered, "Uuuh…actually she didn't…"

For a moment, the Nuff looked a little crestfallen.

Zara quickly completed Zak's sentence, "…Actually, I'm sure she did! She talked about many of the Nuffs. WiseyNuff was definitely among them. You sometimes use other names, and it's a lot for us to remember!"

He brightened up a little. "I understand. So tell me how is she, and why did she send you here?" He was hoping to hear good news.

Zak and Zara didn't know what to say at first, and both felt uncomfortable. Then together they described what had happened and how she had disappeared. They gave him as much detail about the incident as they could.

He was clearly having difficulty accepting it.

"It doesn't make any sense she is a superior swimmer." He told them that he and Elizabeth had been on many missions together and he remembered distinctly her swimming ability. "Elizabeth has great water power."

"Missions, what kind of missions, and what is water power anyway?" Zak was curious.

"She never mentioned to you that she's an X-IT."

"An exit, what's an exit…" Zak didn't understand at all.

"An Extraordinary Interdimensional Traveler. An X-IT. She really never told you."

"Um…she kind of told us." Zara didn't know how to put it.

"Kind of?" Wisey was pushing for more

"Well, through telling us lots of stories."

"Yeah, but we thought they were just fairy tales." Zak shrugged.

"Well, Zak did! I always knew she was talking about her adventures."

Wisey muttered, "Fairy tales, hmmm? Did she ever mention that both of you are also X-ITs?"

They shook their heads and just stared at him as he continued, "Well, you are, otherwise, you wouldn't have been able to get here. The vibrational field of the geodes only responds to the DNA energy codes of X-ITs."

"Are you serious?" Zak asked. "So, when Zara pressed enter, what happened?"

"You accessed a portal in the InfiGrid and entered a vortex that led you through a passageway, which lies outside of the time-space continuum."

For a moment, Zak looked even more confused. Zara, on the other hand, felt the same kind of excitement she did when Grandma Elizabeth used to tell them stories. She really liked WiseyNuff.

He continued, "It is a corridor between worlds that allows interdimensional travel, but it can only be entered by those with the power and energy codes of X-ITs."

The wise old Nuff moved closer to them because what he had to say was very important.

"You two have that power and can travel to other galaxies, even to parallel universes."

The young adventurers were dumbfounded as they tried to take in what they had just heard.

"Grandma Elizabeth, and your grandparents, Zak, are X-ITs but your parents are not. It always skips a generation." He paused.

"The stories they told you are real and are intended to prepare you for a lifetime of interdimensional travel."

"Wait just a minute!" Zara said excitedly. "Are you saying we can go to other planets and even to different galaxies?"

"Yes, I am, and you already have—you're here on Quomos!" He smiled. "Not only that, but you don't miss out on anything back home. No one knows you are gone because you are in a time-space vacuum."

"That is so wild!" Zak was no longer holding back his newly found enthusiasm. "You mean we can be in two places at the same time?"

"In a way, yes. All you will feel when you get back to Earth is a moment of what we call *drift*, when you forget for a second what you were about to think, do, or say." He paused. "I am surprised Elizabeth didn't tell you all this."

"Maybe she was just about to but she never got the chance before she…er…went missing…" Zara's voice trailed off.

Zak saw that she was struggling, and continued to describe the night that she disappeared, "The divers said it could have happened to anyone."

Wisey looked perplexed. "Yes, but it is hard to imagine that it could happen to Elizabeth; not without me knowing."

Zara agreed, "I'm having a really hard time with it too, in fact…"

Zak and his logic jumped in, "Yeah, but those riptides can sure get a hold of you and then that's it, you're pulled out to sea and never seen again." He sounded very matter-of-fact.

Wisey stopped abruptly and looked at him very closely, pushing his nose towards Zak's face. "Are you telling me they never found her body?"

"They couldn't, they looked all over," Zara said, beginning to believe that maybe she was right.

Wisey smiled. "Ah well, you know you had me worried for a moment."

Again, his nose twitched as he tugged on his left ear.

"And you're not now?" Zara asked

"Well, not about Elizabeth but about something else; something that, if used for dark purposes, could destroy all that we know.

Zara looked at Zak as WiseyNuff's smile was replaced with a frown. She knew what she was about to say next was significant.

"On the night that she disappeared, she had just started to tell us about a secret and a sacred key, when we…er…had to…well…er…go and do our homework." She looked at Zak appealingly. "See, we should have stayed."

The old Nuff had a sense of urgency about him. He'd learnt all he needed to know for now. "This is very grave we have to gather the clans. Come, follow me."

Chapter Eight

Yorazz had sent word to the chiefs of the four Nuff clans that there was to be a summit in the Universal Hall, the largest of the dome-shaped buildings in the city. The dwellers knew of the X-ITs presence after they had been captured earlier, so the streets were humming with excitement.

Zak and Zara's minds were buzzing with questions by the time they arrived at the big dome. They had tried their best to keep up with Wisey who, for his years, had been moving at a very fast pace. Every now and again, the two of them had to break into a jog just to stay alongside him, especially as they were also trying to absorb their surroundings in more detail.

Everywhere was covered in the purple half-light that made the landscape appear a little eerie. In the distance, were two ranges of mountains, which were very different in shape from those on Earth. The ones in the foreground were like giant molehills and were dark mauve, while the ones in the background were steep and spiky and seemed higher than the Alps and the Rockies. Zak thought they looked like they had been painted in, like the backdrop on a stage. They were pale purple with grey streaks, and he was questioning again whether this was for real or, had they landed right in the middle of a movie set. He felt a sharp pain in his brain but it only lasted a second. Before he had a chance to say anything, it was gone. He put it down to the collision he'd had with the large Nuff at the canal.

As they reached the gathering place, the door to the domes opened like the wings on a fly, and the three of them walked in.

"We call this building the Universal Hall," WiseyNuff announced.

The X-ITs noticed that as well as Nuffs and Yobuns, there were some other strange creatures and an assortment of robots present in the hall. Before they had a chance to ask Wisey about them, he pointed towards a small group clustered together. There were no more than six of them but they were beyond weird. Their heads were shaped like a three-leaf clover and their faces covered in short fuzzy grey fur. They wore dark grey cloaks that fell differently, depending on the roundness of their little bodies and the length of their dumpy legs.

"Those are Zybuffs," Wisey said. "They were once wizards of technology. The reason their heads are so big is that they spend much of their time thinking and analyzing things. Their language is hard for us to understand, but SmartyNuff acts as a translator. They speak in some kind of mathematical code, and we have been working on understanding it for zytags. Just as we think we have broken through, they jump to a higher level of sophistication."

There were other unusual-looking characters in amongst the Zybuffs and Yobuns. Wisey didn't talk about them, and Zara guessed they would learn more, later. As she looked around, she saw that the Nuffs themselves were all different sizes, and their fur was in many colors. Their basic shape or form was similar, and each of them had the same diamond shape light embedded in the middle of their foreheads. Zara had spotted that this came in four distinct colors; red, yellow, green and blue, although WiseyNuff's was colorless, almost translucent.

A table in the shape of a nonagon floated in the middle of the hall. It didn't have any legs and seemed to be held in place by an invisible force field. Hovering above it was a hologram of the galaxy swirling around. The light wasn't very bright but every star and every planet was easy to see as they drifted by.

There were three Nuffs sitting on unusual stools that seemed to hover above the ground. A fourth Nuff was pacing around as the X-ITs were brought over and introduced by Wisey.

"This is Elizabeth's granddaughter, Zara, and her friend Zak, they're here to help us find our missing brothers and sister."

The two adventurers from Earth gave each other a sideways glance; they had no idea what he was talking about.

"Welcome to Quomos, known throughout our galaxy as the Purple Planet, for reasons that are clear to see. My name is StrongyNuff and I am the chief of the FireHerder clan."

His voice was gruff and he was more muscular than the others they'd seen. His fur was golden and he had a face that was more lion-like. He had a muzzle and a long tuft of fur that hung down from his chin, like Wisey's, only it was thicker and curled up at the end. The fur on the top of his triangular-shaped head was styled into a wave shape, and

Zara thought that he looked quite handsome. The diamond in the middle of his forehead was red.

The elder Nuff then introduced them to the other three, "This is CoolyNuff."

Through their earpieces, Zak and Zara thought his voice sounded almost Spanish and they smiled at each other as he started talking. Cooly's fur was beige and the light in his forehead was blue.

"You are welcome here. My clan is zee WaterWhisperers."

The next chief to be introduced was SmartyNuff. Wisey described how she was the one he'd mentioned earlier who could crack the codes of the Zybuffs better than anyone else. She was petite and athletic with silver and white fur, a long elegant neck, and only a short tuft under her chin.

Her cloak was red and yellow and well fitted to her small body. She smiled at the visitors.

"It is nice to meet you, I am the leader of the AirSpinners." Her voice was light and crisp and the diamond in her forehead was yellow.

The fourth Nuff was way scrawnier than the others and he had nicks in both of his ears, probably from fights when he was younger. His fur was dark grey and scruffy, and his bottom jaw protruded giving his face a different shape. His cloak was decorated with random bits of metal and held together with a piece of bone. He also had a ring in the upper part of his ear and a tattoo around the green light in the middle of his forehead.

"I am WeirdyNuff, clan chief for the EarthTamers, you can call me Weeze." He grinned and winked at the same time.

Zara thought that he was probably a whole lot of fun as he gestured to one of his clan.

"We need more hover-stools for our guests."

Three additional floating stools appeared from nowhere and screeched to a halt next to the nine-sided table. Zak and Zara thought that they looked like giant chocolate-coated marshmallows hovering above the floor making a kind of humming noise. They both sat down and joined the chiefs of the four Nuff clans.

The inside of the Universal Hall reflected the same kind of energy as the rest of the planet. Things weren't quite right and it was all in a state of ongoing decay. In here though, Zara intuitively picked up a much stronger vibration behind some kind of veil. Looking around, she could see an almost ghost-like impression of how it used to be.

Seconds later, she was propelled into a parallel reality. Beyond the veil, it seemed like everything in the Universal Hall was richly colored and alive. She saw giant flying bugs that lit up like fireflies and joined together to form the brightest chandelier she'd ever seen.

Lining the domed-shaped ceiling were beautiful white feathers that gently moved to create a kind of air conditioning system. She knew somehow that each one had been carefully picked and placed there because of its size and style. As she watched, she was sure she heard one of them sneeze, and she smiled as those close by ruffled up a bit and fluttered excitedly, before moving back into a regular rhythm. The one that had caused the disturbance turned a delicate shade of pink, reflecting its embarrassment.

A waterfall flowed out from one of the walls. Halfway down it changed to streams of silver rays and as it reached the floor, it turned into golden glitter that sparkled in the sunlight. A collection of letters that formed a living alphabet were busy arranging themselves into a sentence, and as they floated past she saw they were spelling the phrase, *If somebody loses, nobody wins*. A special kind of music played in the background and there was something magical about this place.

It was the big, strong Nuff, who broke her trance.

"So it's perfectly obvious to me what has happened to Elizabeth. She's been kidnapped probably by the same person who mesmerized us into banishing the StoneKeepers." Strongy was convincing.

Gasps of surprise echoed through the dome-shaped structure.

"Kidnapped?" Zak said softly to Zara.

Zara was feeling smug and relieved.

"Told you, didn't I—but you didn't believe me."

The other Nuffs went on murmuring.

Strongy continued, "…and I say we can't just sit around and do nothing."

"Wait a minute," Zak spoke next. "Why would anyone want to kidnap Zara's grandma?"

Strongy didn't hesitate, "For the Key, of course."

"What key?"

Zara answered Zak's question, "He's talking about the Sacred Key that Grandma was going to tell us about." She turned to face StrongyNuff. "Aren't you?"

"Oh, that key," Was all that Zak could think of to say!

"Yes, the InfiniKey. It's the Key to the Wellspring of Everlasting Energy, and in the wrong hands, it can do untold damage. And that's where it is right now in the wrong…"

Smarty interrupted him, "Come on, Strongy, we don't know that for certain."

"Well then, SmartyNuff, who else besides Yezzadar could have taken her? We have to go to Scartuss now, find Elizabeth, and get the Key."

"And then what?" It was Cooly's turn to speak.

"We find the others and reclaim the Key to the Wellspring of course, and bring life back to Quomos."

"I was afraid you were going to say that." CoolyNuff was ill at ease.

Strongy was convinced he was right. "What's the alternative? Leave things as they are? Our crops can't grow very high. Our rivers don't flow very fast. The air is almost stagnant and our dead can't pass through the Gateway to the other side. This is an opportunity to make the sun rise again and put things back into balance."

Cooly wasn't letting go. "There are no guarantees."

A hush fell over the hall as WiseyNuff got up and walked around twitching his nose and tugging on his ear. When Wisey spoke, all present listened attentively. "There are no guarantees but when the Universe gives you such signs it is only wise to see where they lead, and in this case, I believe we must follow them."

He continued, "The remaining half of the Key was given to Elizabeth for safekeeping. We knew she would take good care of it and she always has. There is no reason to think that has changed."

StrongyNuff wanted action. "Yeah and something has happened to her now, otherwise they wouldn't be here. They're the ones we've been waiting for," he said, pointing to Zara and Zak.

Yorazz stepped forward onto the main floor and in a loud rasp, "I don't think we should do anything. We need not rush things. Who has a problem with that?"

Zara couldn't hold herself back anymore. "I do," she blurted out. "I want my grandma back. Does anyone have a problem with that?"

She stood firm, strong, and determined on the outside and was shaking like a jellyfish on the inside. Her knees were knocking together, but nobody noticed.

Wisey smiled to himself.

Strongy put his arm up. "See, that is the kind of courage it takes to right an ancient wrong. Let's take a vote. Who's with me?"

A whole load of the crowd yelled 'YoHa' and placed their right paw in the middle of the upper part of their chests.

"And, who's with me?" Cooly called out.

Fewer present shouted YoHa and raised their arms.

Feeling defeated, CoolyNuff gave Zara an awkward look, but she didn't notice. She just wanted to do whatever it took to find her grandmother, especially now it could also help the Nuffs get their planet back to normal.

They left the Hall and headed to a smaller domad to get some food before preparing for the mission to Scartuss, home of the Nuffs archenemy, Yezzadar. Zara sat next to Smarty while Zak was with Strongy at the other end of a funky horseshoe-shaped table that again, just hung in the space, unattached to anything. The residents of Quomos were enjoying each other's companionship while they drank down some colorless broth and chewed on, what appeared to be, fruits and vegetables. Zak and Zara were the only ones there who didn't readily start eating because the food to them looked very unappetizing.

The odd-shaped bowls contained some pea pods only instead of green, they were grey. Orange, cabbage-like leaves were laid alongside and appeared to wriggle their way under the pods as if to hide from view.

"They taste delicious, try them," Smarty prompted Zara.

"But, but aren't they alive?"

"Well, yes and no, they're quite fresh so they are still full of energy. What you are seeing is the vibrational force coming from them, which means they are rich in goodness."

Zara wasn't sure and looked down the table at her friend. Zak was listening to StrongyNuff, coaching him how to eat.

"C'mon, try it! It tastes better than it looks." Strongy bit down on a pod and chewed the grey, pea-like things inside. "Go on, she's watching you and you don't want her to think you're afraid, do you?"

Perhaps in the past, Zak really wouldn't have cared less but he was feeling more protective of Zara, and somehow sitting next to this particular Nuff made him feel stronger and more masculine. He picked up a pod and chewed on it, rather noisily, as Zara watched him. He smiled proudly and realized that it didn't taste that bad after all. Zara was impressed and began to eat as well, only in a more delicate way, by following Smarty's example. She had opened the pod and removed the peas throwing away their covering.

"The boy, how long have you known him?" SmartyNuff was curious to find out more about the two of them.

"Zak?"

"Uh-huh."

"Pretty much all my life since we were little kids."

"So what is he to you?"

"Oh, we're just best friends, that's all." Zara had never thought about Zak in any other way.

"So what happens when you get older?"

"Huh, well, I don't know, it's not like that. I guess I haven't ever seen him as anything other than a friend." She felt a little ill at ease.

"Maybe it's time to start."

Zara suddenly sat up very straight as she became aware of something under the table. Something was brushing up against her legs, something that at first was comforting but then alarming. It had been a good three years since Grandma Elizabeth's cat had died, and that was the last time she remembered this happening. As hard as her grandmother had tried to keep Luna from crawling under the table during mealtimes, it had never worked. The moment food appeared she would take her place and wrap herself around the legs of those sitting down to eat, just waiting for a crumb to fall.

Only, Zara knew that this wasn't Luna, and she felt herself go cold as she saw the tip of a silver tail disappearing under the table. She bent over to see where the cat had gone to, but there was nothing there.

"Did you drop something?" Smarty asked, a little startled by Zara's abrupt movement.

"No, no, I just thought I saw a cat and it brushed up against my legs."

"We don't have cats on Quomos, but maybe it's a sweepet."

Zara felt a moment of relief. "What's that?"

"It's a little creature that cleans under the table as we drop things on the floor. They're kinda active at this time of day, especially if they're hungry."

"This one had a silver tail," Zara said, hoping to have her fears taken away.

"Hmm, I can't tell you what that was, sweepets don't have tails. Maybe you..."

Zara didn't hear the rest of what Smarty had to say because she was listening to another voice. *All is well I am with you. No harm will come while you are protected.* She didn't know where it came from, but for now, it calmed her angst. She felt a soft buzzing sensation coming from the pendant hanging around her neck, hidden under her shirt.

Zak was talking to Strongy. "How do you know when to eat? It always looks the same around here."

"It won't be like that much longer, I guarantee you."

"But in the meantime…"

"All you can do is go with your instincts, they'll never let you down."

Strongy looked at Zara, but Zak didn't get what he was talking about. He looked at her too a little confused, as his logic tried to understand what *instinct* really meant. He'd spent a lot of time thinking about it but had been unable to work it out in his head. Zara looked over at him as he chomped down on some more pea pods. She wished she could have a little time with him alone to talk about what was happening. It didn't look like that was going to be possible, at least for now.

CoolyNuff walked over to where they were sitting. Zara welcomed the distraction from her own thoughts, and as she looked up at him, it was clear to her why he was known as the cool Nuff. He had an air about him that was clear and calm, almost nonchalant. His eyes sparkled and the diamond on his brow was a deep aqua-blue, like the color of a glacier.

"Brother, that was a good speech, you deserve the name StrongyNuff. You definitely won them over."

"Ah, yes but you really are the better speaker, I just had reason on my side."

"Passion too, brother. Let's just hope the Great Mystics are on our side too."

He was talking about the ancient ones who had entrusted the Nuffs with the InfiniKey. They had brought them to Quomos all those zytags ago when their planet of origin had been hit by an asteroid and suffered from a series of extreme phenomena that left it uninhabitable. The circumstances that the Nuffs found themselves in now, were very different, and Zak and Zara were about to learn more about why the two of them had been transported to the Purple Planet.

"When do we leave?" Cooly continued.

Strongy was quick to reply, "As soon as we've completed the training and gathered enough provisions."

"I will be there," Cooly said as he started to leave. Then he turned back.

"One thing more, while you are preparing do you mind if I take our young guests outside and show them around."

"If they want to go with you, sure." Strongy continued eating as the two X-ITs looked at each other welcoming the opportunity to leave the food where it was, and follow CoolyNuff.

"Great idea, we'll go." Zara just wanted to get out and was still feeling very uneasy after her *under the table experience.*

"Mmmm-hmm," Zak agreed with his mouth full.

"Good, I know you will find it informative."

Chapter Nine

CoolyNuff led them out of the city to where the ground was more undulating with rocky outcroppings, giant pod trees, and snake-like vines, which grew over and around everything. The three of them headed in the direction of some foothills, that served as a small mountain range and provided protection to the more densely populated area they were leaving behind them.

Zara felt better outside, she'd never really enjoyed being surrounded by walls for too long since the time she and Zak got trapped in a cave when they were kayaking. They had been exploring the pirate's caverns under the cliffs near Hope Cove and had got caught by the rising tide. The current was so strong that as hard as they tried to paddle against it, they kept being pushed back into the rocks. The only thing they could do was to wait until the tide turned, but they were in the cave for several hours and the space above their heads had grown very tight before they paddled to freedom.

The two of them now walked side by side, a few steps behind Cooly. Zak was curious to learn more about Yezzadar, who he'd discovered was a master of technology with a robotic army called the Terrortribes.

He was eager to know, in more detail, what this character was all about but now wasn't the right time. Suddenly, as these thoughts were running through his head, he heard a high-pitched sound that sent a sharp pain right into the centre of his brain. It was more intense than the one he'd had earlier, which he'd put down to his brush with the oversized Nuff alongside the canal. He turned really pale and looked at Zara. "Did you hear that?" he whispered.

"Hear what?"

"The high-pitched squeak."

"No, I heard nothing like that." She was surprised at the pain-filled look on her friend's face and reached out taking hold of his hand.

"Are you sure you're okay to go on?"

The pain was gone as quickly as it had come, and Zak felt he'd made a bit of a fuss about nothing. "Yeah, sure, I'm cool." He liked that she was holding his hand.

Zara caught herself and pulled it away.

"Zak, there are some things that we seriously need to talk about when we get back from here."

They both agreed they needed time together with no Nuffs around.

After some more minutes of walking on flat ground, the path became steeper and they started up a trail on the side of a small mountain. A little further on, the natural formation of the rugged landscape started to transform. From a distance, what had looked like just another outcropping of rugged rocks, turned out to be a mass of fallen rock columns and some giant rounded stones covered again in wild vines.

"This was our most sacred place. It is the Wellspring," CoolyNuff declared.

"Looks like nobody's been here for quite a while," Zak said dryly.

"Exactly."

Cooly explained that much of the tension between the clan chiefs, which they had witnessed in the Universal Hall, had its roots here.

A little farther on, they reached the edge of a small plateau. In the centre, were some more fallen columns heaped haphazardly on the ground, with two very large flat stones either side of the pile. Zara and Cooly carried on walking around them while Zak stopped to investigate further.

"Zak, what are you doing?"

"What are these platforms for?" he shouted out to Cooly.

"Oh, those are for the Guardians of the Gateway."

"What happened to them?"

"Nobody knows; no-one even remembers what they looked like anymore, they were gone before the *long night* fell."

Cooly and Zara continued to an area that was shaped like a baseball diamond, surrounded by several large boulders. After a few moments, Zak caught up with them. Zara couldn't help thinking that the energy of the Wellspring was like Stonehenge, the ancient burial site on Salisbury Plain. She felt a knowing chill run through her.

He told her what the place was all about. "This is where our souls pass through the Gateway to the other side."

"You mean this is where you…er…come to die?" Zara asked.

"I suppose you could put it that way, but it's not how we think of it. We see it as a time of renewal and rebirth. Anyway, it's not important now. There has been no regeneration for deca-zytags since we stopped the planet's rotation."

"You did what?" Zak could hardly believe what he was hearing.

"We wanted the sun to always shine. We wanted more warmth, more light. We wanted our crops to grow faster and more luscious."

Zak was astonished; it just didn't make any logical sense. He started asking Cooly a whole bunch of questions. Zara was distracted and walked on towards the side of the mountain, which was covered with a mass of carvings that looked like hieroglyphics. She'd always been able to see things others couldn't see, and pick up on energies that others didn't feel. At first, she thought it was normal but when she tried talking to her parents about it, they told her that she had an overactive imagination. The only person who really understood her was Grandma Elizabeth. It was part of their close bond.

Zara moved in to get a better look at the engravings. Some were symbols, while others were figures. She recognised the Nuffs and the Yobuns but there were different beings portrayed that she hadn't seen before. There were other versions of the big flying creature that had rescued them earlier, and she was fascinated to understand more about the Nuff's world. She had learnt from Smarty that the big bird, which had carried them to safety, was called a dodon. It was part of a menagerie of other alien-looking creatures. Some drawings were of weird-looking spaceships and flying saucers, all covered in graffiti. She giggled as she saw something that looked like a cross between a skunk and a kangaroo with oversized feet.

Zara reached out to touch the carvings, and when she did, the whole wall started to come to life in 3D, and all the images began moving. She jumped back wondering if she'd done something terribly wrong, when suddenly out of nowhere she heard a voice.

"It's interesting to discover what our eyes can see when our hearts are open."

She was startled. She hadn't noticed WiseyNuff sitting on a large rock watching her as she moved closer to look at the glyphs. He dropped down to stand next to her with such agility that he would have put many younger Nuffs to shame. She instantly felt at ease in his presence and couldn't help but notice that he looked more at peace here and, more youthful.

She turned around to see where Zak was.

"All is well, CoolyNuff is with him. There's no need to worry," Wisey answered her question before she had a chance to ask it.

"What you are seeing tells you the story that is known to us as *The Legend of the InfiniKey.*"

He paused and pointed to the wall.

"We moved here as a family generations ago."

As Wisey talked, Zara saw it all unfolding in front of her eyes. The Nuffs were happy-go-lucky beings and each of them had the same mark high in the middle of their furry chests, which glowed and pulsated. Some had cloaks on their backs but every Nuff had the diamond-shaped light, in the middle of their forehead, in one of four different colors. The X-ITs had noticed these on all the Nuffs they'd already met, only here their lights appeared to be much brighter.

"We call this an enervisor," he told her, pointing to the light on his brow. "It allows us to read energy in non-ordinary ways. When we see through our enervisor, all things are woven together with filaments of light and connected, like one vast tapestry. When we see through our other eyes, everything is separate."

Wisey described how each of the four Nuff clans has a special relationship with one of the elements.

"The role of our WaterWhisperers' is to keep the natural springs fresh, and take care of the rain and the ocean tides. Their enervisors are blue. EarthTamers have green enervisors and are responsible for keeping the land fertile and the planet free from serious earthquakes."

He looked to check she was listening. "Our FireHerders enervisors are red and these clan members calm the volcanoes and gather the flames when there is a risk of fires getting out of control. Lastly, the AirSpinners have yellow enervisors and their role is to keep Quomos free from pollution and ensure that the hurricanes, typhoons, and tornadoes aren't too destructive. The color of the enervisor is how you can tell which clan we each belong to and what special powers we have."

Zara looked at the moving wall and at the Nuffs working in the fields, farming fruits and vegetables that were very different from those on Earth. There were some long, thin plants with gold leaves and nut-like things growing in bunches halfway up their stalks. In other fields, thousands of sky blue tomatoes grew on mini-palm trees. Then there were vineyards full of emerald green fruits the size of ping-pong balls, hanging from vines.

"Those are grooglies. They're a very special fruit that we often take with us when we go on missions. They have magical properties but they are not as plentiful now."

Wisey looked away for a moment to recapture his thoughts but before he'd got them together, he was interrupted.

"What are you doing here, WiseyNuff?" Cooly and Zak had joined the two of them.

"I might ask you the same question," Wisey retorted.

The leader of the WaterWhisperers was cool. "Just showing our visitors around, to give them a bit of our history."

"Aha, one of my favorite subjects but, I prefer the term *mystery*."

Zak sidled up to Zara and pointed to the glyphs on the wall.

"What are these funny drawings?"

She turned to her friend. "Well, they're kinda like a movie of their history…or rather a mystery."

"Zar, movies are movies because they move! These are just carvings."

Wisey winked at her and tapped the top of his chest. Zara knew that Zak couldn't see the wall in the same way that she could.

"I was telling Zak about our mythology and what happened here," Cooly said with pride.

"Maybe it's not as mythic as we think," Wisey said before continuing.

"Legend has it that the Sacred Key to the Wellspring of Everlasting Energy or the InfiniKey was given to us Nuffs for safekeeping after a fracture in the fabric of the Universe, called *The Split*. It was a moment in time when the web of connection between all beings was broken, and the One became many."

The X-ITs were curious to hear more.

"Fear dominated our galaxy and wars broke out as beings wanted to take what others had. Nothing was ever enough. Holding onto everything became a way of life. Our covenant was to protect the InfiniKey against those who might use it for their own selfish motives. We were told to put it in its rightful place only when the many understood the true essence of power. Then and only then, could *The Split* be healed, and the connection restored."

They were listening attentively and there was a long pause before anyone broke the silence. Zak spoke first.

"Huh, so instead you used it to try to streeeetch daylight." He liked the words that he'd chosen to describe what they'd done and smiled at Zara. She didn't smile back because she thought he was being disrespectful.

"Well, that is one way of looking at it." Wisey took it in the spirit in which Zak had intended. "Yes, we broke the covenant."

"So, what happened next?" Zak was all ears, this was the kind of story he enjoyed listening to.

"Every clan had a StoneKeeper, a Shaman, who worked with the clan chief. As partners, they balanced the physical and spiritual dimensions of our world. It was the stone and its keeper that gave each clan the full and awesome power of their element. Then on that fate-filled day deca-decazytags ago, before the long night fell, the four StoneKeepers and the clan chiefs gathered here with the desire to alter the natural cycle of darkness and daylight."

As Wisey spoke, Zara heard a popping sound and the story started to come back to life. Only, she was shocked to find that she was no longer standing, watching the mountainside, but had been sucked through a veil into another reality.

At first, she panicked, not knowing what had happened. She could feel her heart beating fast and couldn't see very much of anything because it was so dark. *What's going on, where are the others?* Then the same familiar voice she'd heard earlier whispered, *I am here no harm will come to you.*

There was a smell of something burning and a lot of strange mutterings. As her eyes adjusted, she suddenly realized she was standing right in the middle of the experience that WiseyNuff was describing. Still scared, she knew deep down she would be safe. Whoever or whatever it was that was answering her questions would protect her.

It was so weird, she felt like she was in two different worlds at once, as if time was of no importance and there were just multiple levels of *now*. For a moment, she thought herself back to being with Zak and stood there alongside him, gazing at the mountainside. Then she focused again on being in the full experience of WiseyNuff's story. With the same odd popping sound, she was once more sucked through the veil, surrounded by Nuffs and other strange creatures.

Zara relaxed a little knowing she could choose her reality, and started looking around. As far as she could tell, the mountains were covered in luscious vegetation as the scented smoke from the fire pit encircled the arena. She could hear many different sounds coming from the crowd as they waited for the ceremony to begin.

The Wellspring was in its original state. It was a magnificent outdoor temple with all of its grand stones standing in perfect symmetry. Each one was covered in glyphs similar to the ones she had first seen on the mountain face. The stones were curved at the top and radiated an energy that made them seem to be vibrating with life, even if it was at a very low frequency. In the centre of the diamond-shaped arena, was another kind of stone; it was a giant amethyst geode like the ones in Grandma Elizabeth's loft, only bigger. It lay flat on the ground and was open in the middle forming a gateway into the earth that was the entrance to an underground tunnel filled with bright white light. Zara strained to see what was standing on the platforms either side of the gateway so she could tell Zak. All she could make out were two ghostly shadows that made her shudder.

There were Nuffs all around her but they weren't wearing any cloaks, and all of them had the same symbol in the middle of their furry chests. At first, she couldn't make it out and then, to her amazement; she saw it was the same shape as the pendant around her neck, only bigger. It was Grandma Elizabeth's $\mathcal{E}$. *But how can that be?* She wanted to be sure and stared at a few of them. Zara saw that on some Nuffs it faced one way while on others, it was the mirror image, and looked like the number three. On some, it was silver and on others, it was gold. Hmm, *maybe Grandma is more famous than I know.*

As she looked on, she saw what she knew had to be the four StoneKeepers approaching. She moved in closer to get a better look, as they all positioned themselves at the four points of the diamond. Nobody seemed to notice she was there. Each one of them was holding a long staff bearing a large colored gemstone, held in place by some kind of elemental force. She focused her eyes as the EarthTamer stepped forward and took his place facing the centre of the diamond at the eastern point. His staff was made of living vines twisting around and draping a beautiful emerald green stone at its apex. Some of the vines were trying to climb up the StoneKeeper's arm and he kept shaking them off. Zara smiled to herself, it looked kind of cool, as if they were somehow excited to be at the ceremony.

The StoneKeeper for the WaterWhisperers entered the sacred space and stood a little distance away, at the southern point. Zara was trying very hard to make out its gender but was unable to do so. She could see that its staff was liquid and shaped like an elongated turquoise wave. It made a whooshing sound as it kept breaking and reforming, throwing out a fine white mist at the top that sprayed over a blue-green crystal.

She immediately recognised it as an Aquamarine, her grandma's favorite gemstone. *I bet she'd know what the others are if she was here.* Elizabeth had worked with the energy of these kinds of stones since the time she was a young hippie. She knew the properties of all of them.

The FireHerder was the next of StoneKeepers to move into position. It was a female Nuff and she stood on the western side of the diamond, holding a staff made of dancing flames. Zara could feel the heat but for some reason, the flames didn't seem to singe her fur. Their orange and red tips flickered as they wrapped themselves around a rich ruby-red colored garnet that was hidden by the glow.

The last to take his position, at the northern point, was the StoneKeeper for the AirSpinner clan. As he walked to his place, the dust from the ground underneath his staff was spinning, forming an army of tiny dancing dust devils that followed him into the diamond-shaped arena. Zara could see that the staff itself was made of wisps of clouds with stars circling the stem. At the top, suspended in mid-air, there was a large golden yellow stone, which Elizabeth would have told her was a citrine. It sparkled as the light from the fire-pit caught it.

The night was quite dark as the four of them stood in the ceremony, surrounded by Nuffs and other beings that inhabited Quomos. Zara could sense that no one really felt comfortable. She could see that the energy fields around their bodies were very tight, but she didn't understand why. The cold and shivery feeling that ran through her let her know that something was about to go horribly wrong, but there was nothing she could do to stop it from happening.

She was aware of a presence as something brushed past her face, then another and another. Whatever it was, it made a soft pinging sound that reminded her of Grandma Elizabeth's wind chimes. They didn't feel threatening, just annoying, a bit like mosquitoes. She pulled her arms up and started moving them around to swat whatever it was. It didn't work because they were having too much fun with her, so in the end, she just let them play. Then all of a sudden everything stopped. She took her hands away from her face, amused and a little relieved.

A deep silence fell over the gathering as the StoneKeepers positioned their staffs in such a way that they were suspended above the four ornately carved cornerstones that marked the points on the diamond. Stepping away, they released their hold on these organic creations, leaving them floating in mid-air, just as a hooded cloaked being approached the centre.

The sense of anxiety and agitation was intense as everyone watched a fifth Nuff place his staff above the centre stone in front of the mouth of the Gateway. It was more elaborate than all the others and was formed of two large hissing serpents. They were stranger than anything Zara had ever seen before. Instead of snakeskin, one was covered with golden feathers and the other with silver fur. The two of them intertwined like strands of DNA and twisted together in such a way as to create seven spaces between their writhing bodies. Each of the gaps was filled with a different colored crystal stone; first red at the bottom, then orange, yellow, green, turquoise, blue and purple. The reptiles' deep black eyes stared out at the crowd, while the crests above their heads touched at the top to form the perfect opening for the final piece of the sacred puzzle.

Zara could smell the scent of the fire more strongly now as the hooded Nuff removed a small gold and silver artefact from underneath his cloak. He held it high above his head so all could see the horizontal figure of eight, which she knew at once, was the InfiniKey. The sacred object was growing larger and larger as it caught the firelight, revealing an intricate pattern of carvings. Then, with great reverence, this statuesque Nuff positioned it in the space between the serpents' crested heads. It fitted perfectly. Once it was in place, the real magic began to happen. As the Nuff stepped back, shafts of light started to jump from one StoneKeeper's staff to another, illuminating the gemstones and sending streams of lightning bolts zooming around the arena.

Colored light forms, some sinister and others serene, danced as if they were alive, continuously changing shape and creating a sound and light show the likes of which Zara had never seen before. All those gathered, were standing with mouths open and eyes wide. They watched as the as the light beings shot up into the sky and then down to the ground weaving a tapestry of images that were beautiful and dreadful both at the same time. Finally, everything coalesced in the centre. The InfiniKey grew brighter and brighter casting a gold and silver light that was so dazzling the gathered crowd had to cover their eyes to stop from being blinded.

Before they had a chance to open them again the ground started to shake, gently at first but then more violently. Zara was frightened and for a moment was tempted to go back to join the others but she didn't want to miss a thing. In the beginning, only the smaller stones fell.

Then when the quaking grew stronger, the larger ones tumbled and the open-air temple began to fall in on itself, crushing some and injuring others. She didn't know what to do or where to run to—she wanted to help the ones who were trapped but it was too dangerous. Then she heard the voice again. *Move closer to the centre and no harm will come to you. Remember this is their destiny you cannot rescue them from themselves, it's their time.*

Zara cringed as she saw the scene of chaos and devastation. Fissures started opening in the ground and some of the Nuffs fell into them. Others were running in all different directions trying to avoid the falling debris. It was mass panic and the screams of some of the smaller creatures echoed through the night, as those rushing to get out of the temple trampled them. The noise was deafening as the rocks beneath their feet cracked and the columns tumbled, smashing against the mountain's crusty floor. Zara found it hard to maintain her balance as she watched the four StoneKeepers abandon their staffs and head for higher ground.

Wisey continued to describe the situation to Zak on the other side of the veil.

"The only one who remained unruffled was the Nuff in the centre of the diamond. As he watched the Gateway between the worlds seal itself shut, he knew exactly what he had to do. He stepped forward and braving the blinding light, he grabbed the InfiniKey from the serpent staff. His body went into a series of convulsions before he collapsed to the ground, holding the sacred object tightly in his hand. The quaking stopped immediately and as it did, the night gave way to the first signs of day."

"So, it sort of worked?" Zak asked.

"Well, they thought so when the purple glow of dawn's glimmer appeared on the horizon."

Zara was captivated as the story continued to reveal itself. After the hooded Nuff had removed the Key, the ground settled, and the beings began to return. There were dead and wounded lying around and some were freeing those trapped by the fallen debris, while the purple light intensified.

After coming to terms with the extent of the devastation, some Nuffs let out a muted cheer as they waited for the sun to rise, believing that the ritual had worked. But their excitement was short lived. Soon their expressions changed as the gravity of everything that had happened became clear.

Wisey explained. "The synergy of the stones and the InfiniKey stopped the planet's rotation at dawn. The sun was just rising and, since that time it has not climbed high in the sky above Quomos again. It just rolls along the horizon. Sometimes it hides completely for many zytags and we live in darkness; this is as high as it ever gets. But this was not all that happened here on that fateful night." He paused before continuing.

"Until that time, we had always been able to renew ourselves in an ongoing process of death and rebirth by stepping through the Gateway to the Wellspring of Everlasting Energy. After this ritual, it sealed itself shut and now many souls are trapped on Quomos unable to pass through to the other side."

Zara shuddered again as she saw the ghost-like disembodied souls of those who had been crushed, floating above the site with agonized expressions, searching desperately for the opening. She wanted to run over to the Gateway to see if she could pull it open, but there was a force holding her back. She struggled against it, but after a few minutes knew she had to surrender. This was not what she was here to do.

Zara turned around just in time to see the StoneKeepers reclaim their staffs. Only now, they were no longer vibrant with energy. The vines were dried and stiff; the flames didn't flicker; the wave was frozen and the stars didn't shimmer. All that remained was a very faint glow emanating from each of the magnificent stones. The four StoneKeepers moved into the middle of the diamond where the body of the fifth Nuff lay lifeless and face down in the dust. To save the Nuffs from annihilation, he had made the ultimate sacrifice. They stood over him honoring the courageous act that had likely protected their lineage. Then with great respect, the WaterWhisperer bent down to retrieve the Key that was lying beside him.

Staring at the sorrowful scene in front of her, Zara took a deep breath, hardly believing her eyes as he held it up for the others to see. Only half of the InfiniKey remained. It no longer looked like the symbol of infinity but more like the number three; or turned around the other way, the letter ε. It was the mark that was on each of the Nuff's chests and…exactly the same as Grandma Elizabeth's pendant!

Zara quickly reached up to check that it was still hanging under her tee shirt. It was, and she only breathed out again, once she had found it was safe. Seconds later, she was back with the others, hoping that no one had noticed her trembling hand as she fumbled around.

Seemingly unaware, Wisey continued with the final part of the story, "Once they had come to terms with what had happened, some wanted to try the ceremony again, but we only had half of the Key. Different clan chiefs have gathered since then, but nothing could be done."

He scratched his ear and tugged on the tuft of fur under his chin. He had something very important to say. "You see, not too long after the collapse of the temple, the four StoneKeepers disappeared. Since then, we've been on many missions and travelled the Galaxy far and wide but our search has led us nowhere. We cannot grow strong again until they are back with us for they help us to fully feel our feelings. SaddyNuff, BaddyNuff, MaddyNuff, and DarkyNuff are vital to our way of life; without them, there can be no peace for us or for our planet. Worse still is that when they are separated from the rest of us as well as each other, they become the extreme of what they feel. Saddy is filled with sorrow, Baddy becomes overcome with fear, Maddy's anger turns to rage, and Darky expresses all things shadowy."

Zak was listening but a little confused. "But why would you want all that feeling stuff, aren't you better off without them." He'd been struggling a bit with the thought of Zara moving to London and didn't like how he felt, so he had tucked it all safely away.

"If we deny any part of what we are as Nuffs, then we can never be happy. We will always be missing something and nothing will ever be enough, so we must bring them back. We think that Yezzadar knows where they are, but he holds a deep hatred towards us and is a powerful adversary."

"Did the stones disappear with them?" Zara asked, with a little tremor in her voice that made Zak look at her sideways.

"Yes, and that is why our enervisors don't shine as brightly anymore and we have lost much of our elemental power. We have to wear our safe-suits, these cloaks, to protect us. The shame of what we did, led us to feel unworthy of the trust that was placed in us by the Great Mystics. So, we gave the remaining half of the InfiniKey to a visiting X-IT. It has been passed down through many generations on Earth, and Elizabeth has been its guardian for zytags; that is until now."

Zak was intrigued. "So StrongyNuff wants to go to Yezzadar's planet, find Zara's grandma, get the Key, and try the experiment again?"

Cooly replied, "Yes, but it's too dangerous. Yezzadar has an army that would be hard to overcome. If we do go to Scartuss, get the Key and hold another ritual, without the other half and the StoneKeepers, we could be in a much worse place. For deca-zytags, we have learnt to live in this purple dawn, after all, it's not completely dark. So, if you two go back to Earth, Strongy will relax and then we can get things sorted."

Zara wasn't at all happy with this suggestion.

"And, what about Grandma, you don't really think we will leave without her, do you?"

"Okay, but if Yezzadar has kidnapped her you may be risking your own lives by staying here."

Zara put her hand up to her chest and felt a surge of confidence.

"I'm not going home until we find her, whatever that takes."

CoolyNuff shrugged his shoulders while Wisey had a knowing look on his face as if he knew something that was unknowable to other Nuffs.

As the rest of the small party began walking towards the path, Zara turned one more time to look at the mountainside and found herself drawn back into the other reality. As she glanced around, she was blown away by what she saw. On one side of the fallen temple, there was a massive army of large silver cat-like animals, the Agapanterrans led by their Queen, Sylvameena. They were poised to attack an equally large army of huge golden bird-like creatures, on the other side, commanded by Aigledor Sovereign Ruler of the Auriandrons. In the middle, standing in front of the Gateway, Zara saw herself holding Grandma Elizabeth's pendant high above her head.

She looked around at those gathered there and caught sight of Zak with WiseyNuff, but her vision was limited. Hard as she searched with her eyes, she couldn't see her grandmother. Zara gasped loudly and brought herself back through the veil. She desperately wanted to check it out with Wisey, but he'd gone with the others back to the city. Much as she would have liked to follow them, she felt compelled to return one last time; but whatever was there a moment earlier, was gone. She willed it to open up again but nothing happened. All that was left was a wall of rock with a series of static symbols and drawings. *Was it just my imagination? Maybe this is Grandma's secret that she wanted to tell me? If only I could find her, she would know what was happening. I have to ask WiseyNuff about Aigledor and Sylvameena...*

Her thoughts were interrupted when a stone fell to the ground from a small outcropping above her head. She spun around and saw something dart behind a rock. It was charcoal silver and it was very large. She froze. Seconds later, she heard the flapping of giant-sized wings and the screeching of a bird followed almost immediately by the roar of a big cat. To Zara, it was a familiar sound. She'd heard it in the graveyard at Elizabeth's funeral.

The young adventurer felt anxious and confused. Her senses had been bombarded with so many different sights and sounds she decided not to linger longer, and so legged it to catch up with the others. She was now running as quickly as she could, across the rocky terrain, to rejoin them as they made their way down the mountain. Zara was shaken up, wondering if she'd taken one risk too many. Upon reaching Zak, she got as close as she could, hoping to feel a little safer. He was busy talking to CoolyNuff, so she stayed quietly by his side as they walked on.

Zak was animated. "Can't wait to meet this Yezzadar character he sounds like a reeeal baaad guy. Now at least I kinda know why we're here, maybe we can give him what he deserves."

What he didn't know, and neither did anyone there, was that a sinister presence had been watching every move they'd made. It had heard every word they'd spoken almost from the first moment the two X-ITs landed on Quomos. If Zak had known this, his mood might have been quite different.

Chapter Ten

"Get out of my way, spikemonkey!" It was Yezzadar shouting at a Tussite as he kicked it across the floor of his headquarters. The little porcupine-looking creature was just busying itself, but it made the mistake of getting too close and became an easy target for the mean and mechanistic-minded recluse. He had been watching, with great interest, all that had taken place at the Wellspring. He was able to see everything from the comfort of his home planet, Scartuss, in the notorious Sedah's Belt on the dark side of the moons.

Yezzadar was a gross-looking being. His four eyes protruded from a face that was angry and cold. The upper ones were larger and a yellowy color while the lower ones were brown. They were more like normal eyes although the part that should have been white was bloodshot, and the pupils seemed to dart around in a strange way. A greyish scaly skin covered his face and he had no hair to speak of, just two odd-shaped lumps on either side of his head.

He was dressed in an armored robe that stretched almost to the ground and was made out of a metallic substance. It had giant thorns all over it. The boots he was wearing were black, shiny, and heavy-looking, making him seem taller than he really was. A thick silver-like chain hung around his neck supporting a huge triangular medallion suspended from a silver ring. It carried the portrait of a creature that brought a deep and ancient dread to the hearts of the furry beings from Quomos—a steely black beetle.

Yezzadar knew that there was very little that really scared the Nuffs, but they had never overcome their fear of these six-legged bugs. So, for zytags, he had been building a huge army of mechanical beetle-like robots known as the Terrortribes. He had experimented with them on less-inhabited planets, and talk of their weaponry had spread throughout the galaxy.

The grey-faced being had watched everything that had been going on, almost from the moment that Zak and Zara had arrived on The Purple Planet. He saw the meeting at the Universal Hall with StrongyNuff and the others. He cackled as the youngsters from Earth tried to eat the Quomethean food. And...he had just witnessed the entire storytelling at the Wellspring.

He was feeling smug as he sat in his control room spying on all that was happening on Quomos. Like WiseyNuff, he knew there was a lot more to the arrival of the X-ITs. After all, he had been one of the main architects in making it happen; he just didn't think they'd get here so quickly. Now, he had to make sure that the search for Grandma Elizabeth and the missing StoneKeepers would take them on a wild goose chase, so he could turn his plans into reality. Yezzadar knew he had to do everything he could to stop the Nuffs from saving Quomos, whatever the cost and the consequence. He had to prove his superiority and implement his fantastic strategy.

After all, he had worked hard to build these battalions of stylish beetles, which were kept in several large hangars not far from his headquarters. There were now thousands of them and soon he would finish the development of a chip that would allow a new level of cleverness. His coleoptera-technology would permit each robot to clone itself at the push of a switch, which only he controlled.

There were several prototypes of these computerized creatures designed to master all the elements, but the ones already in production were less than five feet tall. They had three antennae sticking out of their very small heads that allowed them to receive instructions.

Yezzadar had wanted them to be bigger but he couldn't stabilize them above this height. They stood upright on two of their six legs, which had heavy trotter-shaped feet to keep them steady. The other four legs were fancy weapons. One of these was a GuppaGun that spewed out an oil-like substance that paralyzed the enemy. A single drop on fur or flesh, of this vile smelling stuff, immobilized the victim, penetrating deep into the central nervous system.

The mechanical wizard was proud of himself and of what he'd achieved. There was no way that he was going to allow the Nuffs to regain their power. Not now. He had come too far and his plan was almost complete. Yes, there were some minor corrections that still had to be made to the Terrortribes operational programme, but with fear on his side, he was confident he would succeed. All he needed to do was to be sure that his spy remained undetected for as long as possible.

As Yezzadar gazed out across the dark sprawling landscape of Scartuss, a trickle of green saliva dribbled out of his open mouth. In the distance, he could see a glimmer of soft warm light coming from a small building. It made him smile. It was like a single diamond in a field of icy black coal. The thought of what it contained was the only thing that brought him any sense of peace. *One day,* he thought to himself, *I will be able to give her everything and then she will love me again.*

The surface of the planet was rough with very little life of any kind, only a few types of cactus-shaped plants that thrived without sunlight. Darting across his vision he could see the planet's other main residents known as the Scartusians. They were long, dark, wisp-like creatures that moved above the ground with great urgency. There were thousands of them living here, and Yezzadar had an unspoken agreement with them—*we won't mess with you if you don't mess with us.*

So far, it had worked well and he had no wish to do anything to upset them. Soon after his arrival on this dark and stark planet, he'd seen them swoop down and devour a hostile visitor in less than two seconds, like piranhas stripping the carcass of a cow.

For a moment, he was distracted by the distant glow as he thought of her, but then he pulled himself together and returned to focus on the task-at-hand. He twisted around and looked again, with all four eyes, at the main screen in the darkened control room. There wasn't much light because he'd been in the dark so long, he didn't need it.

Scurrying across the floor was a cluster of the only other living beings on Scartuss, the Tussites. They had always worked with Yezzadar, not because they liked him but because they enjoyed being busy. Tussites were round-bodied with dangerously long quills. Their dark brown spikes were the source of the oil-like venom used in the guns named after this noxious stuff—guppa. These creatures had small flesh-colored faces with eyes that glowed in the dark. They walked on their two hind legs most of the time but were just as comfortable on all fours.

Yezzadar watched the screen closely as the small group on Quomos climbed down the mountain path after their time at the Wellspring. He was looking forward to watching the preparations for their trip to Scartuss; it would provide him with more entertainment as they practiced their moves.

Chapter Eleven

CoolyNuff escorted Zara and Zak to a domad to get some sleep and some much needed time on their own. Despite not being able to tell whether it was day or night, there seemed to be a definite rhythm to life on the Purple Planet. Once inside, the X-ITs climbed onto the soft, round mattresses that looked like giant white marshmallows with spongy pillows. It was quiet in the domad; the air smelled clean and fresh with a hint of lavender, which reminded them of Grandma Elizabeth's cottage. Everything was happening so fast, it was the perfect opportunity for them to talk. They hadn't had time alone since their ride on the dodon.

"Zar, I've been feeling a little weird almost since we landed here. Sometimes it's as if there is this like...er...thing wriggling around in my head," Zak said, sounding a little vulnerable.

"Ugh, that sounds horrible...are you sure?"

"Well, it's like there's this buzz that every now and again gets so intense that it hurts. It's like something is crawling in my brain and when I..."

He suddenly paused mid-sentence.

"Wait!" He leant forward listening for something. "It's gone. It's just stopped!"

Zak looked surprised as if he was waiting for it to come back. He was almost straining himself to hear it. Then a smile crossed his face as he realized that it just wasn't there anymore—at least for now.

"So that's eNuff from me." He laughed. "Get it?"

Zara looked at him, she didn't find it funny. He decided to change his approach.

"Okay, Zar, so tell me what's up?"

Zara's voice was a little more hesitant than usual.

"Well, like it's a lot to take in, and we still don't know where Grandma is. Everyone seems nice, but sometimes I feel it's just one of those dreams. There's a part of me that's like pretending it isn't real, and if it gets too scary all I need to do is wake myself up."

Zak wasn't used to her being this way and didn't know what to say. Being more down to earth, he just said it how he saw it.

"It's very real and it could be dangerous. I'm not too sure I like the sound of this Yezzadar dude or his Terrortribes."

He paused as if he was waiting for something, and when it didn't happen he carried on.

"StrongyNuff wants to get the planet fixed, and he thinks we can help them."

"So do I." She was clearer now.

"It's gonna be risky."

"Yeah, I know, but that's okay. In a weird way, this is the best thing that could've happened. We're on an adventure just like the ones Grandma told us about."

Zara sighed and with all the hesitation now gone from her voice, added, "We will find her Zak and she'll be really proud of us!"

She suddenly remembered something.

"Zak, I saw Aigledor and Sylvameena again."

"Whaaat? Where? When?"

"When you left the Wellspring."

"C'mon, someone else would have seen them?"

"I know this may sound weird but I saw them twice. I think…er…one of the times might have been about the future. They both had these huge armies and we were standing in the middle in between them."

"Yikes, so what happened?" He was pretending to be interested.

"I came back to the mountainside."

"Huh?" He didn't ask from where. "And the second time…"

"Just after you left, I…um…saw them fighting like they did in the graveyard, they were behind those big rocks above where we were standing."

"Did you actually see them?"

"Well…er…sort of but not exactly…they were mostly behind the rocks."

Zak didn't know what to make of what she was saying. It sounded more like the game again. He decided to brush it off. "Well, next time, tell me right away. I'm wiped, let's get some sleep."

Back on Scartuss, Yezzadar pushed one of the hundreds of buttons on the console in front of him and turned his back on the big blank screen. He left the control tower, followed by a trail of Tussites. He wanted to visit the hangars to make sure his beloved Terrortribes were turned up to max potency.

Chapter Twelve

The X-ITs woke up at exactly the same moment. Zara was full on.

"Zak, I saw Grandma. She was with that guy again in a dark place and there were some weird-looking creatures with spikes. She was trying to tell me something. I could hear her, but she couldn't hear me...although I swear she looked straight at me."

Zak was about to reply when a chill ran through him that made the hairs on the back of his neck stand up. He didn't know what it was but was sure there was someone else in the domad that he couldn't see. He looked across at Zara and was about to ask her if she'd felt the same thing when suddenly the round door to their sleeping quarters opened upwards. Wisey was standing in the doorway, with three other Nuffs. One was Weeze or WeirdyNuff, and the other two they hadn't met before.

"Will you join us? We have more to show you," Wisey said with a twinkle in his eye.

Zara couldn't hold herself back.

"Wisey, I had a dream. In it, Grandma was on this dark planet with a horrible-looking man...er...creature-like thing. They were talking and..."

"Ah!" said Wisey. "There are dreams and then...there are dreams. Some dreams are clutter clearing, but others are a lot more than that."

Zara liked what he was saying.

"You had a lucid dream. It's like we are awake in another world at the same time as we're asleep in bed. These are cosmic journeys and teach us a lot about the bigger universe. You see the soul never sleeps it..."

She interrupted, "Oh yes, that's totally real. I have these kinds of dreams all the time and this was definitely one of them."

Zara knew he understood. "I'm sure she's alive."

"Of that, there is no doubt." He smiled as he tugged on the fur on his chin. "We just have to find where she is."

Zara felt happy, she was starting to trust herself. Zak's uneasy feeling passed quickly, although the stuff in his head a moment earlier, had left him spooked.

"Follow us and we'll give you some instruction. We have to get ready for the mission, but first, this is BrightyNuff, she will come with us."

The X-ITs introduced themselves.

She bowed her head then, lifting her eyes, gazed directly at the two visitors from Earth as if she was looking right into them. Like Smarty, BrightyNuff had silver and white fur with some cool markings. Her enervisor was red, so she was a FireHerder, and a member of StrongyNuff's clan. She was sparky and upbeat. Zara liked her right away.

Wisey continued, "And...this is ClearyNuff, she can see things others cannot see. She is a seer and a visionary."

The X-ITs saw immediately that she was an AirSpinner because the diamond in her forehead was yellow. Her face was more like that of a small cat, and she smiled and nodded when introduced.

The two of them were taken through a covered hallway made of the same spongy as stuff that was in their domad. It was shiny and white and though it looked very slippery—it wasn't.

After a few minutes, they found themselves in a strange dome-shaped building full of what looked like moving maps, but with nothing on them other than a few grey lines. The walls and ceilings were all painted white and in the background, was a purring sound that sounded like some kind of music.

As they entered, Brighty gave them each a futuristic-looking sweatband with a crystal in the middle. She helped them to place it over their heads with the crystal in the middle of their brows.

"These are your enervisors." Wisey smiled. "Now you'll be able to see things more as we do, but you must close your eyes."

At first, they thought this was a little strange, after all, how could you possibly see things with your eyes closed! But as they shut them, the walls came to life with all sorts of pictures and images like a gigantic 3D movie screen. They were in a virtual world. The room was alive with scenes, sensations, sounds, and smells from different realities. It was as if they were inside a vast holographic universe and nothing like they'd ever seen before.

"Wow, this is wicked!" Zak said a little louder than he meant to.

WiseyNuff was smiling. "We call this the MetaDome. In here, we have access to all different realities. It sits on an energy vortex that links us directly into the InfiGrid, an electromagnetic field that contains an infinite source of vibrational energies."

"It's incredible. I'm blown away it is sooooo amazing," Zara blurted out.

SmartyNuff spoke next, "We believe that all beings throughout the whole Universe are part of one big family. Look carefully, and you will see currents of energy connecting all of us together. They are very delicate, like a web of the finest gossamer threads. You can't normally see them, but they are always there."

Zak and Zara screwed up their faces with their eyes still tightly closed. At first, they couldn't see them. Then after a few moments, they saw what looked like shimmering threads of light, all over the place, connecting everyone. They were beautiful and reminded them of how sometimes, in the early morning dew on a sunny day, all the blades of grass appear to be connected by rainbow-colored spiders' webs.

"Do you see like this all the time?"

"After a while, you learn to focus on some parts and not others, so your senses don't get overloaded," Brighty answered. "Now open your eyes."

As they did, everything faded. Zak quickly closed his again just to check it was all still there.

The X-ITs were impressed and wanted to find out more about the world of Nuffs.

WiseyNuff was pleased with their reaction. "This is only one of the special powers you have. Brighty will teach you how to read energy fields."

Zak was curious. "Yeah but like how does this stuff really work, and can we...er...use it back home?"

"You've had super sensory abilities or SUSAs ever since you were born, but only a few schools teach you how to use them. There's a whole world of magic and mystery when you fire up the power of imagination."

Wisey described how X-ITs possessed certain gifts of awareness that let them use their senses in ways that other humans did not. He talked about how on Earth most people work with only five senses and don't even know that they have more. He said that some of them are scared to go beyond the basic ones because they defy logic.

"As X-ITs, you are multi-sensory humans."

Zara didn't understand everything he said, but she knew that she had sometimes seen things differently from her friends. She could often tell what was going to happen in the future, especially when she and Zak were together.

"It is time for you to sharpen your SUSAs so that you can fulfil your roles as Extraordinary Interdimensional Travelers."

Zara was sure that they were already improving as she closed her eyes again and looked through the enervisor. She wanted to find out more about what it meant to be X-ITs and hoped deep down that her grandmother was going to be there to help them.

ClearyNuff, who had disappeared for a bit came back with something, that looked like cookies and milk, knowing the X-ITs would be hungry. They tasted strange, like a blend of butterscotch and cheese. It didn't matter; Zara and Zak scoffed the lot. It had been a long time since the grey peas.

"So run it by me again, why are we here?" Zak still wasn't sure and wanted a rational explanation.

"Well, the reason is twofold," Wisey said clearly. "The first is that we need you to help us find our missing StoneKeepers. Three of them disappeared during the fall of the purple haze, and the fourth one has not been seen since the night of the ritual."

"And the second reason?"

Turning to look at Zara, Brighty answered, "You are Elizabeth's kin and it is part of your destiny. She holds the Key to the righting of this ancient wrong and has been preparing you for this moment all your lives."

Wisey also glanced over at Zara but knew that to say more would be of no value at this time.

Could he know I have the Key with me, she thought to herself, *and if he does, why doesn't he say something?*

BrightyNuff went on. "We thought we would have enough energy reserves to keep us going until the time was right for the Key's return, then we could take off our cloaks and reclaim our power. But since we've been unable to find the StoneKeepers, we don't have the energy we need to regenerate. All our supplies are running low. The absence of sunlight has taken its toll on us."

"Huh! So, you wear your cloaks as safe-suits to prove you are strong enough, or bright enough, or wise enough. Get it, Zar, they're the Nuffs!"

"Zaaaaak…"

Before she could say anything, Wisey looked across at them. "Without our safe-suits, we feel less powerful. There are some, as you have learnt, who would prefer to stay this way, within the safety of the known even though it doesn't bring them joy. They fear change and would rather live a secure and predictable life, where every tomorrow is like yesterday."

He turned to Brighty. "Others, like StrongyNuff, have fire in their hearts and believe that this is the time when we can transform life on Quomos, reclaim our full power, and bring renewal to our planet."

Then the wise Nuff paused thoughtfully for a moment.

"What is in one of us is in us all. Each being holds a unique piece of the Universal jigsaw puzzle that makes up the whole. Some will act and others will wait, but all choose the role they play whether they know it or not. It is only by having the courage to live true to our hearts, that we will find peace. Once we reunite with the missing StoneKeepers and stay in tune with the rhythm of life, we will find harmony again."

Zara sort of understood what he was saying because she had heard her grandma speak in these ways. "Of course we will help, we have always wanted to have these kinds of adventures."

Zak was a little more hesitant. "Well, umm, Zara has, but I guess I'm here too and there is some cool stuff going down. So yeah, I'm in…for what it's worth. I'm still not sure about all this harmony stuff though!"

Chapter Thirteen

They left the MetaDome and walked down a small hill to where the ground was much flatter. In front of them, Zak and Zara could see a big archway that looked like a giant chicken wishbone. It was huge, standing over 30 feet high. The X-ITs were curious to know what kind of bird it came from.

The answer was fast in coming. Just as they walked into the Dodons' den, they were faced with an even bigger version of the bird they'd flown in on. It landed only a few feet in front of them. At first glance, Zara counted a dozen and they were at least the size of a jumbo jet.

"Let's take you to meet Captain Bushawoo, he's the leader of the SuperDodons." BrightyNuff had taken the lead.

Despite their size, the feathered giants waddled in a dignified way once they had folded all four wings—they had two on either side. The *Super* version of this species must have been at least twice as big as the two-winged bird that had brought them to the city. Zak couldn't help wondering what their nests and eggs must look like.

He turned to Zara. "Can't see them perching on the branch of a tree back home, can you?"

She smiled and dug him in the ribs with her elbow. "Silly!"

Captain Bushawoo greeted them in a funny-sounding language, which he quickly changed so that the visitors could understand. He was kindly-looking and had clearly experienced a lot. His beak had quite a few scratches on it, and some of his red and yellow tail feathers were missing. Despite all of this, Zara couldn't help thinking that he was a fine-looking old bird and wanted to hear about his adventures.

"Are you here to get ready for the mission to Scartuss?" Captain Bushawoo asked knowingly, looking at BrightyNuff.

She answered, "Yes, we want our Earth friends to learn more about what they can expect. We need to prepare them for the journey."

"Well then, let's take them to the redwing area so we can get a better handle on what equipment everyone will need for the trip."

With that, Captain Bushawoo morphed into a rather sleek carrier that hovered above the ground with some kind of engine on his back end. Zak and Zara stood mesmerized as they watched the big bird transform itself. Then they just looked at each other and laughed. The SuperDodon muttered something and they all got in.

The Dodons' den was huge and far more than just a place for these feathered giants to hang out. As they moved through it, they could see a load of odd-looking beings going in and out of different domed buildings.

The bright-eyed Nuff explained in more detail. "This whole area is a sort of massive training camp for all kinds of activity. Ever since we became known in the Galaxy as *The Warriors of the Purple Planet*, we have worked hard to develop

71

skills and metaphysical methodologies that help us to protect others from harm. This has given us abundant strength and finesse on all levels, but nothing like we could have if we can bring home the missing StoneKeepers."

She went on. "In each of the colored domads, we work on different kinds of projects, products, and prototypes. In the orange one, they are developing advanced modes of transport, but they are all transmorphations. They'll be designing some morphing maps to help the SuperDodons change into some new forms of carriers."

She paused and turned to look on the other side of the pathway.

"They won't be like those mechanical pieces of junk over there." Brighty pointed to what looked to the X-ITs to be ultra modern spaceships and sleek all-terrain vehicles. But they were all covered in dried vines and dust.

Zak didn't understand. "They look really kinda futuristic. Why are you leaving them to rot?"

"We're trying to live without many of these machines, they're unnecessary."

Zak was shocked.

The FireHerder gave her reasons. "If the AirSpinners had their way, it would be machine mania. Luckily, we have strong leaders in the other clans who want us to live more organically, without all that stuff. All we need to do is supplement our natural abilities with computers and robots. We don't need weapons. "

ClearyNuff, who didn't react to Brighty's comments about AirSpinners, took over describing the tour. "That green domad houses all the research and development work on gadgets."

Zak's eyes lit up. "It would be cool to take a look in there." He was keen to test his tech know how, and at the same time was feeling a little unsure as to whether he could really make a difference.

They pulled up nearby and stepped out of Captain Bushawoo who immediately returned to being himself! He had always found transmorphing to be fun, though he had to admit that it wasn't as comfortable anymore. He was getting a little creaky in places, and his feathers took a while to settle down after these experiences.

Cleary was delighted by Zak's response. "Well, as soon as we've got you familiar with the equipment for Scartuss, you can help us with the P44Ti."

Before Zak had a chance to ask anything, she answered, "That's the prototype we've been developing to help us annihilate the Terrortribes."

Zak's eyes lit up again!

Zara, meanwhile, was with Weeze when they stepped inside the green domad. It was made of some kind of leafy membrane and was far bigger than it looked from the outside. Now that she was more comfortable with her super sensory abilities, Zara used them to see how it had looked before the decay crept in. It was very bright with large circular platforms like giant DVD's hinged onto the walls of the building at different heights. There were walkways that appeared when needed, linking the disks to each other, and Zara thought that it was such a great use of space.

All over the walls, she could see *liquid art*. It was constantly changing shape and color, and was created from some kind of crystalline substance. Some of the pictures were very abstract and others resembled places and things. Nothing lasted for very long before changing shape again. Unknown to her, the pictures were collages of the collective thought forms of all those in the domad!

Once again, there was a mixture of beings, some they hadn't seen before. Most of them were staring right back at Zak and Zara.

WeirdyNuff or Weeze helped them out. "Those tall ones are the Cratts. They are complex machines, although their language programme is pretty simple." He pointed his long third finger. "The one over there will tell you the purpose of the different equipment we are taking to Scartuss."

After making some introductions, a lanky sand-colored machine, with very long legs, a short body, and a small head covered in stylish antennae, led them over to a bench, which like everything else, was alive. The Cratt sounded a bit like he was talking inside a pipe as he explained what they were looking at. He pointed to a rather classy backpack and began describing how it worked.

Weeze put one on. "When we go on a mission, we take one of these full of *NuffStuff*. It holds everything we need and more than you think." He smiled his weird and crooked smile.

The Cratt continued by picking up some wristbands made of amethyst crystals like the ones inside Grandma Elizabeth's geodes. "These are called confidometers, and depending on how many of the crystals light up, you can measure the level of confidence of a being." He said, looking at the purple stones.

They were nice-looking, and although Zara wanted to try one on, she was afraid it might show that she was feeling nervous. So instead, Brighty took hold of it and placed it on her own wrist. It lit up like a set of fairy lights!

"See, that's how it works," she said, feeling happy that all of the crystals were glowing.

"Yes, that's why they call you BrightyNuff!" Weeze couldn't resist.

Next, the Cratt began to describe a piece of equipment a bit like a flowery torch or flashlight. It was gold with bright yellow lightning bolts up the stem, with a long stalk.

"This is an Aurabooster. It gives strength to those who have lost confidence and need some energy to get back to normal."

Turning to Weeze and with his agreement, the Cratt pointed it towards him and a beam of golden light spurted out of the Aurabooster. For a moment, there was a halo all around WeirdyNuff, causing him to grin broadly.

"Can you give me a blast too please?" Zara asked hopefully.

Weeze picked up a second Aurabooster and pointed it at the X-ITs. An oval-shaped light formed around their bodies giving them a real buzz.

SmartyNuff explained what was happening. "Around every living being, there's an egg-shaped field of light. You can see it through your enervisors. Some beings have bigger ones than others. Most of the Nuffs have energy fields that reach as far as their outstretched arms in all directions. Humans are almost the same."

Weeze took over. "When the life force is drained, these fields become much smaller and thinner. Some even have big holes in them making us vulnerable to shadow forces. Auraboosters give back some of what's lost, so the darkness doesn't take us over."

"I could do with one of those at school," Zara said half-jokingly.

"Yeah, me too..." Zak added.

"You won't need these by the time you're finished here. You'll see," Weeze said reassuringly.

The X-ITs were both feeling revitalized as the Cratt began describing the other gadgets that would be in the backpacks.

Zak wanted to test everything.

"There'll be a training session on how to use all this before leaving for Scartuss."

Zak was clearly impressed by the technology so far and looked at Zara with a big grin.

The Cratt had done a great job of explaining the gadgets and was now over with some other Cratts, doing what Cratts do, and no doubt sharing what it was like to talk with the humans!

The X-ITs and their hosts went back outside, and in the distance saw that there were a number of other Nuffs being instructed in different activities. As they got nearer, they could see that they were actually fighting with one another. They recognised CoolyNuff immediately. He was sizing up SmartyNuff ready to attack. Then he lunged at her but she leant to one side, squatted down, and easily hurled him over her shoulder.

"No, no. NO!" Strongy was doing the instructing.

"How many times do I have to tell you to go in low so they can't use your momentum against you?"

Cooly nodded as Smarty helped him to his feet and they tried the manoeuver again from the beginning. But he did the same thing a second time and Zara felt bad for the fallen Nuff.

"He seems hopeless at this." Zak was comparing it to his video games, where just by flicking the controls you could get the players to perform the way you wanted.

Zara disagreed. "No, he's not, Strongy will show him how to do it you wait and see."

She was confident that CoolyNuff would learn the moves. She didn't know that this kind of combat was not the strength of the WaterWhisperer. As she watched, she started playing with her pendant and thinking about her grandmother.

Leaning over towards her, Zak whispered, "Do you really think it's part of the InfiniKey?"

Zara was shocked.

"When did you work that out?"

"When we were up at the Wellspring and your voice wobbled."

"Oh, but you didn't say anything."

"I'm not as geeky as you think I am, Zar."

She felt a bit bad that she hadn't told him. "It could be the half that was left after the ritual. The one that was given to a passing X-IT."

"Shouldn't we tell one of them?"

"Do you think they'd be as eager to rescue Grandma if they knew?"

Zak didn't answer he was thinking about what Zara had just said, and he was watching intently as Cooly faced off with Smarty again.

The leader of the WaterWhisperers lunged at his counterpart from the AirSpinner clan, this time staying low, but she ducked down just as she'd done the time before. The result was painful for both of them; Cooly's head struck Smarty's knee, and in unison, they yelped in pain. Zara winced but StrongyNuff growled with exasperation. He tried hard not to show his frustration too much and calmed down once the fighters picked themselves up off the ground.

"Okay, alright, fine. Let's skip the next round and go on to the robots. We'll practice moves on a couple of the mock-ups of Yezzadar's Terrortribes."

Zak was ecstatic. Just the thought of seeing these things, was enough to really get his attention.

"So, you don't have weapons like we have on Earth?" Zak asked.

Strongy explained. "Well, in a way, yes. We are our weapons of choice. What you just saw is how we go about defeating our enemies."

"Huh, really?" Zak didn't sound too impressed.

"We don't use your kind of weapons and we don't need to kill our enemies. We prefer to use our skills to defeat our enemies. Cunning, illusion, and superior intuition are the best weapons—it's much more powerful this way."

Brighty quickly added, "And it's much more fun to outfox them and to see them defeated in ways where they don't really understand what happened—you wait and see." She laughed.

"The only exception," Smarty spoke a little more seriously, "is the P44Ti prototype. This is a grand-looking weapon but it won't harm a living being. We will show it to you, and you can help them to make it work, so we can all gain mastery over these robotic creatures."

Zak turned to Zara and spoke in a whisper, "All this other stuff about the InfiniKey is sorta okay, Zar, but now we're about to see the real deal."

She knew from this he wasn't going to say anything about her pendant and so she smiled at her friend. He was jazzed and wanted to get to grips with the P44Ti. He was even more excited at the thought of seeing Yezzadar's mechanical models.

With all that was happening, he didn't have a moment to think about what might be going on inside his head. In fact, he had completely forgotten about everything that had happened earlier.

Chapter Fourteen

Zak didn't have to wait long to get what he wanted. A few short steps away, there was another building that was a little different from the other domads; it was more rugged. When he stepped inside, his eyes lit up. As far as he was concerned, just this moment alone made the whole trip worthwhile. Hanging around on large virtual pictures, suspended above the ground were 360-degree images of what he could only imagine were Yezzadar's Terrortribes.

StrongyNuff confirmed what he was thinking. "What you see all around you are detailed drawings of the Terrortribes. We have been developing the prototype of a gadget to exterminate them for some time now."

Zak gazed at the portraits—they weren't very pretty, and their weapons were just as ugly, although from his point of view, kind of cool. Each illustration contained a mixture of words and equations. Some were side views and back views, while others were the full head-on version. You could see them from every angle.

There were other Nuffs in the workshop working alongside some Yobuns. Zara was glad that Yorazz, their leader, was somewhere else, as she didn't get a good feeling when he was around. In the middle of a large bench, lay a silver object that everyone was looking at. It was simple and sophisticated both at the same time.

Strongy beamed. "What you see here is the P44Ti—it is a beautiful piece of equipment that we have been working on for zytags."

It was clear to see that Brighty wasn't impressed.

They all walked to the bench. Strongy continued, "You can see the quality of this weapon. It is in a class of its own!"

Zak was hooked. "How does it work?"

"It sends out a vibrational sound wave that when properly focused, can interfere with the Terrortribes' guidance system, and stop it from working! It also packs quite a punch."

"Cool, let me take a closer look." The X-IT was really surprised by what he found. "Er...how weird I've been working on something a lot like this at home. I've called it a VibaZappa! This could...er...like do even more than what you say."

During the summer, Zak had made a smaller version that sent out a vibrational sound wave. He used it to destabilize a small mechanical army that he'd been building for the last couple of years. He was amazed at the coincidence.

Zak walked towards where the Terrortribes' portraits hung.

"Um...let's look at these drawings. Is the back of the beetle curved?"

"Yes," Strongy replied.

"How stable are they on their...er...two feet?"

"Well, we think there are some vulnerabilities, we just haven't found them." Strongy scratched behind his ear. "Let's just take a look, they're over here."

He took them to where there was a gauzy vine-like membrane covering something and pulled it back revealing several beetle-like robots lying face down. They all looked a little scuffed and battered.

Zak was awestruck. "Oh man, this is…er…well, like amazing…"

"We call this the *fight* simulator," Smarty added. "If you want to, you can test the P44Ti or what you call the VibaZappa, but first we need to practice some moves on the Terrortribe models."

Another EarthTamer, known as NottyNuff, had now caught up with the rest. He didn't look nearly as confident as the others as he joined Cooly, Smarty, and Strongy. The remaining two had returned to the MetaDome with Wisey.

Walking around the creatures, Strongy talked a little more about their creator's pride and joy. "Yezzadar fits these things with all sorts of different weapons. This one here is a GuppaGun—the quills it shoots contain a poison that on contact affects the whole nervous system and you are as good as toast unless we find the antidote. This arm is a saw."

Just as he finished his sentence, Smarty jumped back. "Hey, one of them moved."

Strongy dismissed it. "Impossible!"

Zak came to her defense and stepped closer. "I saw it too, but no big deal, most likely static in one of the circuits."

"Are you saying you know how these things work?" Strongy was curious.

"Well, not exactly but how hard could it be to figure out for someone who got to the 15th level of *Fatal Fantasy* before it was even halfway out of the box?"

Strongy cocked his head, thoroughly confused by what Zak had said, and brushed it off. He wanted to get the battle started. So, he went over to check the controls while the others took another look at the P44Ti.

Zak turned around and was surprised when he saw the robots standing in front of him. They were bigger than he thought and he took a step backwards when they appeared so life-like. They were certainly ugly, and their weaponry was threatening enough.

"We're ready, Zak. Over there, can you work the controls?"

"Sure, you bet!"

He moved to the panel with lots of flashing lights, while the three Nuffs crouched down ready to attack.

"What about the weapon?" Zak asked.

"What weapon?" It was Strongy.

"The one we were just looking at. The P44Ti."

"That? It's for Yobuns. Nuffs don't need it. Remember what I said? We're our weapons of choice."

"You're kidd…Aaaaah!" Zak grabbed hold of his head. Zara and Strongy ran over to him.

"Are you all right?" they asked with concern.

"Yeah, yeah, it's just a little headache, it comes and goes."

Zara took his hand. "Are you sure? You don't get headaches!"

Zak nodded. "I'm good, and I don't want to miss this."

StrongyNuff was pleased. "Yeah he's fine, let's get back to the fight. Are you ready Zak?"

He nodded and hit some switches.

Yezzadar's Terrortribes came to life. One of them lurched at Smarty, and she rolled away from it, taunting it at the same time. Then it lunged at her again. Her plan was to make sure the beetle-like robots crashed into each other. Another one of them shot some flames at Strongy but he dodged the initial discharges. Then the blasts kept coming closer together and the X-ITs were convinced he was going to get hit. But, he held up his paws and moved the flames away from him, causing them to make a sharp turn and shoot onto the back of the robot bearing down on NottyNuff. The fiery tongues fried it, and it came to a dead stop.

Zak's jaw fell open.

"How did he do that thing with his hands…er…his paws?"

Zara answered, "He's a FireHerder, that's how."

"A what?"

"A FireHerder. See how their enervisors are different colors. Well, not only do they help them see things, it shows you which one of the elements they have mastery of; fire, earth, air or water. His is red, which makes Strongy a FireHerder, so he can play with fire. Don't you remember Grandma told us about them?"

"Oh, she did…yeah, yeah, of course."

Smarty was busily engaged with another robot that was spewing thick clouds of grey gas at her. With tai chi-like movements, she sent the gas back into its face, blinding it and causing it to crash into the wall.

"Yes!" Zak shouted.

"Smarty's an AirSpinner, see?" Zara pointed out to her friend.

NottyNuff was on his way over to congratulate her on her moves, but just as he got there, he let out an agonizing scream. He'd been hit in the back of the leg by a dart from a GuppaGun. He collapsed, writhing in pain, and then just lay there immobilized.

Strongy was shocked. "Huh? Is he just faking it? How can Notty be hurt, these are just mock-ups, shut 'em down, Zak."

The X-IT tried to do as he was told and hit the controls, but two of the remaining Terrortribes just kept on coming.

"Zak, I said shut 'em down, he isn't faking it."

"I can't. It's like there's a hidden programme in the controls. I can't override it." He tried again but with no response.

A third and fourth robot then started spewing acid as Smarty, Strongy and Cooly did incredible acrobatic moves to avoid the vitriol. With amazing teamwork, they pulled the wounded Nuff away from any further danger.

In desperation, Zak left the controls, grabbed the prototype weapon, and headed towards the four robots. Zara tried to stop him.

"Zak, what are you…"

Zak ignored her.

The P44Ti was a lot lighter than he had expected and was great to hold. *Nice,* he thought to himself, *it even feels warm*. He focused and then fired it. Immediately, a strange vibrational wave came out from the nozzle of the weapon. It hit one of the Terrortribes right in the centre of the chest causing it to fall onto its back with a loud crash. Strongy looked up and gave the X-IT an approving look.

Zak was on an adrenalin rush but it only lasted for a second before the sharp pain in his brain suddenly returned. This time it was the worst it had ever been. He winced and tried to shake it off determined to fire the weapon again. He lost his balance for a moment, getting it back just in time to see the three remaining mechanical beetles coming towards him.

The X-IT was struggling to stay upright, as the pain got worse. One of the Terrortribes lunged out at him with serrated pincers, while the other one began firing the GuppaGun. A dart flew out grazing Zak's arm and causing him to drop the weapon. It landed right at the feet of the other robot. Luckily, the venom didn't get him, but the dart hit a watching Yobun, who was paralyzed, instantly.

Ignoring the pain in his head and his arm, Zak dived to grab the fallen weapon. He rescued it seconds before the heavy foot of one of the robots crushed it.

Strongy yelled at him, "They're the real things. Zak, get out of the way!"

But he wasn't going to stop. Like action man in a movie, he rolled over and blasted another, leaving only two standing. He jumped to his feet, fighting against the pain in his brain and, facing the robot. Zak focused all his energy as he steadied himself, aimed the machine, and pulled the trigger. The same vibrational wave shot out, and the giant beetle toppled backwards, falling to the floor with a loud clunk.

The last one turned and struck out again, just catching Zak's sleeve and tearing his shirt. He let out a groan as the ache in his head nearly blinded him. He had to keep it together for one more moment and focus his aim on the single spot where he knew these mechanical monsters were vulnerable. It had worked with the first one, or was that just luck?

A second later, through a haze of pain, he fired again, but the creature turned to deflect the wave. Zak quickly got his sights lined up one last time and pressed the trigger. He watched as the final Terrortribe started to fall to the floor. This and a loud cheer were the last things he remembered before collapsing right alongside Notty, the comatosed Nuff.

Chapter Fifteen

Back on Scartuss, Yezzadar had returned to his control tower only to see several of his beloved creations staring out at him from the big screen. He was furious that Zak was holding the P44Ti and was aiming it at his precious Terrortribes.

"No, this can't be happening. My plan was perfect."

He ranted and raged, desperate to do something. He kicked a couple of hovering Tussites across the control room and did everything he could to distract Zak—but it was a difficult challenge. Zak was far from a willing victim.

"This boy's pain threshold is much higher than I had expected."

Yezzadar had tried to break Zak, but he wasn't winning.

Unknowingly, he helped him to find the exact point on the Terrortribes, where they were vulnerable. Just below the centre of their breast-plate, was the only spot on their armour clad bodies where if zapped, would cause them to lose balance. Once they fell on their backs, they were helpless to get up again. The last thing Yezzadar saw before the screen went blank was the ceiling of the building as the final Terrortribe tumbled to the floor. He had been watching everything through the eyes of the unknowing bearer of his hidden transmitter—Zak.

Meanwhile, on Quomos Strongy was shouting orders.

"Get me some transport…now."

He picked up the young human and carried him urgently to a waiting shuttle, then rushed him to the blue domad, the centre for medical emergencies. Once they'd established it wasn't guppa, the head surgeon knew exactly what to do, but it was a risky procedure and one that took a lot of concentration. First, he had to find the exact point where the brain-bug had lodged in Zak's head. Then he had to use a very fine instrument to remove it, without damaging the cerebral cortex. The operation was extremely delicate and required extraordinary precision, with the expert help of a couple of Cratts.

During the procedure, Zak felt himself float up into the corner of the hospital room and found he was looking down on himself. His body was lying motionless while the surgeon worked on his head. He saw the whole thing from above.

Wow, how can I be in two places at once? Never mind. This is wild. He flew out of the room to find Zara who was with Smarty, pacing up and down.

"Zak, Zak, are you okay…" she said, suddenly feeling his presence.

The petite Nuff reassured her that it wouldn't be much longer. Zak was smiling and was quite impressed by her concern. *Hmmm, she really does like me, I wonder if…*

The next thing he knew, he was back in the corner of the ceiling watching the rest of the operation from across the room. *I wonder what is going to happen when it's all over.*

He awoke with a jolt and felt a dull ache in his head. He reached up to find a patch of his hair had been shaven away. WiseyNuff and the surgeon were with him.

In the tray by the side of his bed, only inches from his face, was a long and skinny charcoal grey maggot wriggling around. He looked at it with disgust and tried to find something to crush it with, but the surgeon stopped him.

"You don't want to do that. This is what was causing your headache."

"Yuck, this? Howwww?"

"It was inside your skull."

Zak's eyes widened as the surgeon put the squirming maggot in a small clear container.

"It's a living creature but it's also a viewing device. It lets someone from a distant location look through *your* eyes."

Zak stared up at Wisey.

"Wwwhat happppened?" he asked, his voice slow and shaky. "I remember feeeeling this pppain when I was firing at the Terrortribes and then…"

"Well, somehow and at some point after you arrived here, you were implanted with this brain-bug. It starts out much smaller when it first penetrates the skull and allows the viewer to see the images you are seeing. It lives on grey matter and gets bigger and bigger. So the pain gets worse and worse."

He paused.

"There was a small hole, no bigger than a pinprick, on the side of your head next to your ear where it entered—all the surgeon had to do was to find out where it was lodged and go in and remove it. It's not the first time it's happened, but you weren't to know what it was."

"Bbbbut who put it there?"

"We don't know, but probably the same someone who replaced the robots, with the real thing."

The door opened and Zara ran up to the bed and gave Zak a big hug. "Are you all right? I can't believe you did that…"

"Well…er…"

StrongyNuff, who was now standing at the door behind Zara, interrupted Zak. "I can believe it. You fought those robots like you've been doing it forever."

"Actually, I have…"

"You have?" Strongy and Zara were surprised and blurted the question out in unison.

"Sort of, in video games."

"Well, whatever video games are, they prepared you well, and you are very skilled."

"I wish you could tell that to my mum."

Zara wasn't quite as impressed. "Zak, that wasn't one of your video games, you could have been killed."

He looked up at her and their eyes met for a moment. Then Zak felt uncomfortable and didn't know what to say, so broke the gaze.

"Did you see what they took out of my head?" He pointed to the brain bug in the container.

"Eeeeewwwww, how gross." She backed away as if he still had something wrong with him.

"Let me see that." Strongy scooped up the jar. "This little sucker is going to prove I was right."

Zak and Zara looked at him quizzically as he left the room with a big smile on his face.

Wisey wanted to know more. "When did you first experience the headaches?"

Zak thought for a while. "When we were at the meeting of the clans with Strongy and Cooly."

"That's what I thought," said Wisey. "So whoever it is, has been watching us all this time, and knows everything."

Zak started to apologize but Wisey stopped him. "Nothing happens without reason. And I am pleased with your bravery. In honor of your courage, we have named the new weapon the VibaZappa after your own discovery."

Zak beamed with delight and couldn't stop smiling, even though his head hurt like crazy. He turned to look at Zara. "How are the others doing?"

Wisey answered, "Not very well. We are testing the substance from the darts to find its chemical composition. We know that it affects the central nervous system but we don't have an antidote yet."

There was something else troubling the wise old Nuff. Someone had replaced the simulated models with the real thing. He had lots of questions spinning around. *How had this happened without anyone knowing?*

Where did these deadly robots come from? Who or what was responsible? For now, they remained in his private thoughts, and he wasn't sharing them at this stage. "There is much to do, I must leave now."

Just as he left, Smarty arrived.

Zara turned to her. "He's going to be okay so we don't have to worry."

She smiled but seemed very uncomfortable. She looked down at the floor.

"What's the matter?" Zara asked.

"You two have to go home." She was obviously a reluctant messenger.

Zara was defiant. "No! Not until I find my grandma."

"It's been decided. It's for your own good. It's too dangerous for you here. As soon as Zak is well, you will go."

With that, she turned away and left the room.

Zara was angry. "Zak, I'm not going home, I'm going on the mission whatever it takes. I'll find out what's up, and come back for you." She hesitated for a moment. "You will be alright now, won't you?"

"Yeah, sure I will, but shouldn't we do what they say?"

"No!"

"Er…oh okay…go then." He didn't know what else to say. His head was still aching but it was a low, dull thud and fading fast.

She left and went to where she knew the briefing would take place. Zara was darting in and out hiding behind plants and trees, all of which were delighted to see her. One put its branches around her, and she had to politely untangle the embrace before moving to the next one.

Everything was alive on Quomos, even if the energy wasn't nearly as strong as before the long night fell. She giggled to herself *that would have been more like a bear hug if life here were back to normal.* With her developing powers, she could see clearly through the veil at how lush it was. There were frilly caterpillars crawling up the leaf-filled bushes, while exotic birds flew overhead diving in and out of the trees looking for a snack.

Zara soon reached the MetaDome and hid amongst the branches of an old silvery windmill tree near an opening she could see through.

WiseyNuff was speaking, "There is still much preparation to be done before taking off for Vivo. You will need a briefing and some instructions in order to be ready for this important mission."

Vivo, why are they going to Vivo, Grandma's on Scartuss?

A strange blue-bat creature was perched on Wisey's arm. "Chuttnee has just come from the laboratory where Strongy had been analyzing the brain bug found in Zak's skull."

She shuddered just at the thought of the grey maggoty creature wriggling around. Her SUSAs were getting stronger by the moment and so she tuned into Strongy to see what had happened.

Immediately on leaving Zak's room, the leader of the FireHerders had gone to prove he was right, and that Yezzadar had kidnapped Elizabeth. Although her *seeing* was blurry at first, Zara watched as with the help of a Nuff scientist, they placed the bug on a smaller version of the nonagon table with a galaxy map floating above it. Suddenly, a light flashed from one of the stars, illuminating the source of the brain bug's signal.

"There goes your theory, Strongy. The signal's not from Scartuss it's from Vivo."

"Let me see that." He stared at the map. "He's clever. I'll give him that."

"What do you mean?"

"Yezzadar figured out that when we found Elizabeth was missing, we'd rush to Scartuss. So, he moved her over to Vivo. Huh…thanks to you, that's no longer a secret and he's going to be seeing us a lot sooner than he expected. Besides, we need a trip to Vivo to pick up more provisions. It may be an odd-looking planet but at least they have light and food."

The X-IT now focused her attention back on the team gathered in the MetaDome. In addition to Wisey, the mission members included Cleary, Brighty, Weeze, Smarty, and Cooly. Strongy would be joining them shortly.

Zara thought that Weeze seemed to be a little troubled because he was acting strangely. *Hmm, maybe that's why they call him WeirdyNuff or perhaps he's got pre-mission jitters.* She smiled and felt quite charged up as she looked on. There was no doubt in her mind she was going to Vivo!

Wisey began by explaining how they would travel in two morphed SuperDodons that would convert into SpaceJets. The first would carry the seven Nuffs—Wisey would stay on Quomos while the second craft would be used as a cargo vessel to take some essential equipment and a few extra Cratts.

Cooly spoke next. "Just as well, we're not taking the X-ITs."

Zara scrunched up her face angrily at first and then smiled to herself. *Little do you know!*

Wisey continued, "Vivo is a long way from here, and we have to pass through the *Vostos*. As you are aware, this is an energy void in the InfiGrid and it challenges all who pass through it. But don't worry, we will watch out for everyone."

There were a couple of Cratts and some Zybuffs busy at work with the equipment. A large screen came on with an image of a morphed SuperDodon. As with all their morphings, the eyes were always somewhere and Zara could see them just below the nose cone.

The shape from the top was long and sleek, but the side view was more like a fatter version of Concorde. There were a few windows along the side and a very large curved one that stretched across the front of the craft like a huge sun visor. Inside, there seemed to be quite a lot of space as there were only a few controls. As the picture zoomed, Zara couldn't help grinning. The whole of the inside, as well as the seats, were covered in red and yellow feathers. *It really looks quite comfortable*, she thought to herself.

Wisey turned in the direction of where she was hiding, and with a twinkle in his eye and without speaking said, *it is*. For a moment, she thought she was busted and quickly ducked down further out of sight, but no one came over so she lifted her eyes again.

"Now we would like to give those of you new to Vivo, a little more information on the planet itself and the beings who live there." It was ClearyNuff.

Zara pulled down her enervisor and saw an orb appear on one of the floating maps. Then bit-by-bit it zoomed closer until she could see Vivo clearly. It was similar in places to some parts of Earth; and as it was enlarged even further, she could see potholes and caves on the surface and in the rockscape—lots of them.

Cleary described the Vivoans as being easygoing friendly folks and spoke of a giant creature in their mythology called Dreadzog. He lived in the tunnels under Vivo and brought fear to all who went there.

"It is likely that Yezzadar has hidden Elizabeth underground because he knows they will not get curious and explore these catacombs."

Her voice became a little quieter. "More recently we have heard of another tunnel dweller who the young Vivoans have named the FrightGeist." She warned of the damage that had been done to many by this sombre apparition. "It's very different from the creature who has been there since the beginning. This one lures the children in and then drains their energy to give itself strength. We think it is one of Yezzadar's servants, but from what we understand he has some other helpers."

Cooly continued in his strong accent, "We hope that some of the Vivoans will 'elp us to locate 'is lair. Then we can smoke 'em out—as Zak would say!"

Although he always seemed a little flippant and didn't want the X-ITs coming along, Zara found him to be intelligent, in a non-intellectual way. There was something mysterious about his cool outer personality. She wondered what it was he was trying so hard to cover up.

The leader of the AirSpinners, SmartyNuff spoke next. "We have to be really careful not to be tricked into believing someone wants to help us when they are actually serving Yezzadar's cause!" She warned.

"We'll all have to be very vigilant to make sure we don't get sucked into the FrightGeist's dark doing."

Zara suddenly caught another glimpse of Weeze, who quickly disappeared. He seemed quite different than when they had first met in the Universal Hall.

Wisey then spoke in a serious but calming tone. "Next, we need to talk about what happens on the way to Vivo as you pass through the notorious Vostos. Let me tell you a little about what to expect, so it is not too much of a surprise. For some of you, this will be a reminder as you have already lived through the experience, but all others listen to what I have to say." He seemed to turn towards Zara as he spoke. She ducked down again.

"Sometimes, when we don't understand something we make it bigger and more frightening than it really is." He looked around at all the Nuffs gathered there. "This experience will not be completely new to many of you as you have been preparing in Dreamtime for a while now. You will remember there are times when you are about to fall asleep but you are still alert. It is like you are neither awake nor asleep."

Zara nodded to herself.

He described how only the physical body rests when we are asleep. "Our life-force or, what humans call the soul, continues its adventures even when the body is deep in its sleep state. Sometimes we can get stuck in between worlds in different places. We start to see things, like strange creatures, or other beings. They can even appear to be in the room, and around our beds. Some see monsters while others see angels. Some only feel there is something or someone present, while others hear voices. Usually, at times like this, we either wake ourselves up or drop into a deeper slumber to escape. Unless of course, we want to be in this space in between sleeping and waking."

Zara knew what he was talking about and had sometimes asked Grandma Elizabeth about these kinds of things. As she stood in the tree, she could feel some angst creeping in and saw the concern on a couple of the Nuffs' faces.

"So what happens in the Vostos?" two of them asked at the same time.

Wisey continued, "Every being experiences the journey through the Vostos in different ways. It depends on what we're afraid of. In this energy abyss, we face ourselves, and our deepest fears. The force of what happens to us depends on how well we know who we are. If we are always happy, we will meet our sorrow. If we think we are kind, we will face our meanness. If we think we are unworthy, we will find our self-esteem. All of the opposites come out of the shadows to help us release the grip that fear has on our lives, and reclaim those parts we have denied."

He looked around and saw that all were listening very carefully, except Weeze, who was nowhere to be seen. "In the Vostos, we are pushed to let go of everything that stops us from being who we really are. If we are holding on loosely, then it is not so hard. But if we have become afraid of all that we don't understand, then we will get an intense reminder. In the abyss, we meet that which frightens us so that we can take our power back from the fear, and turn our energy up to maximum potency."

"How long does it last?" ClearyNuff wanted to know the details.

"Well, it's time out of time. For some beings, it is just a flash, and for others, it seems like an eternity."

AirSpinners always liked things to be crystal clear. "So what you are saying is that the time it lasts depends on the distance between who we think we are and our true self? You're saying that when we are in the Vostos we get to see what really scares us, then it won't hold us back anymore!"

"Yes Cleary, exactly, so we can rid ourselves of all that represses our true essence. The way to pass through it is to do nothing. It is best to look at it as if you are watching a movie, with you as the main character. You have to trust in the Source to guide you through."

"We will be there wiz you," Cooly said to reassure them, and to hide his own angst.

"We won't let any harm come to anyone," Brighty added.

Suddenly, there was a strange slurping noise, and they all turned around to see Weeze straightening his cloak. He looked a little spaced out, but he soon pulled himself together. Zara was now convinced there was something strange going on with him but didn't quite know how to check it out, especially from where she was standing!

She was certain that he wasn't whom they'd called WeirdyNuff at all—at least not the one she'd met earlier. *Maybe there are two of him but how could that be as they're dressed the same. Maybe this is just part of his weird factor.* Whatever it was, she didn't like what she was feeling. *Maybe he's the spy.*

Zara stayed hidden in the tree a little bit longer while the team went through some more details about the mission. Just as she was climbing down, she felt a drop of water, fall onto the back of her hand. She wiped it on the leg of her jeans unconsciously and then did the same thing a second and a third time. She was in a hurry to get back to Zak and brief him on what had happened. She didn't notice that it wasn't raining.

Chapter Sixteen

Back in the blue domad, Zak felt restless and was tossing and turning. His head still hurt and he just wanted to sleep it off.

"Can somebody give me some help?" He was feeling frustrated and eventually managed to get the attention of a Nuff nurse. "I can't sleep, 'cos it's never light and it's never dark…"

"You'll get used to it—the rest of us have."

The nurse left and Zak noticed something moving by the window. As the shape got clearer, he saw that it was Zara. She put her finger up to her mouth, before he could blurt anything out, and climbed in. She jumped down to the floor, hurrying over to his bed, and leant over.

"They're going to this planet called Vivo, they think Grandma is there."

"Huh! I thought Yezzadar was on Scartuss."

"No, that was just to fool us. And they're moving up their next trip. They're leaving very soon. And…"

Zara hesitated for a moment not quite knowing how to put it.

"Yeeessss?" Zak was staring up at her.

"Well, I'm going!"

He looked at her curiously. "Do they know?"

"Well…er…not exactly. But I'm sure Wisey does!"

"Zara, this place is dangerous. They put weird stuff in your head. I could have died and…"

"I know; I KNOW…and I'm still going. That's all there is to it."

"So what if Grandma Elizabeth did drown?"

"She didn't."

"Okay. But do you remember when my grandpa died? It was the worst thing that ever happened to me. Then my mum told me there was one thing that would have been worse."

"What?"

"If I'd died before him. She said there's an order to life, the older ones go first, but before they leave they give us all they can to help us through our lives. Your grandma's already given you a lot. Can't it be enough?"

Zara was surprised at how profound and philosophical Zak was being. Maybe the brain bug did more damage than they first thought. She understood what he meant, but it didn't make any difference.

"Zak, she's still alive and I have to find her."

She started to move towards the window.

"Zar, what's that silvery stuff on your jeans?"

"What? What are you talking about?"

"Those silver smudges down your legs."

She stared down and touched the stuff; it was cold and tacky. Her mind flashed back to the water that had dripped on her hand. A chill went through her. She focused her *seeing* back to the windmill tree by the MetaDome. As she tuned in to her SUSAs, she saw that the moment she climbed down from the tree and rounded the corner, it started to shift its shape. First, it changed into something formless but then, it turned into a very sleek feline.

"It was Sylvameena. I was standing in Sylvameena."

"What? C'mon, how can you have been standing *in* Sylvameena?"

"She was a tree and she knows everything. She knows they are going to Vivo. Zak, I have to leave, NOW."

She gave him a quick hug and before he could say anything else, she had jumped out of the window, leaving him even more worried and restless than he had been earlier.

Chapter Seventeen

The room was dark and bare except for a few candles sitting on a long table that was made out of some kind of metal. The three-legged high-backed chairs, in which they were sitting, were of the same material and looked very uncomfortable. It smelled musty and dank as the two of them looked across at each other, surrounded by strange corrugated bronze-colored walls.

"More—what do you call it—wine?" he said to her in a raspy voice leaning across to pour the liquid out of a metallic flask.

"Not around you Yezzadar." It was Elizabeth.

"Oh, come on, you've known me a long time. I'm not all bad."

He filled the goblet held by Zara's grandma.

She was dressed in a long robe that fell to the floor as she sat pretending to enjoy the dinner that had been prepared for them. It looked even less appetizing than the food on Quomos.

He taunted her. "Do you know how few *grapes* there are in this part of the Galaxy? And…how few creatures I would even want to share a beverage with?"

Yezzadar took a drink from his goblet and Elizabeth reached for hers but knocked it over.

"Oh dear. Silly me."

"Don't worry accidents happen…"

As he turned, the candlelight caught him revealing his expressionless four-eyed face. He had no features to speak of and the sallow scaly nature of his skin, with irregular lumps, made him look more weird than sinister.

"If that *was* an accident…"

Elizabeth was indignant. "Of course, it was. Those were prescription sunglasses I left on the beach. Everything's blurry without them."

"I'll have the Tussites grind you a new pair after we've had dinner."

"That's most hospitable."

They sat in silence for a moment then Yezzadar blurted out, "Elizabeth, it was an emergency."

She saw it differently. "That's a matter of opinion depending on your perspective. Isn't it?"

"Maybe for you, it wasn't urgent. The life cycles of your planet haven't been drastically disturbed; at least not yet anyway. You know I can help them on Quomos."

"C'mon, Yezzadar, you don't want to help them, you just want power over them."

He looked away for a moment and was about to say something, but then changed his mind. "Look we both knew something had to be done."

"So what are you suggesting?"

"No more rituals and magic Elizabeth, it's time for MACHINES."

He reached down and touched something, causing the wall to open with very little sound. The other side was a warehouse filled with row upon row of inactive Terrortribes on hangers, dangling above the ground like clothes in a closet. There were hundreds of them. Some were just like the ones that Zak had defeated, and others were very different.

"I am perfecting some all-terrain types and have designs for others that can walk on water," he said in a dry but enthusiastic tone of voice.

Elizabeth was not impressed. "They're just weapons."

He smirked. "They can be, but they can serve a higher purpose too. And who better to set things straight than you and me?"

Yezzadar now moved around to Elizabeth's side of the table. She drew her aura in tightly, as he hung over her. "We're both warriors, my dear. You're not that different from me. We belong on the same side."

She pulled away as much as she could. "What are you drinking? Suddenly we're going off to war together?"

"Well, it might come to that."

"Yezzadar, what do you want from me?"

"I want what's best for the Nuffs and for Quomos."

"Shouldn't they be the ones to decide how to get their planet back in balance?"

He wasn't happy with what she was suggesting. "They've had their chances and they've messed it up. Look at the state of decay. Please, please…come to your senses and help me to help them."

She didn't reply.

Yezzadar, walked around the table sighing with frustration as he closed the wall with him on the other side of it, leaving Elizabeth alone in the room.

She wasn't sure how long she'd been there in total as there was no time to speak of. She had done her best to help Zara see that she was still alive, but she wasn't sure how much had got through. The electromagnetic field on Scartuss was quite different from anywhere else and messed up some of her energetic impulses.

Elizabeth was still her spritely self and had no intention of remaining captive for much longer. She'd managed to seduce him into releasing her from the force-field cage he'd put her into at the beginning. Now she was sure there must be a way to escape from the building.

Zara's grandma went over to where Yezzadar had been sitting, hoping to discover the lever that would open the wall. After a few moments of searching, her eyes landed on a lens-like thing on the leg of the table. Waving her hand across it did nothing. *It must be some fancy pulse recognition system,* she thought to herself. She gazed around at the ceiling and the walls. *There has to be another way out of here.*

Chapter Eighteen

Zara got back to the loading area just in time to see Captain Bushawoo and a second SuperDodon land on a large platform and transmorph. She just stared at them. First, their bodies became more angular, and then apertures started to appear along their sides. Finally, their wings became more streamlined, and they turned into the stylish SpaceJets she had first seen on the pictures at the MetaDome.

She watched from behind a bush as the Cratt they had met earlier was handing all the Nuffs a checklist. "Taaake a looook at this. Now...teeell me if sommmetthing is miiissing." He sounded, more than ever, like he was speaking down a pipe.

Strongy read the list out loud, even though the Cratt's writing wasn't that easy to decipher on the rough wriggling tile that he handed out:

NuffStuff - <u>Vivo Pack</u>
1 Aurabooster
1 Confidometer
1 Bubble Builder
6 Stealth Juice
3 Choffles
Assorted Nuff Nosh
Basic Survival Kit

After a brief recap of the contents, each of them picked up their backpacks. The stylish bags were all in different colors depending on their clans, but the design was the same, with a large $\mathcal{E}$ in the centre.

Strongy went first. As a FireHerder, his bag was red. Cooly collected a blue one. Smarty and Cleary were AirSpinners, so their two were yellow. Brighty's was red, while Weeze, the only EarthTamer, got a green one.

Zara then saw Chuttnee, the little blue bat-like creature that Smarty had said was their mascot. It was clear to her that he must be going with them and she giggled to herself, *maybe he carries a bat-pack!*

Her thoughts were cut off when Strongy started to talk. "Now that we have our stuff, let's all get on board and go nail this guy once and for all and maybe find our missing StoneKeepers."

New data had just come in from Vivo describing how things on the planet had changed a lot since their last visit, and it wasn't for the good.

Zara could see Yorazz, leader of the Yobuns walking towards the ship with his own heavy backpack.

Strongy saw him coming. "Yorazz I'm surprised to see you, given what you said at the meeting."

"Yes, well...er...there were other considerations." He glanced over his shoulder to see his mate walking away, and quickly stepped onto the ship. Strongy did his best to conceal a smile.

Wisey had walked with the others to the launch platform, along with two Nuffs who would support the team from Quomos. He wanted to wish them a successful mission and had made sure that the Cratts had a couple of spare backpacks and several VibaZappas, just in case.

As they stepped into the morphed Captain Bushawoo, Weeze let out a terrible burp and almost fell over with the force of it. Cooly helped the staggering Nuff to stand up, and they climbed on board.

Zara now knew that there was something majorly wrong. She just didn't know what. She continued to watch as the last Nuff climbed on board the SpaceJet, and the gangway folded upward.

She suddenly felt someone next to her and jumped with surprise.

"Okay so let's do it, let's go nail this guy once and for all, and...find your grandma, huh?" It was Zak. He'd been crouching down, a few feet away, behind another bush.

Zara gasped then chuckled. They started running towards the transmorphed dodon and leapt into the equivalent of the wheel well, just before Bushawoo's undercarriage folded in.

She was delighted to see him. "Well, so you changed your mind."

"About?"

"About my grandmother, what else? You've realized that she's still alive."

"I still have my doubts...but somebody's got to keep an eye on you. And, I was worried that..."

Before Zak had a chance to finish, there was a loud roar as the engines fired up. Flames burst out of the SpaceJet's tail as it started to taxi. The two of them were jostled around and Zara was tossed right into Zak's arms. She felt a twinge of something that took her by surprise; but then after an uncomfortable moment, she straightened up and broke the embarrassing silence.

"Do you smell something?"

"Wasn't me."

"Me neither."

The SuperDodon lifted off and, disappeared into the purple sky. Zara turned to Zak.

"It's going to be a long trip. Oh, and I need to tell you what happens in Vostos."

Chapter Nineteen

Yezzadar was busy in his workshop still unhappy that he couldn't talk Elizabeth around to being on his side. *She'll see it my way sooner or later,* he thought to himself. *The problem is I can't tell her everything—not yet.* He was a master of mechanics and spent hours in his workshop building and refining things to prove his superiority. He hadn't always been revengeful but circumstances were driving him deeper into the darker side of his nature.

He looked up at a row of Terrortribes and then back down at the one he was working on. He had a remote control glove on one hand as the robot in front of him held a metal rod in its claw. Yezzadar moved his gloved fist in a crushing motion and the Terrortribe did the same, pulverizing the rod.

He was pleased with himself and began to remove the glove, but suddenly became aware of something in the factory with him. He looked around and then turned to where the robots were hanging. Reflected in the metallic bellies of all of them was an image that wasn't there a moment earlier—a large panther-like creature, an Agapanterran.

"Sylvameena!"

He watched her reflection, in hundreds of his beloved creatures, as she morphed into her humanoid form.

"I must know Yezzadar, where is she?"

"She's here."

"And where's the InfiniKey? Does she have it?"

"She hasn't told me yet."

"Then I suggest you enhance your interrogation techniques, or maybe I need to help you."

He didn't want her help.

"She'll tell me sooner or later, don't worry." He wasn't as confident around Sylvameena. She was clearly pulling the strings.

The Agapanterran moved in closer.

"Sooner, Yezzadar, sooner." Implying that he needed to use more extreme techniques.

"Torture never accomplished anything."

"Maybe, but it will make *me* feeeeeeel better." She licked her lips.

"Alright, alright follow me."

He guided her through the vast hangar to a place where the entrance lay between the two buildings and then waved his gloved hand across a lens. The wall opened into the room where he had been eating dinner with Zara's grandmother, a short while earlier. It took a moment to adjust to the light.

"Elizabeth."

He looked around feverishly.

"Elizabeth, I know you're in here, there's no way to get out."

Sylvameena knew better. "Idiot. She's gone."

The light from the factory caught a bronze multifaceted mobile hanging from the ceiling revealing at least a dozen images of Sylvameena's face as she morphed back into her natural feline form.

She growled loudly. "I'll find her. You know this planet, she can't have gone far."

Sylvameena growled again, and Yezzadar jumped back a little scared.

"Listen to me, everything is going to be alright. I've got a spy on Quomos."

"A spy hmmm? I hope he serves you well. Because if he doesn't then…Anyway, I was there myself and I didn't see any spy."

Yezzadar was not sure what to say next. He looked down and it was like the whole of the floor was a vast image of Sylvameena's face and form. He didn't know where to turn.

"He's there and I'm getting information all the time. They're going to Vivo and I have a plan."

"Tell me something I don't know."

A drop of sweat ran down his cheek.

"Sweating are you, or is that a tear?" She laughed.

Outside, the landscape was rough, rugged, and hostile.

The constant threat of the hungry Scartusians was enough to bring fear to the strongest of souls. Elizabeth looked back at the structures that had housed her from the time she was kidnapped. In the distance, she saw the door of the hangar open, *he must have found out I'm not there.*

She watched as some of the earlier versions of the Terrortribes marched out into the near darkness. Although their weapons weren't overly sophisticated, they were dangerous enough. It was imperative that she find a hiding place in amongst the boulders where they couldn't reach her. Before going any further, she grabbed a sharp stone and cut the bottom off her long robe. Although it protected her legs, it impeded her movement and she needed to travel as quickly and as deftly as she could to get away from her pursuers.

A little further, Elizabeth reached an area of wasteland with some high rocks in the distance. *If I can make it over there, then maybe I'll find a place to shelter.* Before she was even halfway across, a whooshing sound went past her ear and a spikey-looking dart landed on the ground just ahead of her. A smoky acid-like substance emanated from the vibrating tip, it was guppa! Another just missed the top of her head followed by a third and a fourth.

The spritely hippie stopped and turned around to see a very large Tussite, standing upright not far behind her, with quivering quills. He was sizeable but he was alone. She stood firm and, in her mind's eye, planted a strong silver grounding cord that went from the tip of her tailbone right to the centre of the planet. It travelled up her spine and joined the energy from another golden one that went from the top of her head, way beyond the dark starlit sky above. She felt strong and connected, then stared right into the eyes of her attacker. The Tussite blinked not knowing what to do. Finally, before it pulled out another of its quills, it backed down and on all fours turned and walked away.

Hearing the clattering of the Terrortribes getting closer, Elizabeth knew she didn't have long before they reached her. Not far away, a loud howling sound spooked her but also gave her the motivation to move even faster into the cold dark night. She ducked down behind a large rock just as one of Yezzadar's robots came into view. It stopped, and as its head swiveled, it scanned the surroundings, but it didn't pick up her vibration, so soon moved on.

She went in the opposite direction and started climbing up the rocks. They were slippery and she slid down more than once. Another of the Terrortribes had chased her but lost its footing on the rocks, and fell over. Now she was out of their reach, at least she hoped she was. Zara's grandma soon found a trail that was well worn. It made the going much easier for a short while, and weaved in and out of the rocks until it ended in front of a cave. *I can hide in here for a while until I get a sense of what to do next, the Terrortribes can't get to me.* She moved further into the rather unusual grotto until she hit her foot on something.

Looking around, she saw clusters of strange oval-shaped luminescent rocks in different parts of the cave. They were about the size of a football and were protected by larger rocks that resembled the ones she'd climbed over to get here. *This has to be somebody's home because they are placed too perfectly to be a natural formation. But whose is it?* She got an uneasy feeling and didn't have to wait more than a few seconds before there was another horrible growling sound. The answer was right in front of her, framed in the entrance to the cave.

It was hideous with bulging eyes and razor-sharp teeth. The wispy-looking reptile was ready for a fight and, Elizabeth knew exactly what she was dealing with. Scartusians took no prisoners and stripped their prey to shreds, devouring every piece of them, bones and all.

She grounded herself again imagining the gold and silver cords and stared at the creature. Elizabeth's blue eyes reflected the glow of the luminescent rocks making them even more intense. The cave dweller tried hard to turn away, but couldn't. Instead, it adopted another strategy; it closed its eyes. It knew the cave intimately; living on the dark planet strengthened its other senses. It opened its nostrils and began sniffing. It had caught Elizabeth's smell and was coming closer. She backed up further into the cave aware that she was now at a disadvantage.

The Scartusian lunged, narrowingly missing her and causing her to hit the back of her calf on a rock. Elizabeth sat down hard on her bottom, but was up again in a flash, as the creature sensed her every move.

She was still backing up, as the reptile got closer, still with its eyes shut, but now with its jaws wide open revealing oversized razor-sharp teeth. *Ouch,* her spine hit the wall at the innermost point of the cave; there was nowhere else to go.

No stranger to danger, she thought quickly and feigned a move in one direction, then ran as fast as she could the other way. Elizabeth headed for the cave entrance, fooling the Scartusian, but only for a second. It was faster and it was angry and had no trouble beating her to the opening and blocking her way out.

Zara's grandma stumbled and fell but not before, she noticed a pile of boulders close to her right foot. As the creature made its final approach, she kicked out the keystone and scrambled out of the way. Exactly as she'd hoped for, her action caused all the boulders to come crashing down on top of her attacker crushing it under a mass of rock. There was a long moment of silence as the dust settled. Then suddenly, just as she thought it was over, the head of the Scartusian broke through the rocks. Elizabeth, almost exhausted, grabbed a boulder to defend herself against another attack. The creature stretched its neck, opened its mouth, and took one last gasp before falling backwards, lifeless. She stared at the dead Scartusian. Wiping the dust off her face with the back of her grazed hand, she knew she had to have a lot more cuts and bruises, but nothing that wouldn't heal.

As she stood up, she saw that there was a new problem to deal with. The rock fall had blocked the entrance to the cave and the boulders were too big to move on her own. So, climbing up on one side of the rock pile, Grandma Elizabeth searched for the best place to start working her way out. Suddenly, a loud cracking sound came from the back of the cave. Then a second one a little closer, down below from where she was standing. She knew she wasn't alone but what was it? It happened again and again. Then she became aware that the sound was coming from the luminescent rocks. Only they weren't what they seemed to be. Instead, they were the eggs of the Scartusian she had just killed, and they were hatching.

Unfurling from the football-sized broken shells, were miniature versions of her attacker but even these were almost half the size of the deceased parent. For a moment, she froze, staring down at the growing numbers of creatures crawling over the boulders towards her. They were clearly hungry and searching for food.

Chapter Twenty

The bright yellow and red seats inside the dodon SpaceJet were soft and feathery, and the temperature was cool. The walls, on the inside, were skeleton-like made from the ribs of the big bird. StrongyNuff and ClearyNuff sat apart from the other team members, on an elevated platform, in front of a large screen. The rest of them were in rows along the edges but could see what was on it even on the lower level, because of its curvature.

Weeze and CoolyNuff were sitting alongside one another chuntering in their own private language. It was Weeze's first mission and he was feeling the pressure. He told Cooly how he hadn't felt like himself for the past few days and thought it might be stress. He had been seriously out of sorts and, although he was a little better, he still didn't feel great. Zara's intuition had been right but at this point, she had no idea how right it was.

A couple of Cratts were at the controls when Strongy got up and started pacing.

"How much longer to the Vostos?" he asked the bigger of the two stringy Cratts.

"Two point three; no, two point two; no, two point four tacs."

"Can't you speed him up?"

"Speed no. Speed no good. Speed kills. Kill him."

The strong Nuff was growing impatient; after all, he was a fighter, not a dreamer. This period of non-action was making him irritable. He walked down to the rear end of the craft, trying to burn off some of his pent-up frustration. He'd just turned around to head back to the front when he heard a noise. He stopped and moved towards where he thought it was coming from; it sounded like *coughing* behind a flap in the corner.

The ginger-colored Nuff assertively lifted the flap to reveal a large pouch. In doing so, he caused the release of a thick cloud of green-colored gas, right into his face. He quickly swished the smelly substance away with his arm. Once the fumes had cleared, he could see clearly. Staring up at him, were the two stowaways.

"What are you doing here?" he asked sternly as he helped them out of the pouch. "You couldn't stay away, huh?"

Zara was coughing. "What was that yucky green stuff?"

Strongy reminded them. "Well you know this ship is a living thing, don't you?"

"Yeah." Zak nodded.

"Well, you hid in a part of the Dodon's body that…no one would really choose to hide in."

Zara looked at Zak while holding her nose. "Oh yuck!"

The Cratt commander had made his way down to the rear of the ship to find out what was happening. "Turn back to Quomos…turn back to Quomos."

StrongyNuff wasn't even considering it. "No, keep going."

The Cratt was surprised. "The Vostos! The Vostos!"

"They'll just have to go through it like everyone else."

The Cratt went back to the front. "Like everyone else, like everyone else."

StrongyNuff winked and shrugged his very broad shoulders. He turned towards the X-ITs. "Good pilot, lousy conversationalist."

Zak looked at Strongy curiously. "Whoa, so wha-what's this Vostos?"

"Don't worry, from all I've seen, you'll be just fine. Now go and sit over there," he said, pointing to some spaces between Cooly and Smarty, before returning to the elevated platform.

"So you came anyway?" SmartyNuff smiled at Zara.

"I have to find my grandma; it's not negotiable." She'd heard her father use the phrase in the past and felt strongly that nothing was going to get in her way. For a moment, her thoughts flew back to Earth and her parents. *I hope they're okay and aren't worried. But if WiseyNuff is right they won't even notice we're gone.* Then she remembered what her father had said about Grandma Elizabeth living in *la-la land and wanting Zara to see the world.* It made her feel angry and all the concern faded away, strengthening her resolve even further.

"I understand but you know I had to tell you, not to come?"

Zara smiled and nodded at her friendly companion.

Meanwhile, Zak had sat down next to Cooly who, at first, turned away. It didn't stop him from tapping him on the shoulder. "So...uh...CoolyNuff...tell me what's this Vostos thing?"

The WaterWhisperer looked at him but didn't say anything.

It was Zara, who picked it up. "You're scared, aren't you? But you've been through it before."

Cooly turned and looked her straight in the eyes. "Yes, that's *why* I'm scared." He then let his gaze settle on Smarty, prompting her to answer Zak's question.

"The truth is, we're all scared even though we don't want to be. The Vostos shrinks time and space but there's a toll to pay."

Zak reached into his pocket and pulled out some coins. "I've got some money on me."

Zara felt embarrassed and wanted to poke him in the ribs big time, but he was across the aisle.

Cooly was irritated. "Not that kind of toll. It's psychological. It messes with your mind."

With that, Zak turned visibly pale. The WaterWhisperer had certainly got his attention. The young human had always prided himself on being strong-minded and in control of his emotions. A few years ago, he'd decided that logic was the best way to deal with all the feeling stuff that didn't make any sense. He'd just reminded himself of how important a decision it was after he heard Zara would be moving to London. He couldn't afford to be soft; he thought it made him weak. But he was scared now.

"Wha-what kind of things happen to your mind?"

CoolyNuff turned away again and so Smarty answered, "Most of us have two sides—the side everyone sees and another that lies in the shadows, hidden from public view. In the Vostos, your shadow side comes out to meet you and for everyone to see."

Zak shifted his weight and leant over to Zara. "What do you think your shadow side is all about?"

She thought for a moment. "Don't know, what's yours?"

Zak shrugged his shoulders. "I don't think I have one."

Zara rolled her eyes skeptically. "We'll see."

The flight had gone very smoothly, which was not surprising as Captain Bushawoo was a competent interplanetary flyer. He was renowned for being a debris dodger, and so far had elegantly managed to avoid some meteorites and assorted space trash that floated across his path. Right now, everything was calm. There was little else for the travelers to do but graze and doze while they waited for the craziness of the Vostos to arrive.

They didn't have to wait too much longer. There was a sudden bump and the screen became a mass of swirling gases and all the stars disappeared. The first sign inside the ship was when ClearyNuff started talking gibberish. The normally crisp and clear speaking Nuff was spewing out verbal garbage. Part of her still knew what was happening and so she left the control platform and joined the others down below.

Zak and Zara watched as she struggled with what was going on in her mind. No one could really see how deeply confused she was as she faced the part of herself that made no sense at all. The struggle was hard, and her face was twisted with pain. Her yellow Enervisor almost lost its entire color. Her ability to reason was gone, and her mind was full of crazy ideas that were foggy and muddled. Cleary felt like she was on the edge of madness as she tried to become, what WiseyNuff had called, *the witness of your own experience.* But it wasn't easy to go through this kind of thing and not feel afraid. She didn't even look like herself.

There was a second bump.

Zak and Zara heard sobbing and saw it was CoolyNuff. He was in some kind of hallucination and shaking wildly. It looked like he was having a fit. Unknown to them, he was facing the part of himself that was uncool—a real geek. He could see it towering over him—it was so huge and nerdy. He couldn't understand how this could have anything to do with him. After all, he was smooth and sleek and this other part was one huge fashion mistake. He just stared straight ahead. *How can I be this way, surely this can't be me, but* aaaaagh *maybe it is.* He watched and wondered. Then he felt a power surge going through him; it was making his whole body tremble.

Zak looked across at Zara. "We're in the Vostos."

She didn't answer so he scanned the other Nuffs. Several of them were now thrashing around, obviously in pain, while BrightyNuff was laughing uncontrollably, like a maniac. Inside her current reality, everything seemed so dark, she couldn't find her way. The light had gone out as the blackest feeling, she'd ever known, surrounded her. It wrapped itself around her like a blanket of ice. She could feel it pulling at her very essence and shaking her to the core. There were things screaming at her in the dark. They were faceless and formless, but they were there and she knew it.

Zak didn't get it. "Hey, Zar, I don't see what the big deal is, nothing's happening to me. Are you okay?"

Zara didn't answer.

He looked around again and noticed Yorazz was sitting right at the end of the row. He was shaking and sweating profusely. Zak kept watching. The skin on the yobun's face started stretching to such an extent that it cracked and, in a few seconds, it was all gone like a smashed boiled egg. Then, the membrane covering what was inside the shell, peeled away to reveal the head of a vile-looking, red-colored reptile, with four tongues lashing out and licking four large black fangs.

Zak's eyes widened as he turned to Zara. "Look over there; look there." He pointed but got no response from his best friend. It was as if she didn't even know he existed.

Pleading with her, "Zarrrrah, please look over there." She didn't react at all.

He turned again to look at Yorazz and saw that all the Nuffs were now cracking open. Inside their skins were all different kinds of creatures.

One was a shabby hyena-like monster with a big grin on its face, gnashing its teeth, and with saliva dribbling from its jaws. Another was a giant black ant with furry antennae and two enormous pincers that made a clicking sound. A third was a bat-winged water hog with twisted tusks and a long pointed snout, that was telescopically unfolding towards Zak. All of them were moving in his direction.

He was desperate now as he turned to Zara. "Can't you see them?"

Again, there was no reaction so he jumped up. "C'mon." He went to grab her but his hand went right through her. He was horrified. The monsters were getting closer so all he could do was run to the back of the craft.

"Help, help." But the Nuffs just stayed where they were as he ran past them. It was as if he didn't exist. Zak looked behind. The monsters were gaining. He turned to run even faster and came face to face with a huge, white, hooded figure blocking his way. He stopped in his tracks as it removed its hood to reveal a skeletal face with a few bits of flesh hanging off it. He screamed.

There was nowhere to go. He was boxed in from both directions until suddenly he saw the flap covering the pouch that he and Zara had hidden in earlier. He lifted it up releasing the same green gas as before. It caused him to cough madly as he dived through the aperture to escape his hideous tormentors. To his surprise and then to his horror, it wasn't the same pouch. Instead, he had leapt through the opening, straight into outer space. He was falling away from the SuperDodon. As he watched it disappear into the distance, he screamed, dropping like a stone through the intense blackness.

Zara, meanwhile, was desperately trying to open her eyes but it wasn't working. She decided it was best to stop struggling. She could hear the birds singing in the garden, as she woke up in her little room at Grandma Elizabeth's cottage. The smell of lavender was wafting in through the open window, and it was a lovely sunny day.

Elizabeth popped her head around the door and said good morning, with a breakfast tray containing a bowl of cereal and a glass of orange juice. As Zara yawned and wiped her eyes, her grandma asked, "How did you sleep, my dear?"

"Not so well, Grandma, I think I've been living in a dream for a long time."

She sat on the edge of the bed. "Do you want to tell me about it?"

Zara shook her head still looking towards the window. "It was just another one of those dreams, but it was very real."

"Why don't you tell me about it? You know it makes you feel better."

"O-Okay, Grandma. Well, there were these funny types of creatures and they wanted me to give them the pendant you gave me. They were all asking for it."

"You didn't give it to them, did you?"

"How could I? It was only a dream."

"Let's have a look just to be sure." She leant over and started undoing the top button of her granddaughter's nightshirt.

Zara put her hand up. "Grandma, what are you doing?"

"The pendant. Now!"

Zara was shocked and as sleep finally left her, she saw that the eyes looking at her were not those of her grandma. She struggled to pull away, and as she did Sylvameena growled.

"Give...it...to...me," the Agapanterran shouted as she morphed out of being Elizabeth into her normal silver humanoid shape, with her amber eyes blazing. Zara rolled out of bed and darted for the door with Sylvameena hot on her heels. She shot down the landing as fast as she could and headed for the stairs. Once at the bottom, she rushed to the front door and tried several times to unlatch it. She gave it one last giant tug and it started to open. Aigledor was standing on the doorstep. A sense of relief flooded her as he, in his humanoid form, held out his hand to help her...or so she thought.

"The pendant, Zara. Give it to me."

She didn't know what to do. She felt like sitting down and putting her head in her hands, but she couldn't let either of them have it; it was too precious. Instead, she placed her hand on her chest just as she heard Sylvameena growling behind her. She ducked down and scampered between Aigledor's legs, out into the garden. Looking back quickly, she saw the two of them morph into their animal forms as they launched themselves at each other. The now familiar sound was still horrendous to hear as they fought again for supremacy.

Zara ran down the path only to be confronted by an army of silver Agapanterrans blocking her way. She heard a loud screeching sound and looked up to see a flock of large golden birds swoop down and begin attacking the big silver cats. She backed away and hid by a tree watching as they tore into each other ripping their opponents apart.

There were hundreds of them everywhere. In the distance, she could see that the battle was destroying the village. Flying bodies were snapping electrical and telegraph poles. As they fell, a frayed end of an electrical wire sent a spark flying and set fire to the thatched roof of one of the cottages. She watched as it spread, but there was nothing she could do except watch. Pillars of smoke rose into the sky, as these age-old enemies destroyed more cottages and their surroundings.

All Zara could do was to scream.

The next thing she was aware of was Zak holding one of her hands as SmartyNuff held the other. The small Nuff was doing her best to comfort her. "It's all right. It's okay we're out of the Vostos."

Zara blinked her eyes a couple of times and shook off her experience.

"So, what was it?" Zak was right up close.

"What was what?" She pulled herself away. He was crowding her.

"Your shadow side. The part that nobody's ever seen!"

"It wasn't really about me." She was a bit dazed.

"Well, what was it about?"

"The future, I think. So, what was yours?" She wanted to deflect the question.

"Mine. Well, mine wasn't much!" Then he shrugged. "No big deal really."

With that, he got up and walked over to the Commander Cratt. "Just out of curiosity, when we come back, do we go the same way?"

"Same way, same way."

"Are you saying there is no other way?"

"Other way's slow, too slow, way toooooooo slow."

"But don't you think it might be worth the extra time? You know to see different scenery on the way back? Going the same way is so boring."

The Cratt gave Zak a curious look. "Sure, sure."

Zara, meantime, was settling down with Smarty. The others were preparing for the remainder of the journey and recovering from their various experiences in The Vostos. She had learnt that Chuttnee had simply hung upside down in his sleep state in a special little area where he always hung out on missions!

The remaining three Nuffs had passed through without any major events and had done their best to take care of the other team members. No one knew how much time had passed or how long they'd been *in it*, but they were through now and would soon be on Vivo.

Suddenly, a loud howling sound abruptly shattered the calm and made everyone jump. Weeze had appeared from the back of the craft like a being possessed. He was tearing at his fur and screaming with terror. His eyes were red, and his body was twisting and jerking. His green enervisor had no color left. He was shaking and screeching wildly until CoolyNuff got hold of him and threw him to the deck. Smarty and Brighty joined in, helping to control the crazed Nuff.

Zara and Zak sat perfectly still, thinking it was probably best to stay out of the way, at least for now. Weeze was lying on the floor with the three of them holding him down. There were horrible slurping sounds coming out of different parts of his body, which was now shaking violently. He fought with the others to get control, as his red eyes glared up at them.

From the platform, StrongyNuff could see what was really happening. He called out to the others. "It's a Dangroid—you've got to get it out of him before it's too late. You know what you must do."

They did. It wasn't the first time they'd faced this revolting reptilian parasite that took its life force from a living host and then tried to take it over completely in a moment of weakness. SmartyNuff stared into Weeze's bloodshot eyes trying to lure the vile creature out. If it was to survive once it was *seen*, it had to find a new host. It usually went to the one with the strongest will. All they had to do was to catch it as it made the jump from one to the next. It wasn't an easy task.

For a brief moment, as it emerged from the now unconscious Weeze, they saw the charcoal grey lizard with horrible red eyes and a long, forked, slime-covered, orange tongue. In a nanosecond, the angry Dangroid leapt into Smarty before CoolyNuff could grab it. She doubled up in pain and fell to the floor. She passed out immediately, staring straight ahead with the same bloodshot eyes that a moment before had been looking out from the other Nuff.

Strongy was now standing behind Cooly, as they both looked into the pools of blood redness. This time the Dangroid looked even more grotesque as it leapt out and jumped towards StrongyNuff, hoping to take him over. But it wasn't quite fast enough. Cooly nudged Zak who leapt up, conquering his earlier fears, and together they grabbed it, wrestling it to the floor.

It was slimy to touch and wriggled, violently hissing and slobbering. It was monstrous, thrashing its tail against Cooly and giving him a nasty cut on the side of his furry face. It almost broke free as it let out a spine-chilling scream that shook everyone there, but this time it wasn't going anywhere. They knew they only had to keep it captive for a short while before it lost its power and shrank into a helpless little tadpole. They just had to stay focused.

All of them watched for what seemed like a very long time as it went from being a full-grown parasitic lizard to a tiny powerless tiddler.

They were still in a state of shock, with the adrenalin flying around their bodies when they put it into a sealed, biodegradable container. Later, they would eject it into space, where after a while it would decompose.

Zara checked in with Smarty to see if she was okay.

"I'm okay just a little shaken up but he didn't have me for long!"

The young X-IT then went over to Weeze, who was still quivering and looked like he was in another world. She stroked his head and reassured him that all was going to be okay. "It's okay WeirdyNuff you're safe now it's gone."

"I knew there was something going on inside me I just didn't know what it was."

"Well, I can tell you it turned up your weird factor a lot!"

"Then you must tell me what I was like so I can build it into my routine." Weeze winked at her.

She smiled back at him. "It's a deal."

Zara had known from the second time she'd seen him that something or someone had *possessed* him. *Next time,* she thought to herself, *I'm going to trust my intuition and check it out.*

Strongy congratulated Zak and the other Nuffs on their performance.

"That was some Dangroid! I don't think I've ever seen one that big before." He turned to look over at Weeze, who with Zara's help was now sitting upright, and lightheartedly added, "Your weirdness must have fed him too much."

They all laughed!

Meanwhile, ClearyNuff, who had stayed on the platform during the episode, now stepped down. "Well, that was one surprise we could have done without after passing through the Vostos. So how is everyone?"

It was obvious that they had all been through quite an experience and needed to soak it in. There were a few comments thrown around in a light-hearted way to lift everyone's spirits, but they were all very tired.

Zak sat next to Zara who was impressed by her friend.

"Wow, I didn't expect you to join in like that."

"Well I sort of like, had to."

"Why?"

"It's a long story, Zar, I'll tell you one day."

"Okay, no worries." She moved a little closer until they were pushed right up against each other. Zara shut her eyes, falling asleep on his shoulder. It was comforting for both of them after all they'd been through.

As Zak sat there, he couldn't help wondering what they'd got themselves into and hoped that nothing else like this was going to happen again—ever. He knew it was a silly thought to have. After all, this was just the beginning.

Chapter Twenty-One

CoolyNuff got through to Mission HQ on Quomos, and told them everything that had happened in the Vostos. All contact stops in the energy abyss and it took a while to reconnect. Wisey and the others were happy to hear that all on board had come through it in one piece.

Strongy told them of Weeze's Dangroid experience, "You know he's always lived up to his name, WeirdyNuff, but he was acting way more strangely than usual. Now this explains everything!" They all joked about it before moving on to the more serious stuff.

Wisey had a lot of confidence in the team and the way they shared leadership. He reminded them that help was available back on Quomos, and suggested that O, the Galactic Oracle, was a great source of insight if they ever needed a different kind of help.

O lived on Spherus, and was probably the most learnt being in the entire Galaxy. He, or was it she, no-one really knew, had already told WiseyNuff that Zak would help them find the solution to the destruction of the Terrortribes. O also told him that the mission to Vivo was the beginning of the Legend of the InfiniKey coming to life. O knew things that others had no way of knowing and rarely took on a body of any sort. Most beings saw a rainbow-colored arc when O was around.

After a short rest, everyone seemed to have energy again, and they were more positive about the mission. The journey through the void, plus the Dangroid experience, had been hard on some of the team. Cooly was on the platform along with Brighty. She wasn't a qualified flier but an apprentice who was keen to get her SuperDodon license.

Zara was sure her intuition was right! She had noticed back on Quomos some glances passing between the pretty, yellow Nuff and Strongy, but wondered if it was only her imagination. Now, she was certain. She had seen the worried look on his face when Brighty went through her Vostos experience. It took him all his willpower not to jump down from the controls to comfort her. Zara had just seen him give her shoulder a gentle squeeze as she stepped onto the flight platform to join Cooly. She was absolutely convinced there was a romance going on between them, and she smiled to herself wondering if anyone else had noticed.

After a moment, she turned to listen to what Strongy had to say. He wanted the team to get very familiar with the NuffStuff in their backpacks. "Let's check that everything is working so that we can clear up any hiccups before we are faced with a tough situation."

He looked across at Zara and Zak. "I know you want to come with us but it's too dangerous and you don't have our training. You'll have to stay here."

The X-ITs pretended to look disappointed.

"Hey, Zak's pretty mean with the VibaZappa!" Zara couldn't help herself. She had already decided she hadn't travelled all this way to sit inside a transmorphed SuperDodon.

CoolyNuff spontaneously gave Weeze a blast of positive energy from his Aurabooster after his draining Dangroid experience.

"Sweeeet—thanks, guys, I needed that," he quipped.

"Let me know when you need another hit, I'll be happy to oblige," Cooly said with a grin.

The others were getting some last-minute instructions on how and when to use the various gadgets, before placing them back in their custom backpacks. Brighty picked up an unusual-shaped container that popped open to reveal some small cone-shaped bonbons.

"It's time for a choffle to give you the extra zest you need for the mission."

Zak was hesitant, at first, after the grey pea episode but after braving it he couldn't believe how delicious it tasted. The smell alone was like nothing on Earth. He fancied himself as a bit of a choco-connoisseur and this was better than anything he'd ever had before.

"These are great," he said loudly, beaming.

"Well, there are lots more where those came from, but they are very potent so we limit ourselves, otherwise what happens isn't good," Brighty said with a smile.

Zak was curious. Then memories of the smell of the back end of Captain Bushawoo filled his nose. He knew what she meant!

StrongyNuff spoke next.

"Okay, with Vivo not far away it's time to have a more detailed look at the Vivoans and what we might expect."

He wanted to talk strategy and explore how they would go about the mission once they'd landed. They looked at lots of pictures that showed in more detail the strange-looking terrain. Some parts of the planet resembled Earth with its green trees and pools of teal-colored water. Other parts were very different. They had been told that the Vivoans had asked for their help to capture something called the FrightGeist. It was living in the many tunnels on the west side of the planet.

A closer look showed that the soil in that area was made of reddish-yellow clay and some of it had been molded by the weather into bizarre sculpted shapes of different sizes. Some looked like skeletons, where the winds had blown away the loose soil, while others looked like strange faceless creatures. Pointing to that particular area, Strongy began describing what to expect.

"The land is not very inviting. Underneath are many caves that are dark and damp. We think Yezzadar is probably holding Elizabeth in one of them. The Vivoans hate this part of their planet, and worse still, they are terrified of going into the tunnels, so they won't help us to find his lair. This means we have to go in after him if we are to succeed."

The Nuffs just stared at each other, horrified at the thought. Zara hated going underground too and always persuaded her parents to take the bus in London because she didn't want to go down into the Tube. She remembered a dream that she had had repeatedly, where she got stuck under a house that was raised a foot above the ground on bricks. In the dream, she'd be crawling on her tummy underneath it looking for something, but because the space was only a few inches high, she couldn't turn over and no one knew she was there. She went cold as she listened to StrongyNuff talk more about the tunnels. *Maybe staying on the dodon isn't such a bad idea after all.*

The big FireHerder looked at them all. "When we arrive, we will connect with the farmers and pick up provisions as usual. They're not expecting us. We're several zytags early, so it will be a surprise, but we couldn't risk them knowing just in case word got out. Yezzadar has spies everywhere and we want to have the advantage over him."

"SmartyNuff, I want you to take Cooly and Chuttnee while we get the cargo. See if you can pick up on any signs of the signalling device or the FrightGeist. You never know they could be connected. Maybe you can find some recent casualties that can give us an idea of where Yezzadar is hiding Zara's grandmother."

ClearyNuff then took over the briefing.

"We've learnt that this apparition, the FrightGeist, drains the energy from its victims, leaving them full of fear and with no sense of who they are anymore. It takes them a long time to restore their lost life force and sometimes the fear stays with them. What we need to watch for are the ones who have become its helpers. It is hard to tell them from the normal Vivoans. So, use all seven senses."

The team watched as Cleary showed them pictures of the different types of Vivoans. Most of them were about the same size or perhaps a little bigger than the Nuffs. Their hair was thick and they all had either a gold or silver stripe of hair that grew out of the top of their heads and dropped down the back of their necks. They also had hair growing from the nails of their very long fingers. Vivoans were attractive beings with very small features, and unlike humans, they all looked similar with just a few differences to tell them apart.

Zara turned to Zak and whispered. "I still can't believe this is real. I feel like I'm watching a movie."

"I can't quite get my head around it either. But it's real, Zar." He stroked above his ear where his hair had been shaved when they removed the brain bug.

"How will we ever explain this back at home? They'll never believe us." Zara turned again to listen to Cleary.

The AirSpinner with her sharp and insightful logical mind continued, "Through your enervisors, you should be able to tell the difference between those that are working with the FrightGeist and those that are not." She showed two more pictures of other young Vivoans. "At first look, you can't see anything unusual about them. But take another look, this time through your enervisors and tell me what you see."

Brighty was the first to comment, "They look the same on the surface but there is a kind of oily-looking tentacle coming out of the navel of the one on the left."

"Excellent!" Strongy acknowledged her. "Now look even closer." His red enervisor was very bright. As a FireHerder, he thrived on intensity and action.

Weeze spoke next. His voice was still a little shaky after his Dangroid possession. "And that little guy on the left has a black hole in his energy field around the cord thingy as if something is gone."

"Bravo!" Strongy shouted as he pointed to the circle of empty space in the middle of the aura. "These are the telltale signs when you are with one who is under the influence of the FrightGeist. The important thing is not to harm them but to hold on to them until we can free the energy cord they have to the giant. Once this is done, they will no longer be at his mercy."

ClearyNuff continued, "Some others that are drained are just left empty, with their whole energy field zapped. Their auras are colorless. You can't miss them. The confidometers will also be useful to measure how much has been drained."

"Will the confidometers work on those under the FrightGeist's spell as well?" Weeze asked.

"Yes, but instead of turning purple, the crystals will be slightly orange. You may have a problem getting them onto these Vivoans. They don't want to be found out and will try hard not to be identified. Your enervisors and your intuition are your best tools here."

Zara was feeling restless. A growing sense of urgency came over her and she stiffened.

"Zak, I think Grandma's in trouble, she's in a cave and there are all these creatures surrounding her. She can't get out."

"Don't you think you might...er...just be like picking up on what they're saying?"

"No," she said tersely. "I saw it quite clearly but..." she paused. "It's gone now." She felt deflated and withdrew into herself.

The briefing finished and they all relaxed in preparation for Vivo. Since the Vostos and the episode with WeirdyNuff, there had been very little excitement. The exception was when Captain Bushawoo had to steer clear of a large meteorite that was heading right towards them. His sharp eyes and fast action had saved them and given him an ego boost. He was feeling quite good for being so speedy and flexible. *Not bad for an old bird* he thought to himself, as he got ready for the final approach to Vivo.

Chapter Twenty-Two

Meanwhile, back at Mission HQ, the Nuffs were talking about how best to support the team once they'd landed.

WiseyNuff pulled on his ear. "We'll keep contact with them through the commecators. We can listen in to their conversations. The problem is that, the deeper they are underground, the harder it will be to stay in touch. Commecators are good for up to five feet or so below, but any more and they just don't work."

There was a big silence. Everyone knew that the most dangerous part of the mission was likely to be in the honeycomb tunnels beneath the planet's surface.

Wisey broke the tension. "Let's see if we can find a way to strengthen the signals. Maybe we can work with a couple of Zybuffs to determine whether anything can be done."

Approaching Vivo, Captain Bushawoo made his final checks for the landing, and all those on board got ready for touchdown. Strongy made sure that everyone was okay and hyped up.

"Are we ready to get Yezzadar, rescue Elizabeth, and save the Vivoans?"

"YoHa." They punched the air, Nuff fashion.

All of them knew StrongyNuff's priorities, he didn't make it a secret, but they were cool with it. So too was Zara, because she was very clear about hers.

The sky was a deep teal color as they landed in a field cleared for the purpose. It could have been a little smoother but a few bumps added a bit of excitement. Bushawoo had put down here many times before.

It was only a few seconds later that several of the Nuffs stepped out of the aperture on the side of the dodon, and started to laugh. Zak and Zara could hear all the noise from inside the craft.

"What's the fuss all about?" Zak asked, moving to try and get a look at what was going on.

Zara knew instantly. "The sun, silly."

"Oh yeah…"

Some Vivoans approached the Nuffs on horse-like creatures called Tartokis upon their arrival. Some of them were towing carts full of fruits, grain, and veggies. WiseyNuff decided to alert their friends on Vivo, just a short while before they landed knowing that they still had the advantage over Yezzadar.

"You're early. We don't have everything ready yet." The Vivoan was stout and stocky with long, dark hair that had a wide golden streak from the middle of his forehead to the centre of his back.

StrongyNuff took the lead. "Yes, we have other business here. We've heard of your FrightGeist and want to help."

The leader of the Vivoans was grateful and welcomed them.

"Okay team, start loading up what our hosts have already prepared for us."

The Cratts and Yobuns began placing the provisions on the second dodon, a cargo version that was not quite as sleek and colorful as Captain Bushawoo. It had been flying alongside them.

SmartyNuff meanwhile was holding a small pod-like capsule with Chuttnee sleeping inside.

Zara turned to look at her. "You come here for food?"

"We have to. We don't have enough variety with so little sunlight and our poor water supply."

Zak was curious. "So what do you give them for all of this?"

"Nothing."

"All this for nothing?"

Smarty nodded her head. "Yes, we have Elizabeth to thank for that."

The two X-ITs stared at her.

"A long time ago a monotaurus grabbed an infant and took it into the tunnels. Everyone was scared to enter, but your grandmother went straight in after it and saved the life of the little one."

While Zara felt proud of her grandma, Zak was more concerned about the creature. "So what happened to the monotaurus?"

"You'll have to ask Elizabeth that now, won't you."

Zak was impressed. "Wow."

Leaving Zak and Zara awestruck, Smarty stepped out of the craft with Chuttnee and went to where Strongy was talking to a second Vivoan.

"He says that a starship landed here a few zytags ago."

Smarty wanted to know more. "What kind of ship? One like ours?"

"No, it was heavy metal."

The two Nuffs traded worried looks, prompting Smarty to ask the Vivoan. "Where did it land?"

He pointed into the distance. "Over there."

"Well, let's see what our little tracker has to say about that…Chuttnee, Chutt…" Smarty made some chttng sounds and opened the pod. Chuttnee woke up and started chttng back to her. She then pulled out a smaller container with Zak's brain bug inside. The chttng of the little blue bat grew louder and after picking up its signal, he flew off in the direction that the Vivoan had pointed to.

Smarty looked around. "Seems like Chuttnee agrees with you and has picked up the resonance. Now, where is CoolyNuff?"

He was nowhere to be seen. She didn't want to lose time and Strongy agreed she should go on ahead, saying he would join her later. The leader of the AirSpinners was true to her name, SmartyNuff, and was extremely competent, she'd been on a lot of missions and used her powers of rational analysis to solve many a challenge. She'd spotted a small herd of unattended Tartokis, and so jumped on the back of one of them and headed after Chuttnee.

The X-ITs had been watching everything from the SpaceJet, and Zara was eager to act. She grabbed Zak's arm. "C'mon, let's go."

"But they'll see us."

"Not if we go the back way."

"Do we have to?"

Captain Bushawoo had already transmorphed his front end and was relieved to get his bird head back. He screwed up his face just as Zak and Zara jumped in their original pouch. Suddenly the two of them were ejected with force in a thick cloud of green-colored methane.

"Oh, yuck!"

"It's only gas, Zak! Now head for the horses."

The area where they had touched down was a clearing in the middle of the bush country. The vegetation was strange to the eyes of the adventurers from Earth. It was beige-orange, dry and scrubby-looking, the scent in the air smelled like roses! In the distance, they could hear a cooing sound and wondered what birds and other creatures might live here. They didn't see anything—even with the help of their enervisors.

As she ran to where the animals were standing, Zara couldn't help noticing the fur on the fingernails of the Vivoans. It looked so strange, especially as their fingers were so long. One of the younger females had painted hers in different colors, in contrast to their dull-looking sackcloth clothes. Zara thought she might be a bit of a rebel and they may have something in common.

The X-ITs made it to the Tartokis without being noticed. Zak was a little nervous. "Which one are you taking, and which one do you think is the tamest?"

Zara was a good rider and so wasn't as worried. She climbed onto the back of a silvery-white one that was being nuzzled by one that was caramel in color. "Here take this one, these two seem to like each other."

Zak gave her a sideways look.

"Get over it, Zak, and get on."

Tartokis were lovely-looking animals. Most of them were the golden-caramel color, like Zak's, with unusual green eyes. Their manes were long and thick as were their tails, and were the same chocolate-brown color as the dark line that ran along their spines splitting at the tail and then going down the back of each hind leg. The distance between their shoulders and their haunches was a little shorter than a normal horse and their legs a little longer. The others Tartokis were silvery-grey, like the one Zara had chosen. They had bright blue eyes and a black line along their spine, with a black mane and tail.

"These are really pretty animals," Zara said to Zak as they rode off.

She was happy to find that their backs were much softer than they looked but she wasn't prepared for what happened next. As she settled down, she immediately felt a *zing* go right the way through her. She was connected to the Tartoki—it was as if they'd become one. She was a little afraid at first and wriggled around. Then she was sure she heard it telling her, *relax and no harm will come to you.* Zara thought how it reminded her of the way she felt sometimes when she was playing with Jake. She was missing him.

Then she looked over at Zak who was holding onto the mane very tightly. She saw the look of surprise as he settled on his Tartoki and felt the connection. His expression was priceless. Tartokis didn't walk in quite the way that horses do—they sort of bounced along, but it wasn't uncomfortable.

The two of them rode past some kind of houses that were made from all natural materials. Clusters of them were carved into the side of the small hills that were now starting to surround the two riders. The Vivoans had done a good job of decorating the outside of their homes with all sorts of stones, berries, and fancy shells.

Zak saw that there was an abrupt change in terrain up ahead, although he couldn't quite make out what it was. He looked down at the ground and noticed a number of holes of all different sizes; he wondered what kind of creature had made them. The X-IT was impressed by how the Tartokis were masters at avoiding them. Zak was even starting to feel secure as they rode in the direction SmartyNuff had taken a little earlier.

Zara thought about how much she'd wanted this kind of adventure since she was a young girl. She could hear her Grandma Elizabeth telling them over and over again. *My dears, we each create the worlds in which we live. First, we have a dream, and then we think about it becoming real. We put our hopes and wishes into it and open ourselves to the possibility. Before we know it, we take a risk, and there we are alive in what began as only a dream. Most importantly, you have to be sure that you are living your own dream and not somebody else's. Otherwise, you will never find the joy that comes from fulfilling your destiny. Yes, you will feel afraid sometimes, you will feel lonely sometimes, you will feel insecure sometimes, and you will question everything you ever thought was true. Just remember that inside you, you have the power to set yourself free of all your doubts and fears; and, if you want to, you can choose a different dream.* As she rode alongside Zak, she smiled remembering all that Elizabeth had told them. In that moment, Zara knew beyond a shadow of a doubt, that she was living her dream and she would find her beloved grandmother.

Chapter Twenty-Three

Strongy, Brighty, and Weeze were taken by the Vivoans to the town hall, along with Yorazz, to discover more about the unknown Skyship and the FrightGeist. Strongy picked up on their sense of urgency. He wanted to find Yezzadar and Elizabeth, and they wanted to get to grips with the source of danger to their young ones. The connection was obvious to him, and it was important to act quickly and get on with the mission. Brighty, on the other hand, was more interested in finding out as much as possible about what had happened.

PirsittaPinto, a striking female Vivoan, took the lead and filled them in on the history. "When the first child was found, we thought that it was some mysterious virus. We took care of him until his strength returned. He remembered nothing of what happened, but he had this dark mark above his navel."

She showed them a drawing of an almost perfect circle with a hole in the centre. "We didn't think too much more about it until a second...and then a third child disappeared." She described the terrible condition they were in, and how they had lost much of their life force. "We found them in the same state with the same wound. After this, we knew it was something more sinister. So we sat in wait to catch a glimpse of the creature."

"And what did you find out?" Yorazz wanted the details.

"Well, for the longest time we found nothing except more exhausted children. Then we remembered the myth of Dreadzog."

"Tell us more."

"You may have seen, as we made our way here, that there are a lot of small holes in the surface of the planet?"

They nodded in agreement.

She continued, "These are made by creatures called Agapods. They are hairy caterpillars, with the many legs of a centipede. They have a pointed sting at the end of their crusty worm-like bodies that, if it stabs you, can do some harm. It isn't really life-threatening."

Pirsitta described how they grew to a certain size above the ground and then burrowed beneath the surface to live out their short lifespan. "Agapods rarely grow to be more than a few zogas in diameter and about ten zogas in length. They're the size of a fat worm. When they die, their bodies feed the soil and that's the end of them."

"Then who or what is Dreadzog?" Brighty asked.

A younger male Vivoan called JayP took over the story. "The myth describes how one Agapod didn't die but just kept on growing and, kept on burrowing. He is the one that is supposed to have created the vast honeycomb of tunnels underneath Vivo. Only, no one has ever seen him. We call him Dreadzog."

"And you think it is Dreadzog who is responsible for the attacks on the children?" Brighty was curious.

"Exactly that," Pirsitta answered. "Until one day, we heard the sound of a child screaming and as we reached where she was playing, we saw this dark shadow hovering over her. Then something jumped down one of the holes into the tunnels. It wasn't an Agapod."

"So, can you take us to where you think it might be operating?" Strongy asked, eager to stop talking and take some action.

"Yes," said JayP. "We'll take you there right now."

Pirsitta hadn't quite finished. "Since that time, the number of attacks has been growing more frequent and the sightings of the shadow suggest it is becoming even larger."

JayP felt Strongy's impatience building but wanted to add one more point. "Whatever it is, it is using some of the children as its helpers. They set up something called the Energy Drain Zone or EDZ and then lure in other kids who then become the FrightGeist's victims. Once they're in the zone, he drains as much of their life-force as he can and then disappears, until he needs more energy."

"That's very helpful, thank you. Now let's go and see what we can find." Much to Strongy's frustration, Brighty still had more questions.

"You call it the FrightGeist. Can you say a little more about what *it* looks like?"

"Our children named it that, but it is really difficult to describe. It's as if part of the creature is hard and the rest is soft. It has a solid core that is not too big, about your size, but then it has this huge dark ghost-like shadow that hangs over it. It walks on two legs and its energy is very dense."

Weeze asked them to draw a quick picture to give them some idea of what they were looking for. The visual of the FrightGeist made it more real. StrongyNuff was at bursting point and had long reached the end of his patience.

"So, have you got all you need now, huh? Can we move on?"

To his relief, a chorus of YoHas rang out, and they started to gather some more Tartokis and organize the different search parties.

Farther away, SmartyNuff had followed Chuttnee through a bushy forest and out into the area with the odd landscape that they'd seen in the briefing. The holes in the ground here were much bigger and there were several cave-like entrances in between the naturally formed sculptures. Chuttnee's chhhttttrrng grew louder as he approached one of the caves. He was flying backwards and forwards across the opening to the tunnel.

SmartyNuff removed a black slug-like creature and put it around her ear.

"Strongy, Chuttnee's found the source of the signal but it's…umm…"

"It's what?"

Smarty whirled around to see that Zara and Zak had followed her. She quickly took the slug from around her ear and put it back in her pouch, cutting off Strongy without answering his question.

"What are you doing here?" she asked a little abruptly.

"Same as you. Looking for my grandmother."

Zak stared at the mouth of the cave. "You think she's in there, don't you?"

"There's no way to tell."

Zara disagreed, "Oh yes, there is." She jumped off her Tartoki and after hesitating for a moment, she took a deep breath and stepped towards the entrance. She had to get over her hatred of being underground.

Smarty was very nervous. "Don't."

"Why…er…not?" Zara took a step back.

"You…could get hurt."

She knew she had to face her fear and not let it hold her back. "I'll take that chance."

Zara moved into the opening, still a little nervously, with Zak following her.

"Wait…" The chief of the AirSpinners was concerned. "We need to prepare you for this, you must have the proper equipment."

Zak turned. "We took a couple of backpacks, what more do we need?"

The little Nuff didn't answer and looked very uncomfortable.

"What's wrong, Smarty? Really?" The Nuff was feeding Zara's fear and she was getting impatient. At the same time, the X-IT was feeling concerned about her friend.

"Nothing."

"So are you coming with us?"

She shook her head.

"Really?" Zak asked.

"Really!"

Zara shrugged and steeled herself to go into the cave.

"Are you sure you're okay doing this?" Zak asked Zara, knowing about her recurring nightmare.

"Yes, I am. Just don't go too far away from me."

They entered through the mouth of the cave. It was dark inside as they moved cautiously deeper underground. Zak stopped for a moment.

"Cool backpack, huh?"

Zara's mind was somewhere else. "Huh? Oh yeah, what's in it?"

"Nuffstuff. Hey, Nuff stuff…get it?"

"I get it, I get it." Zara paused. "It was almost like she was afraid of something."

"Who, SmartyNuff? Come on, she was willing to fight giant acid squirting robots without a weapon."

"Yeah, I know, Zak, but maybe giant acid squirting robots aren't what scare her."

It took a few minutes to adjust to the changing atmosphere and lack of light. It was a bit creepy, not damp as much as it was just eerie and dark. Their enervisors gave out some light and helped them to *see* when it was dim. What they couldn't see was what was watching them; its silhouette was simply lost in the darkness.

Zara preferred being up front so she could see where she was going. The tunnel was wide and quite dry. They saw how it had been perfectly drilled out by something or someone. There were rocks in a few places, but mainly the walls were made of clay. It wasn't crumbling much at all. In fact, on closer inspection, it looked like there was some kind of gummy film over it that held the soil in place. A little had fallen away here or there, but overall, it was in good shape as far as tunnels go.

The air wasn't very nice, although it was better in some places than others. Zara thought it smelled like the inside of running shoes when you haven't been wearing any socks. She noticed the remains of caterpillar-like creatures on the ground. She didn't know they were Agapods. Only their shells and some hairs were left and she couldn't work out whether they had died naturally or had been food for something else. She decided it was better not to think about it too much.

114

The X-ITs were quiet for a while as they made their way deeper in. Then Zak broke the silence.

"Don't you think it's amazing how much you can see in the dark?"

"Er…yeah, it's not as bad as I thought it would be."

As they continued, they came to a fork in the tunnel. It was an easy decision. They would stay together, and they would take the one on the right. There was much more light!

Before long, the air grew much more dense and damp. It was almost sticky. The smell had changed too, and there were some strange *purgling* sounds. Zara had heard the Nuffs use this word before, it was a cross between purring and gurgling and she thought it was perfect to describe what she was hearing. Chuttnee had flown into the tunnels just before the X-ITs and had gone on ahead. The two of them had lost sight of him. They stopped for a moment and tried to hear where the noise was coming from.

"What do you s'pose it is?" Zak asked, looking around.

"You don't think it's that FrightGeist thingy, do you?" Zara moved a little closer to him.

"Naaah…it better not be."

As they listened, they discovered that the sound was coming from somewhere in the rocky walls up ahead. It was the first place where there was something other than the gummy clay. The closer they got, the louder the noise became. Then, before they had time to do anything to protect themselves, hundreds of small lizard-like creatures with bulbous eyes and long fangs, poured out of the cracks in the rocks. The green-colored crevice crawlers jumped onto the intruders, covering them from head to foot.

Zara screamed. "Zak, they're all over me get them off, get them off."

"Much as I'd like to help you, Zar, I'm kinda covered myself."

Zak grabbed one of them from his left ear and threw it to the floor, then, another half dozen jumped down on him. Zara was trying to get them out of her hair but it was a losing battle. They struggled, hoping to move away from the rocky outcropping, but it wasn't easy. After a few moments, a high-pitched whistling sound echoed through the tunnel, as the space filled up with bat-like creatures.

"Oh no," Zara shouted. "Not more!" She needn't have worried. In seconds, the lizard-like things had scurried into the rocks. Any that were too slow were grabbed by the gumbats and thrown to the ground.

Zak caught hold of Zara's hand, and pointing yelled, "Quick over there."

They ran to a place that was free of rocks, where they watched as their winged rescuers annihilated any remaining crevice crawlers. After they finished their work, the gumbats hung upside down on the ceiling of the tunnel, victorious. Suddenly, from the same direction, Chuttnee appeared with a second squadron, but fortunately, they weren't needed. The Nuffs' blue mascot then flew over to where the X-ITs were checking their injuries.

"Thanks, Chuttnee. Not sure how much longer we could have kept that up!" Zak was rubbing his left ear with one hand and his right cheek with the other. He had two nasty bites that were red, with drops of blood oozing out on his left hand. "They seem to have vampire tendencies except they don't know where to look for the jugular."

Zara couldn't believe how much tougher her friend had become.

"Zak, can you check they're all out of my hair?"

115

"Er…okay. You've…er…got a nasty bite on your chin." He went to touch it but thought better of it.

"Yeah, I know; there's another one on my wrist. They'll heal." She looked down the front of her T-shirt.

"You're sure there are none left down there, want me to, er, check that out?"

She shuddered then broke into a little grin at his second comment, it wasn't like him at all. She chose to ignore it, at least outwardly. "Yep. Let's hope there aren't anymore further into the tunnels."

After a few moments of inspecting each other for any remaining intruders, and thanking Chuttnee for his timely intervention, they began walking on. Zara asked him to join them, but the little blue creature decided he would hang around with his friends for a while.

It was getting hotter as they went deeper. Zak was sweating profusely. "We must be getting closer to the planet's core."

"I don't think so we can still see the light from the entrance. Look over…"

She turned to point back to where they'd come from, but as she did she lost her footing, falling over an edge and sliding down a very long slope into a shaft of utter blackness. Her screams faded into silence.

Zak panicked. "Zara. ZARAHHH."

He ran up and down. The drop looked sheer. He needed some rope, but there wasn't any. After running in circles for a couple of minutes, he headed back to the entrance to see if he could get help. The bat thingies were still keeping the rock dwellers stuck in their crevices, so he passed through the passage without incident. He got to the entrance to find SmartyNuff still hovering around talking to the Tartokis.

"Zara fell. You've got to help."

Smarty stared into the darkness of the cave. She desperately wanted to help but something was holding her back. "The others will be here soon…"

"Not soon. NOW!" Zak was panicking.

"You might only make it worse, wait for StrongyNuff."

"I can't wait, don't you see…"

He looked around wondering what he could use and saw some dry, stringy vines hanging near the cave's entrance. He started to yank at them. Smarty looked on as he desperately tried to break them. She picked up a sharp-edged rock and cut through a couple of them. He looked at her questioningly, it just wasn't logical, but he didn't say anything. As soon as he'd got hold of the loose vines, he ran back to the mouth of the cave. Just as he entered, he turned around.

"Thanks." He disappeared into the darkness, as she stood like a statue staring straight ahead.

Chapter Twenty-Four

Zak found his way back to where he had lost Zara and began tying the vines together to form a rope. There were a few big boulders pushed into a corner on the floor of the tunnel, away from the main thoroughfare. After making sure his makeshift line was secure, he gave it a big yank to see if it would hold his weight. It did. Even though the ground was firm, there were a few loose stones and so he put his foot out tentatively, not wanting to slip into the chasm below. He looked down into the blackness beneath him and started his descent.

Farther down the shaft, Zara's backpack was caught on a small pointed rock but she wasn't wearing it anymore. Instead, she had freed herself from the straps and was clinging to the bottom of it hoping her feet would reach the floor. They didn't.

"Zak. Zaaaaak," she yelled as loud as she could, then paused, waiting for a response. Nothing came. *What do I do now?* Then she realized that something in the backpack could help her decide what to do next. She couldn't just hang around hoping for her friend to rescue her.

It wasn't going to be easy to access it from where she was dangling. Zara was a leftie, so holding on tightly with her right hand, she explored the rock face with her free one. Soon she found a protrusion she could reach and, using her foot, discovered another that she could stand on. Drawing on the strength in her arms and letting out a few timely grunts, she pulled herself away from the backpack. Swinging to the left onto a small ledge, she was able to climb up enough, stretch out, and grab the pack, which was only just within reach.

After opening it, Zara fiddled around and found something that looked like a torch. It was made out of a branch from a windmill tree and had a lens of sorts across one end. She shook it but nothing happened, so she did it again, but still nothing. She opened it and saw inside what could only have been a sleeping glow-worm. Not wanting to frighten it but at the same time wanting it to wake up, she blew on it gently until the little worm started to glow.

Zara shone it around and found, to her surprise and delight, that she was only a few feet above the ground. After placing the backpack over her shoulders, she jumped down bending her knees to break the fall. The landing was good and there were no sprains or strains. With the glowing torch in her hand, she started to walk forward, gingerly. She was nervous that there might be another drop and another shaft taking her even deeper down.

"Grandma, Grandma," she called out, unaware that the same silhouette that was hiding in the shadows when they first entered the tunnel, was now right behind her.

Above ground, CoolyNuff and the Commander Cratt had found Smarty.

"How long ago did they go in?" Cooly asked.

"Just a few zigs."

"You shouldn't have let them."

"And what was I supposed to do? Explain everything?"

Cooly walked up to the opening, avoiding Smarty's question.

"Explain everything, explain <u>everything</u>?" It was just the Cratt doing its thing!

Zak, meanwhile, was full of adrenalin and had begun to climb down the rope that he'd made from the vines, into the shaft below. He hoped it would be long enough as climbing back up was going to be a lot tougher. He was worried that Zara may be lying somewhere unconscious with, at the very least, a broken leg or maybe even something worse. The X-IT didn't want to think about it, so focused his full attention on his hands and feet as he dropped into the chasm.

After a short time, he noticed that although he was moving down the vine, the rock face in front of him was the same. It was the weirdest of experiences. He stopped lowering himself for a moment only to find that the vine he was hanging from, was being pulled upwards. What he didn't know was by what!

"Zara, Zaaaarah?"

There was no reply.

He was worried, scared to look up, afraid of what he might see. When he heard slurping sounds, he knew he had to. His worst fears were realized. There, gazing down at him with half-open eyes, ecstatically chomping on the vine was a gigantic worm-like thing with a frilly-looking mouth, dribbling slime. Its size was about the diameter of the tunnels they'd passed through and was the Vivo creature of myth and legend, Dreadzog. Only he was very real!

The giant Agapod was clearly enjoying dining on the vine sucking it up like a string of spaghetti. Zak did not intend to be anyone's dinner and as fast as he could, he lowered himself down the rope, discovering way too soon, that ropes end. He had a few more moments to consider his options while he dangled far, far above the floor of the shaft with very little hope of escape. It was a desperate situation.

Somewhere, a long way below him, Zara was searching for Elizabeth in the lower tunnels of Dreadzog's giant underground maze.

"Grandma, Grandma, it's me, we're here…"

The young adventurer continued through an area that had lots of short stubby channels, branching off the main passageway. They were all dead ends. She didn't know they had been abandoned because the stalactites and stalagmites would have cut into Dreadzog's body as he drilled through the clay to create his honeycomb home. What she did know was that there was something or someone following her. She could sense it.

Zara whirled around abruptly to confront her stalker, shining the torch right in the face of a copper-haired young man with piercing blue eyes. She gasped. He put his hand up to escape the glare but it only took him a moment to adjust to the light.

"Who are you?" If she was scared, she wasn't showing it.

He replied with the same question, in a voice that to Zara sounded like warm treacle.

"Who are you?"

"I asked first!" The young X-IT stood firm.

A faint orange glow seemed to emanate from inside him.

"I'm Shavolac…and you?"

"I'm Zara." He didn't seem that threatening to her but instead, more mysterious.

He was curious about the young girl from planet Earth standing in front of him. "So what are you doing here and why are you calling out for your grandma?"

"Well…" She was surprisingly relaxed as if she was talking to a friend who she hadn't seen for a long time. After a few moments, she sat down on a rock and told him what had happened from the beginning to the present time.

He listened to all of it.

"I must tell you, this story of yours doesn't make any sense to me. Why go to so much trouble for just one person?" Shavolac was pacing up and down in front of her.

"It's my grandmother!"

"So?"

"Don't you have grandparents where you come from, Shavolac?"

He liked how she said his name.

"My home planet is called Rettosto, and yes, of course, we do." He paused and looked down. "My grandparents tried to kill me."

Zara was visibly shocked and her eyes opened wide in disbelief.

"I'm heir to the throne, and they didn't want me anywhere near it."

"So they tried to kill you? Really?"

He nodded. "They got together and conspired to destroy me so that they could continue to rule and then…"

She didn't want to dig any deeper, so continued the conversation from a different angle, "Is that why you're hiding here? To get away from them."

"That's part of it."

"What's the rest?"

"I didn't want to live in a world where someday I would be a grandfather trying to kill my own flesh and fire."

Zara could really sense his struggle and felt compassion for her new found companion. She guessed he was probably just a little older than her. "You wouldn't have to do that. Once you're the King, you could change the rules."

He smiled at her sweetness. "It's hard for you to understand but it's the way it's always been and it's the way we are. I thought that if I got away from there, everything would change. That I would change. But there are some things that are in our basic carbon cells."

"People can change if they want to really work on it. My grandma has always told me that. You have to be clear about what it is you want to become and then make a big commitment to be it. She says you have to want it much more than you want your old way of being."

He looked at her with his piercing blue eyes, wondering if it could be different.

"No, I can feel it burning! It's always going to be there, this darkness inside of me, this…rage."

The amber glow grew even more intense as the anger rose inside him.

Then the energy coalesced into a fireball in his hand that he spontaneously hurled at the wall of the cave. It exploded spectacularly lighting up the whole area.

Zara wasn't frightened. Her grandma had told her so many stories about things like this, that she wasn't shocked. She didn't feel any sense of danger from Shavolac. "Why are you telling me all of this?"

"You're different."

"I am?"

"Anyone else would have been scared of me, but you're not. You intended me no harm and so you assumed that I intended none for you. That's called innocence."

Zara didn't know whether to take it as a compliment. "People are always telling me that I only see the good side of things that I'm gullible, and if I don't see the bad stuff then one day I'm going to get burnt."

Her choice of words was interesting to him and he was calmer now. Relaxing, he sat down on a rock across from her.

"For me, it's the other way around. All I see is the bad and one day I will be Lord of the AshDemons if I return. Maybe we could make an exchange. I'll trade you some of my rage for some of your innocence."

She didn't know how to respond and jumped off the rock. "I…I have to go and find my grandma so I'd better do that."

"I'll go with you."

"You don't have to."

"I know these caves very well by now and you can see that I can be useful in the dark." He smiled for the first time and she felt something inside her rise again. These feelings were all so new to her.

"There's been some unusual activity down here recently let me take you to where it is."

She was a bit off centre and was hesitant about his offer. "You can just point me in the right direction if that would be easier, Shavolac." Even saying his name gave her a buzz.

"That's okay, it's no trouble. And besides, I'd like to meet a grandparent who doesn't want to kill their offspring!"

Chapter Twenty-Five

The Vivoans had taken the Nuffs to a place where they'd found two drained children only a short while before they'd arrived; Yorazz had returned to the SpaceJet. They searched around to see if they could get any clues about the FrightGeist when suddenly they heard someone crying. Weeze and Strongy moved towards the sound and found a small Vivoan girl lying in the scrub. They had no idea how long she'd been there, but when Brighty put the confidometer on her tiny wrist, there was hardly any color in the crystals.

StrongyNuff turned to Pirsitta and JayP. "It looks like we found her just in time. Weeze, see if there are any more survivors around here."

Brighty pulled the Aurabooster from her backpack and administered two shots. "Look, the crystals are getting more colorful. She's growing stronger and she's not one of his helpers, they're purple, not orange."

Weeze meanwhile, had disappeared into the bushes, so StrongyNuff followed his trail. He almost tripped over him as he lay face down on the ground. "What are you doing, brother, I nearly stepped on you?"

"Ssssh, get down here with me and stay quiet. Look, there are some children and I think they may be the FrightGeist's helpers. They're luring others in."

The two Nuffs watched silently as the children seemed to go into some kind of zombie state and move around in a strange pattern.

"I think they're setting up the EDZ. You know the energy drain zone."

The unsuspecting children from the village had joined the helpers and were playing a game. Unknown to them, they were being drawn bit by bit towards the place where they would soon become frozen with fear and have their life force taken from them.

If Strongy and Weeze acted too soon, they could blow it, but if they waited too long there would be more casualties. It was a tough call.

After a few more moments, the two Nuffs were joined by the Vivoans, who crouched down beside them. After getting a sense of the situation, Pirsitta whispered. "We have to make sure that we not only capture the FrightGeist but that we rescue the corded children who are his helpers. If they escape, they may be lost forever."

"Yes." Weeze agreed. "We don't need to lose any of these guys; they are cool kids and have done nothing wrong. Hey, they're just victims of this Geist's gig."

Within seconds, three of the Vivoan children who had been playing with the others were trapped in the EDZ. The two who were still free hadn't noticed and continued the game until suddenly a huge dark shadow fell over the whole area and they ran as fast as they could.

Everyone there felt the spine-chilling sensation that came with the shadow, and the Vivoans were very afraid. The FrightGeist looked even bigger than ever as it made its way to the frozen children.

"Let's wait a moment longer," Strongy urged.

It seemed like an eternity as they watched the FrightGeist draw closer to his prey. They had to time it just right.

"Now!" shouted Strongy as the sombre shadow stepped into the middle of the Energy Drain Zone.

In the tunnels beneath, Dreadzog was close to inhaling Zak. Looking up, all the X-IT could see was a mouth filled with a scattering of chipped triangular teeth, surrounded by charcoal-colored slimy gums. The oversized Agapod had two skin-like protrusions hanging from either side of his lower jaw that were swaying from side to side as he chomped on the vine. Some saliva dripped down on Zak's face. It stank.

"Okay, you oversized worm, that's it, I am not going to be your dinner."

He began swinging on the end of the vine and noticed some pock-like holes in the wall of the rock face. It was choice time. He knew his next move had to be impeccable or he would plunge into the blackness below.

The vine swayed back and forth gaining momentum, and after a few more seconds, Zak knew he had to let go.

"Time to jump...aaaaah!"

He landed on a rocky outcropping but his left foot slipped on some loose stones and for a moment, he thought he was toast. Fortunately, he instinctively reached out and found another piece of rock that he grabbed to gain stability. It provided him with the opportunity to climb onto a ledge that happened to be the mouth of another tunnel. Taking a deep breath, he scanned his surroundings, not paying any attention to the frustrated Agapod.

"Huh, it looks like I've been dangling inside a cylindrical-shaped piece of Swiss cheese. Whoaaaaaaa..." Zak cowered.

Dreadzog had lowered himself to within inches of where the boy was standing. It was a nightmare scenario as the monstrous worm lunged for his dessert, to find it was just out of reach. In a second, he'd recoiled into his skin to try again. This time as he dived forward he closed his mouth around a protruding rock, chipping off another piece of a tooth and dropping a chunk-sized piece of saliva onto the top of Zak's head.

"Yuck, you're nothing but a slobbering worm but you can't reach me, can you? Too bad you're going to miss tasting some young, earthling flesh."

Dreadzog gazed down at him with a pained look, as another glob of slime dripped from his gums. Zak quickly ducked to one side as it fell into the gaping hole below. He looked up again to find that his pursuer was backing off. Relieved, and after wiping most of the remains of the sticky stuff out of his hair, he climbed further onto the ledge and headed down the tunnel.

He hadn't gone very far when he heard a loud slurping sound coming from another direction right behind him. *I thought I'd got away from him. Maybe if I...*Too late, Zak had reached a dead end. He turned to face the giant Agapod then noticed a smaller tunnel off to his left. With seconds to spare, he darted down it. He hoped the aperture would be too tight of a squeeze for the worm, then quickly realized that all it meant was that Dreadzog had to reduce his circumference and stretch his length.

Zak began running faster as the new slimmed down version of his pursuer speeded up. Within a few minutes, he was back at one of the entrances to the cylinder-shaped chasm and there was nowhere to go unless he could quickly climb up the rock face. A moment of panic swept over him as he lost confidence. Then he stepped onto a narrow ledge that protruded over the chasm below, just as Dreadzog's hungry mouth opened and snapped at him.

"Huh...whaaaat's going on?"

A metallic hand had grabbed hold of the back of his T-shirt and was pulling him upwards to safety. He didn't know what it was but he felt relieved and didn't struggle. After a few moments, Zak could see that it was the elongated arm of the Commander Cratt from the spaceship.

Meanwhile, the Agapod was still desperately trying to grasp his tormentor, wriggling further out of the tunnel in a desperate attempt to grab Zak's legs. Again, he missed but this time the intensity of his momentum caused the whole of Dreadzog's long body to pop out of the tunnel, making a sound that was so loud, it echoed through the underground maze. For a moment, it seemed like he was just suspended in mid-air. Then, hoping to avoid his fate, he flicked his tail wildly against the other side of the cylindrical chasm. It was his last ditched attempt to recover, before falling headfirst into the darkness below.

"What was that noise?" Zara turned to Shavolac after hearing the loud popping sound, which was immediately followed by a shuddering of the floor in the tunnels. "Was it an earthquake?"

"No, I don't think so, but you're safe with me. He put his hand on her shoulder."

Zara felt a zing go through her and didn't know if she was afraid or pleased. What she did know was that she wanted to find Zak and see daylight again. She'd never liked being below ground, but at least now she felt that she'd proved to herself that she was courageous enough to overcome her fear.

"I really want to find my grandma and..." She paused for a long time, "And...she isn't here. I know this is not where I saw her, she's on another planet; I'm certain of it." There was a tone of desperation creeping into her voice. "What if we're too late to help her—she's in a lot of trouble. Do you think we have much further to go to where you saw the activity, it might give us a clue about how to find her?"

"No, we're almost there," he said reassuringly.

A hundred feet above where they were walking Zara's lifelong friend had just been rescued from the slobbering jaws of the legendary Dreadzog.

Zak was grateful and curious. "Commander, what are you doing here?"

"Proooooblem?"

"No, no, there's no problem. But thanks anyway for showing up at a very good time. Er...where are the others?"

The Cratt pointed to the tunnel entrance.

"Ah, right. Well, we need to find Zara, can you...er...help?"

"Find Zaaara, find Zaaara. Where is Zaaara?"

"That's the whole point, I don't know."

"Maybe thaaaat way?" He pointed ahead of them to where some kind of reflection was dancing on the roof of the tunnel. "Maybe oooover therrrrre?"

Zak wasn't good at tuning in, and his enervisor was in the backpack that was hanging on a rock somewhere far below. He wasn't about to go looking for it. So nodding his head, he said, "I guess it's as good as any other. So...let's do it."

Chapter Twenty-Six

Grandma Elizabeth was horrified as she watched the small wiry creatures tear into the still warm flesh of their dead Scartusian relative and devour all but the finest bone structure that created its form. It was a stark reminder of the law of survival. She knew she didn't have long before their focus would shift and the appetite, that drove them to such gruesome behavior, would consume them again. She was next on their menu.

Zara's grandmother climbed as high as she could and found a small opening, which allowed her to get hold of a few rocks that had fallen when the doorway had collapsed. She was stockpiling them as ammunition against her hostile assailants. Deep down she knew that the size of the arsenal she could accumulate would only keep them at bay for a short while. Still, she had to try.

Elizabeth let out a shocked squeal and jumped back, nearly losing her footing, as she suddenly heard a heavy thump come from outside. It was followed immediately by a scratching sound that was faint at first, but then grew louder. It was a bit like chalk on a blackboard and it hurt her ears. She was curious and tried hard to find a space in the rocks to look out. After a few frustrating moments, she gave up because it was impossible to see anything. She turned to face the inside of the cave and saw, to her horror, the baby Scartusians heading in her direction fast; they were clearly still hungry. Picking up some of the odd-shaped rocks, Elizabeth began hurling them at her antagonists.

For each one she hit, another one rose up and dived at her, until she realized she was running short of loose rocks. She knew she wouldn't last long in the cave and decided the second option was her preference.

At least then, she might be able to escape again and get to Zara, who she had *seen* was now in the same galaxy.

"I'm in here, Yezzadar. You win. Get me out and tell me what you want me to do."

He couldn't hear her because he was busy back in his mechanical metropolis, getting his troops ready for action. When there was no response, she pulled on what she thought was the last rock in the pile only to uncover a gold one. She was stunned. For a second, Elizabeth stopped everything she was doing and centered herself. She knew she could only take one brief moment to focus her mind's eye on exactly who or what was making the commotion outside.

Take the gold rock, Elizabeth.

A sense of relief flowed over her.

Take it NOW.

She did as she was told and firmly grasping it, pulled hard. A section of the roof of the cave gave way crushing the nearby Scartusians and allowing her to quickly climb to safety.

Almost out, and still holding the golden rock, she saw the reflection of her rescuer. He grabbed hold of her lifting her out of the way of any remaining pursuers. Elizabeth was trying to remember when they had last been together. In some way, it didn't matter. He was never more than a breath away. Time and distance had no relevance with such a depth of connection. For a moment, as his golden light surrounded her, she relaxed for the first time in what seemed like forever. It was good to feel safe again with Aigledor. She always had.

His voice though, was urgent.

"You must know that Sylvameena is using Yezzadar to get the InfiniKey."

"It doesn't surprise me. When haven't the two of you used us to fight your endless war?"

"You make it sound so trivial, Elizabeth. But we will resolve it one day for sure."

She gave him a long piercing look.

"Dear Aigledor, I thought you understood that you cannot…"

A loud thundering sound filled the air as the two of them looked off into the distance and watched as Skyship after Skyship blasted into the night sky. The direction was clear as they headed towards a distinctive bright purple-colored planet way off in the distance. Their destination was Quomos.

Chapter Twenty-Seven

Zara suddenly breathed a deep sigh of relief. It was so loud that it caused Shavolac to turn around to look at her.

"Are you okay?"

"Yeah, yeah I'm fine. It's just that...er...like I suddenly don't feel urgent anymore. Something's happened, and it's okay." She was picking up on her grandma's energy.

"You look amazing, Zara..."

All the worry was gone from her face and he could see a gold light in her aura. "I'm glad that you feel safe with me."

"Oh, did I just say that?" Zara was surprised.

"No, but well..."

She looked at him and smiled. "I think I can go the rest of the way on my own..."

"I wouldn't want you to get lost, Zara."

Shavolac took her hand and although the expression on her face suggested she felt a little uncomfortable, she didn't resist.

Meanwhile, Zak and the Cratt had been moving in the direction of the strange colored glow that reflected off the sticky walls. It was getting stronger each time they went around a bend in the tunnels.

"There, there, there..."

The Cratt now pointed again, only this time it was toward a large hole in the shaft wall, which seemed to contain something that had all sorts of flashing lights.

Zak saw it too. "Hmmm, maybe there's something..."

Suddenly, they were inside a cavern within the cave, and it was filled with technology.

"Whoa, this is some pretty cool stuff." Zak was looking up at a wall that was covered in machines and he knew what they were.

"You know what this stuff is, Commander?"

"Not Zaara..."

"It's a radio receiving station and that bug in my brain was sending its signal to here."

"Not looking for Zaaaaara anymore then?"

"Of course I am, it's just that...aaaaaghh." Zak started to shiver and shake. "I'm starting to feel kinda funny, not right. Are you feeling funny?"

"Not feeling funny, look funny, not feel funny..."

Zak looked around but only saw the lights, and some shadows until he turned. One of the shadows was getting bigger and bigger until it took over the whole of the cavern.

Scared, Zak started to back out of the other side of the cave together with the Cratt. But his legs were turning to jelly and he didn't even have the energy to speak. He began to stagger and soon fell to his knees. Drained of all fighting power, he collapsed on the floor. The shadow moved closer to do what it always did, steal the life force from others to secure its own continuity.

Just as it was about to draw the chi from Zak, it heard a sound coming from another part of the tunnel.

"Shavolac wait." She stopped abruptly, taking her hand from his.

"What's wrong?"

"I'm starting to feel weak all of a sudden as if…"

Shavolac smiled. "I understand."

"No, you don't. Look!"

She pointed over his shoulder to where a very large shadow had formed and was coming closer.

He turned. "Get behind me, Zara."

She did as she was told as they waited, watching the shadow grow bigger and darker, and feeling the massive drop in the temperature that accompanied the FrightGeist. It wasn't much longer before it appeared and Shavolac hurled his first fireball, then a second. Instead of it having the desired effect, the spectre was just absorbing the energy, making it stronger until it was so huge that it filled the entire cave. Zara collapsed, frozen with fear. Shavolac, desperate to protect her, dived at the shadow and in so doing, started losing his own power.

Upon falling, Zara's shirt had opened and the $\mathcal{E}$-shaped pendant given to her by her grandma was now exposed resting on the upper part of her chest. As the FrightGeist moved towards her, Shavolac found the strength to create one last fireball that he hurled in the direction of the shadow. Instead, it hit the roof of the tunnel creating a reflection on the pendant, which immediately amplified the light. The $\mathcal{E}$ started to glow brighter and brighter until the cavern was filled with blinding white light. The FrightGeist was screaming and writhing as its vast shadow began to shrink. The sound it made was like a death cry echoing throughout the tunnels. It was getting smaller and smaller. Finally, all that was left was something no bigger than a Nuff as it collapsed face down onto the floor of the cavern—drained.

A stunned Shavolac hurried over to Zara and knelt down beside her, just as Zak entered their part of the cavern with the overexcited Cratt.

"Found Zara, found Zara!"

Zak ran over to where she was just coming around in the arms of Shavolac.

She was groggy.

"Zara, Zara, are you okay?" Zak shouted.

"Mmmmmm…"

She stared into Shavolac's blue eyes at the same time as hearing Zak's voice. For a moment, she was totally disorientated.

Zak was relieved and agitated. "Zara, I—who's this?"

She sat up to get her bearings and saw Zak.

"Oh, oh…er…that's Shavolac."

"That's all you're going to say…"

"I…he…"

It was Shavolac's turn to ask questions.

"Zara, who's this?"

"This is my friend Zak."

"And how are we defining friend here?"

Zak was angry. "Zara, who is this guy and why haven't you told him about me?"

"Whoooo am I, whoooo are you, whoooo are we?" It was the Cratt.

Suddenly, a loud groan emanated from where the shadow had fallen moments earlier. It made everybody stop the conversation and turn around to see what was making the sound. Zak, feeling very frustrated with the presence of Shavolac, started to go over to investigate.

Zara wanted to stop him. "Zak! Don't, it's some kind of monster."

"No, it's not; not anymore!"

As he got closer, it became obvious that the FrightGeist had disappeared and all that was left, lifeless on the ground, was a Nuff. Zara and Shavolac quickly joined Zak who was bending down beside the small furry creature. As they gently turned the limp body over, they saw a small flicker of soft green light coming from his enervisor, he was still alive but only just. The X-ITs knew immediately who it was. This was the missing StoneKeeper of the EarthTamer clan and it looked like they had reached him just in time.

Chapter Twenty-Eight

Strongy, Pirsitta Pinto and the others had made their way to where Smarty and Cooly were waiting outside the tunnels. They had rescued the children from the Energy Drain Zone but the FrightGeist had eluded them and jumped down a hole, disappearing underground.

They got off their Tartokis and walked over to the mouth of the tunnels.

"SmartyNuff, have you heard anything from them? How long is it since they've been gone?" Strongy had so many questions. "Did you say that the Commander Cratt was in there too?"

"Yes," Smarty and Cooly answered in unison.

"Well, he's got an earslug so we can contact him. Let's find out what's going on."

"Come in, Commander. This is SmartyNuff, can you hear me?"

She listened and shook her head. She tried again but still no reply.

"So what do we do now? Maybe we have to…" It was Cooly.

Strongy agreed. "Well, we can't really leave them in there, can we? Why don't you go ahead?"

CoolyNuff was puffing himself out to get ready to go where no Nuff had dared to go, for decazytags.

Pirsitta Pinto went over to her Tartoki and produced drawings of the tunnels from a small colorful pouch hanging over its back. The locals always lived in fear of Dreadzog and the tunnels, but many Vivo moons ago one courageous Vivoan had made his life work to draw the architecture of this underground world. Now, as they looked at it they wondered where, in the mass of caves and tunnels, their friends were standing. If indeed, they were still alive.

Suddenly Smarty jumped up and squealed pulling the ear slug out for all to hear.

"Cratt here, Cratt here."

Strongy took charge. "Commander, can you hear me?"

"Hear me, hear me."

"Are you alright?"

"Hey, StrongyNuff, we're down here and need some help." It was Zak.

"Is Zara okay?"

"Yes, we're okay but we think we've found one of your missing StoneKeepers."

They all gasped. "What color is his enervisor?"

"It's green, Zara says he's an EarthTamer." Zak's voice was clear.

Zara was looking at his fading light. "It must be the one they called BaddyNuff?"

Inside the cave, the withered Nuff slowly opened his eyes—he didn't recognise any of them but in a soft voice said, "You spoke my name, I am BaddyNuff."

Zara put the ear slug close to his ear and in Nuff speak heard Strongy tell him that they had come to take him home. The color in his enervisor seemed to strengthen, but only for a moment before he fell unconscious again on the floor of the cave.

After a few more exchanges, they had discovered the whereabouts of those inside the tunnels and gave them directions to move to an area where they would all meet together, with the Tartokis. On the map, it was called *The Hub,* and it was a place where several of the tunnels came together, like spokes on a wheel. It would be easier to lift the StoneKeeper to safety from there, as he was so weak.

The underground crew soon found the path that led to *The Hub* but didn't know which of the five tunnels went through to the outside world. Chuttnee had joined them and was already flying in and out of the different entrances to find the right one, chtttrng as he went.

"Zara, you stay here in the middle with Baddy. We'll see which one gets us out of here." Zak was showing Shavolac who was in charge!

The Commander and Zara's two suitors split up but remained within sight of each other. The only sound, other than the mascot's chtts, was a swooshing sound. Zak was the first to pick up on it. Shavolac was also sure he had sensed some movement in the tunnel where he was standing. After a few minutes, they went back to the centre and shared what they'd found.

Zak went first. "I heard a brushing sound. It could have been some crevice crawlers, but it didn't sound like Nuffs."

Shavolac described the movement he'd detected but Zak didn't show much interest.

He had the ear slug. "Okay, StrongyNuff, we're at the *Hub* are you nearby." There was no answer, so he shook the worm. "These slugs need recharging they haven't had any compost for too long, and they're running out of juice."

Zara couldn't believe what he was saying. *Is this my Zak?* She thought to herself.

Meanwhile, Shavolac had disappeared into one of the tunnels and came back with some information.

"There's no air in that tunnel but there is movement, something is filling it and it is coming this way."

At first, Zak ignored him but then he realized what it was. "Dreadzog."

Zara turned. "What are you talking about Zak, he's just a myth."

"No, Zar, I didn't have a chance to tell you. I thought he was dead but I guess he is still very much alive, as you're about to find out, and...he still wants dessert."

"Huh?" Her face was one big question mark.

The air was still, and growing warmer. It felt like the calm before the storm. A ripple of fear ran through Zara as she heard her grandma's voice. *Your knowing makes it so.* She knew what was about to happen.

Zak tried one more time. "Come in, StrongyNuff, where are you?"

At last, there was an answer. "We're on our way, we'll be there in a few."

"Great but...a few may be too many!" Zak was frustrated.

Strongy questioned him, "Why? Do you have a problem?"

"Yep, his name is Dreadzog."

There was silence.

"What did you say?"

"Der—readzog."

"Oh, that's what I thought you said!"

PirsittaPinto and her two young helpers were stunned.

"So he lives!"

"It would seem that way. Is there anything you know about him that might help?"

They looked at each other. JayP spoke next.

"Well, one of the reasons he lives in this part of the land is because it never rains. Agapods have very fine hairs all over their bodies and they hate to get wet. But the chance of finding any water is impossible—it's desert over here."

Strongy wanted to pass the message on. "Zak, Zara, do you have any water on you?"

"Nope, none left—all out."

Cooly looked across at the Vivoans. "How far away are we from them?"

"Not far at all now, but legend has it he moves fast and he eats intruders."

Strongy stared at his fellow Nuff. "Got an idea, bro?"

"Sho'nuff." Cooly smiled!

Seconds later, a voice from underground said the words they didn't want to hear, "He's almost…"

All they could catch were sounds of shock and horror as the giant Agapod arrived. He filled the whole tunnel, and as he emerged in the *Hub,* he raised himself up, towering over all of them.

Zak hadn't seen him quite like this. His face was the same as earlier, like a maggot with a flowery mouth, bulging eyes and broken teeth, but his vast body was covered with fine little hairs that were almost invisible.

They didn't know what to do or where to go. Chuttnee was buzzing around the creature's head making him even wilder. The distraction bought them valuable time and before they knew it, CoolyNuff was standing with them in the tunnels.

It took him a moment for his eyes to get adjusted before he threw Zak a VibaZappa, and Zara an Aurabooster, both from his backpack.

"Where are the others?" Zak asked.

"Er…well, they might…" He didn't finish.

Shavolac had started hurling fireballs at the creature, shocking Cooly who had no idea who he was, but it gave him the feeling, that together, they would defeat the giant Agapod.

Zak was impressed with Zara's new friend and took a shot with his VibaZappa to add to the attack. All it did was tickle Dreadzog's skin, making him scratch, but it didn't really have a major impact. After all, it had been built to attack the Terrortribes.

For a moment, everyone stopped what they were doing and watched as the massive monster slowly started wrapping himself around the walls of *The Hub* to block all the other openings and prevent any means of escape.

"So he doesn't like water, eh?" It was Cooly. "Okay, so let's see what we can do."

He laughed out loud and told everyone to go to the one tunnel the Agapod hadn't reached. Zara had given BaddyNuff a shot of energy from the Aurabooster, so he wasn't quite the dead weight he had been earlier. With Shavolac's help, they managed to get him to the safety of the one remaining opening. They all tucked themselves well inside it as Shavolac threw some more fireballs until Cooly was ready to take over.

"Stand back, all of you," Cooly shouted as he started chanting in a hushed tone and in a language that no one else present, understood. Then he disappeared and from nowhere water began to flow, slowly at first but then a little faster. The whole of the roof had become like a giant shower head.

Zara was awed and turned to Zak. "Where did Cooly go, has he just turned into water?"

Dreadzog looked equally stunned. His mouth fell open showing to the world that he had only a few tiny teeth left—all the rest were gone! They noticed the long grey whiskers hanging from his chin and realized that the only thing that was threatening about this mythical creature was his size, and the sting in his tail.

The flow became even heavier and soon there was a full-blown waterfall pouring down and filling the space. Everyone was mesmerized as they stood behind the wall of water without a drop touching them. It seemed to stop right at their feet.

The giant Agapod was flailing desperately. He hated his hairs getting wet and now they were drenched and starting to tangle. He angrily wriggled around trying to shake the water off like a dog. It was a losing battle and, it was time for him to give up the struggle. The only thing left was to descend. Dreadzog took one last look at the muddy mess and dived headfirst, as fast as he could, down one of the tunnels. The hairy maggot disappeared out of sight, with the torrent of water following close behind him.

Everyone caught a quick glimpse of the size of the sting on his tail and they were all very happy that they hadn't seen it earlier!

It was StrongyNuff, who broke the silence desperate to know what had happened.

"How's it going down there?"

Zak was a little angry at the lack of support from the other Nuffs but told them what Cooly had done.

Strongy was pleased. "Well, it was a cool plan to bring a WaterWhisperer with us. Well-done, brother Nuff, it sounds like your timing was perfect. Are you coming out?"

"Yep, on our way."

Cooly turned to where Baddy was lying unconscious supported by Zara. He began searching his cloak just to be sure it really was the missing StoneKeeper. A few seconds later, he pulled out a beautiful green crystal that filled his paw, he held it up for the others to see. It was awesome, and although rough cut its energy was palpable, causing Shavolac to back off from the rest of the group.

Cooly leant in closer. "So now we know who this is but…"

Before he had a chance to finish what he was about to say, the supposedly unconscious Nuff, grabbed hold of Cooly's wrist causing him to let out a loud gasp! Zak jumped to his defense but wasn't needed. The drained Nuff blinked several times as if he was coming out from a trance, and then the WaterWhisperer continued, "BaddyNuff? It is you, isn't it? It's me, CoolyNuff."

He nodded weakly as Cooly gently helped him to release his grip and offered him back his paw. "Let's get you out of here and take you home."

Chapter Twenty-Nine

After learning that one of the StoneKeepers had been found and that they would all soon be heading back to Quomos, WiseyNuff had left the control centre with a worried look on his face. He was still asking himself how the *real things* had replaced the two model Terrortribes. He knew that there had to be someone working with Yezzadar, but who was it, and how much did he know? He thought he had seen a couple of the Cratts behaving strangely in HQ, but they were only robots so there had to be some other being behind it all. What if Yezzadar knew that they had found BaddyNuff, he would have to destroy him.

Wisey was also worried because something was blocking the full power of his enervisor. He was unable to *see* as clearly as usual and he knew it wasn't his own stuff getting in the way. It could only be someone who was fully aware of these energies doing this to him, someone who was able to control the dark forces.

He went over to the MetaDome and was met by BiggyNuff. His chocolate-colored cloak was like a puffa jacket with rings around it, and he had on weird boots with hematite heels. Biggy had a huge clip belt around his middle and his enervisor was blue, making him a member of Cooly's WaterWhisperer clan. He was a giant in the world of Nuffs.

Wisey wanted to meet with him alone to share some of his thoughts.

"There are some things that have been troubling me, and I need to tell you about them. I don't want to worry the team on Vivo and so I would welcome your ideas." The older Nuff twitched his nose and pulled on his left ear as he leant further forward.

BiggyNuff felt honored, after all, Wisey was held in such high esteem, and it always felt good to be trusted.

"What's on your mind?" he asked in a soft squeaky voice that was in complete contrast to his big tough appearance.

"There's some being amongst us that is working with Yezzadar—a spy. I hadn't thought too much about it until what happened with Zak and the Terrortribes." His mind flashed back to the domad and the testing of the VibaZappa.

BiggyNuff nodded as Wisey went on.

"There is someone here that tells him what he needs to know. So, I want you to choose two others and to find out what Yezzadar is up to. But there are risks." He reached up and patted him on the shoulder as they turned to look at the moving maps that were filling the space.

"We know that he is on Scartuss in Sedah's Belt which is over here." He pointed to a part of the map that was darker.

"We don't know exactly which planet it is; you will have to find that out. In fact, we don't know too much about this part of the Galaxy. So, in many ways, it is uncharted territory. Most beings prefer to avoid the shadows and stay in the light. Unfortunately, our fear of what lies there gives it more power."

He also told Biggy how they had discovered that the stuff fired from the Terrortribe's gun was something called guppa.

"It comes from a creature called a Tussite, and when you find their home you will find..." He paused. "I think you will find Yezzadar and his Terrortribe factories."

He sighed. "One of the things I have to tell you is that this is a secret mission, and we must not be in contact because of the risk of warning Yezzadar of your visit."

The younger Nuff puffed out his chest to make himself look even bigger.

"Do we know anything more about the Tussites that might help us to locate them?"

Wisey put an image onto the screen of the porcupine-looking creature with its funny face.

"We have an energetic imprint which will allow you to find them but only once you are within a certain distance of their home planet. Unfortunately, we cannot do any better than that."

BiggyNuff shared some ideas and asked a few more questions before leaving the building. Wisey would tell the others that they were going on a Discovery Mission; something the Warriors of the Purple Planet often did to get some data for future adventures.

Of course, it would be necessary to collect backpacks full of NuffStuff and some VibaZappas; there really wasn't a moment to spare. A SuperDodon called Commander Pudrib was to be their transport. She was best known as a *SpaceSpectre* because she travelled at such speeds that all that was left was a ghostly trail. She had won several awards for both short and long distance flying, setting records on different occasions. WiseyNuff also gave Biggy a special commecator to be used only in a real emergency—secrecy was paramount.

Chapter Thirty

On Vivo, they carried the ailing Nuff toward the entrance of the tunnels where the others were waiting. When they got to within a short distance of the opening, Shavolac, who had been walking alongside Zara, hesitated and looked at her.

"This is as far as I go."

"Oh! So you're going to stay down here?"

"For now, at least."

"I understand." She was a little relieved, as she had no idea how to handle the situation with the two of them.

"But I hope to see you again, Zara."

Zak moved a little closer and looked first at Shavolac and then at her. Zara's expression gave nothing away and she moved forward, towards the light, as she thanked him and said goodbye.

The X-ITs emerged from the tunnel with the others, as the heir of Rettosto stood back and watched expectantly. He waited, and for a moment, it didn't seem like she would but...slowly, she glanced back over her shoulder. It was enough for Shavolac, who smiled at her and glowed a little more brightly as he backed into the maze under Vivo.

Strongy, Smarty, and Brighty were there to greet them along with a growing group of Vivoans. The story of Dreadzog had travelled fast and, some had come on foot while others had ridden on Tartokis.

StrongyNuff greeted them enthusiastically.

"Congratulations, you found him. He's been missing, along with the other StoneKeepers for deca-decazytags." He patted Zak on the back and smiled at Zara.

Zara's expression was icy as she stared straight ahead. "No thanks to her."

Strongy followed Zara's accusatory gaze, as she focused on SmartyNuff, who was looking down at the ground ashamed.

She turned back to look at him. "And by the way, where were you just now when we needed help?"

Before Strongy had a chance to answer for himself, Cooly, who was kneeling next to the StoneKeeper, called him over. He was pleased for the distraction and joined the other Nuff to listen to the mumbling sounds that Baddy was making.

"Yezzzzzadaaar..."

Strongy leant in further, clearly concerned. "What about Yezzadar?"

"He tricked me, he tricked you, and he tricked all of us." His voice was weak.

"Where is he?"

"Scartuss."

"Scartuss! But the signal."

"He wanted you to find the brain bug...wanted you to come here..."

Zara was curious. "Why would he do that? Why would he..."

She didn't need to finish, she knew why.

Cooly answered her question, "Because he's going to invade Quomos."

Just then, Yorazz, who hadn't been seen either above or below ground for quite a while, came out of the crowd. Zara shuddered as she saw him and turned around to face the tunnels.

"Zak, no matter how hard I try, I just can't trust him."

He thought she was talking about Shavolac and felt he'd won her back.

"That's okay, Zar, I'll take care of you. He belongs underground."

Zara was confused for a moment.

"Huh, what are you talking about?" Then she realized and decided to let it go. "Oh yeah, okay."

She watched as the leader of the Yobuns came closer and went over to where BaddyNuff was being held by his tribe.

"So you have found him what great news, well done."

For Zara, his words didn't ring true, but no one else seemed to notice. She moved away and took a moment to tune in to her grandmother's energy. *Be aware there is one who deceives you and...* Before the sentence was complete, Yorazz was standing next to her. With an encouraging look, he led her over to join the others who were mounting their Tartokis to return to Captain Bushawoo for the journey home. His raspy voice grated on her as she thought about what she'd just heard from the voice in her head.

"We don't have a moment to spare, Zara. Come, Zak is waiting, follow me..."

Zak was holding the mane of a particularly beautiful silver Tartoki and helped Zara climb on. The feeling she got wasn't the same as the last one, and she put it down to being distracted. As the group rode ahead, she hung back a little. She was trying to get all the confusion sorted out in her head. Stuff was jangling around, with all kinds of thoughts about everything. But rather than getting clearer, it got worse as she felt a surge of anger take her over. *Could it be Shavolac, is he getting to me?*

Suddenly, her Tartoki twisted abruptly and bolted into some high bushes, with Zara clinging on tightly. Seconds later, she was out of sight unaware that Zak had turned around to find her missing. He raised the alarm but as they scanned the immediate area, they couldn't see anything, it was as if she'd vanished into thin air.

Zara was deep in the bush when the Tartoki reared up and threw her off causing her to hit her head on a stone. As she came around, her vision was naturally a little blurry. It took a few seconds before she saw the body of the Tartoki transforming into a massive panther-like creature. It was Sylvameena, Queen of the Agapanterrans.

This was the first time she had been so close to her, but not the first time she had stared into the amber eyes of the Huntress. Zara remembered the silver cat with the golden bird in its mouth, under the hedgerow outside Grandma Elizabeth's cottage. The difference was, she felt safe then.

Now, the X-IT was on her back propped up by her elbows and, in front of her was no ordinary cat. For the longest moment, she held the stare and felt the anger inside her intensify. This creature was behind her grandmother's disappearance, she just knew it, and she knew what Sylvameena wanted. The feline had discovered that the Key was no longer with Elizabeth and roared as she began to transform into her humanoid form, so she could take it!

For a moment, Zara felt panic fill her, so she quickly rolled over to conceal the pendant around her neck, touching it with her hand to give her renewed courage. If

I have to, I will kill her. She was shocked at her own thoughts. Then she heard a loud screeching sound and turned back over again just in time to see a giant shadow hovering overhead, and the half morphed Sylvameena returning to her Agapanterran form.

The big cat roared again as she leapt into the air in an attempt to grab the tail feathers of the Auriandron, and pull him to the ground. Aigledor was faster. Next, he swooped down and one of his talons made a direct hit, cutting a deep gash in her back. She roared even louder at the same moment as he let out a victory screech. The two of them disappeared deeper into the bush to battle it out—one more time!

"Zara, Zara…" It was Zak.

"I'm over here." She stood up a little wobbly at first, soon finding her feet. She waved to Zak and StrongyNuff, who were desperately searching for her.

"What happened to you, one minute you were there and then you were gone. You must have had a maverick Tartoki."

"Yeah, you could say that." And then more quietly, not wanting Strongy to hear. "It was Sylvameena."

Zak didn't know what to say; he didn't get this bit at all and still doubted Zara. "Oh…er…what happened…er…where is she…er…now?"

"Aigledor came to my rescue and they chased each other into the thicker bushes over there." She started watching their forms in the distance. "See over there."

By the time he turned around, it was too late and he couldn't see anything. Through Zak's eyes, there was nothing other than a mass of wild shrubs and dwarfed trees. He helped Zara to steady herself and lifted her onto the back of his Tartoki, riding out together to rejoin the others.

Chapter Thirty-One

It wasn't too long before they were back at the ship saying their goodbyes to the grateful Vivoans. Nearly a hundred of them had shown up to send them on their way back to Quomos. The freight ship was loaded with provisions and the Nuffs knew that they would always be welcome on Vivo. ClearyNuff and Weeze had helped rescue a number of the *wounded* children and had zapped them with their Auraboosters. They'd also shown the Vivoans some cool techniques to restore their energy. The scars, where they had once been corded to the FrightGeist, would always remain but they would get their full strength back.

Once inside the transmorphed SuperDodon, the Nuffs made BaddyNuff as comfortable as possible. Smarty was channeling the rays from an Aurabooster, over his forehead, gradually increasing his power. Soon the green enervisor grew brighter and he was able to talk more clearly and answer the many questions they had for him.

The mood was mixed as they took off. There was a sense of celebration because of finding the lost StoneKeeper but at the same time, they had no idea what to expect when they got back to Quomos. For some reason, all communication had ceased with the team back home and they were concerned they might arrive too late. StrongyNuff was urgent to learn more from the wounded EarthTamer, but Smarty had insisted he wait a while until he was stronger.

They had been flying for some time when she felt comfortable to let him ask his questions. "Okay, Strongy, gently though."

"What happened to you, brother Nuff? Why did the StoneKeepers leave Quomos? Tell us about Yezzadar, bro, tell us what you know."

His voice was still very weak.

"He came to us disguised as a seer and a man of great wisdom zytags ago when WiseyNuff was off the planet at the Intergalactic Coalition…he would have seen through him and known something was wrong, but as StoneKeepers our powers are different…"

"It's okay, take it slowly…" It was the little AirSpinner speaking now.

"He told us that he had had a vision and in it he saw that if the StoneKeepers left Quomos with their stones…the planet would start moving again and it would right the wrongdoing of the ritual. He took us to the planet Scartuss."

"What happened next?"

"Only then did we know it was all a lie…we knew we'd been tricked. He said his vision wasn't true, it had no meaning, and the sun would never rise again high in the sky above Quomos…he told us he couldn't find DarkyNuff, the StoneKeeper for the AirSpinners…then he separated us. He brought me to Vivo and broke me down…my fear took me over and turned me into the monster that I became…I had to steal their energy. It was the only way I could survive."

Strongy was very gentle with his questioning as he could see Baddy was in a great deal of pain.

"Where are the others?"

"I don't know...never saw them again...probably on other planets somewhere in the same monstrous state as you found me...when we do not balance each other out, we become the extreme feeling of our elements. It is only when we are together and the stones are connected that we will ever find harmony again...It's the way of the Universe."

Smarty pulled a feather blanket over him so he could rest, but Zara hadn't asked her questions yet.

"You said he broke you, what did you mean? What did he do?"

The sick Nuff pulled the blanket up further.

Zara repeated herself. "What did you mean?"

Smarty put her paw on Zara's shoulder to quieten her. "Zara..."

"I need to know." She leant over closer. "How did he break you?"

"He locked me away with no light—it was so dark...I started seeing things and hearing things...I went over the edge..."

"So it was the darkness?" Zara stated questioningly.

Baddy nodded.

Zara looked around at the other Nuffs with an angry expression. "You're all afraid of the dark, aren't you?"

Nobody answered; they looked everywhere but at Zak and Zara. They felt ashamed.

She wasn't letting it go. "I figured it out, that's why you wouldn't come into the tunnels. The Commander Cratt and then eventually Cooly, but the rest of you weren't waiting for equipment, were you? It was a lie."

Zak wasn't sure and looked across at Strongy. He appeared irked.

"Is it true?" Zak asked.

"Well..."

"You, StrongyNuff, you're afraid of the dark?"

Zara paced through the cabin, angrily. Zak didn't recognise this part of her and wondered what was happening. She turned to face them again.

"You didn't really care about the crops, you just wanted the night to be gone. And you let them call you *The Warriors of the Purple Planet*? Huh?"

There was a long silence. Then Strongy spoke up at last.

"It was the days of darkness at the time of the skeleton trees, when all the leaves are gone, that we wanted to change; the time when the nocturnal creatures of the world come for us. All we ever wanted was a balance between night and day, no extremes."

"Well, look where it got you, it made everything worse, all because you ran from what you were afraid of, instead of facing it..." Zara's increasing anger seemed to heighten her super sensory abilities and she started *seeing* again.

In front of her eyes, she watched what happened just after the ritual at the Wellspring of Everlasting Energy. It was like being back at the mountainside on Quomos. She felt as if she was experiencing it in real time, as smells and strange sensations bombarded her. There were masses of giant black beetles roaming the landscape, and huge oily snakes slithering between the craggy rocks. She could see swarms of flying insects with red eyes, swooping down over the Nuffs dome-shaped homes. Loud howling noises and terrifying hissing sounds echoed from the

139

blackened countryside. She could hear WiseyNuff's voice in her head telling her there had been many fights between the Nuffs and the creatures of endless night. *It's hard to beat an enemy you cannot see*

Zara looked on as some Nuffs fought off a pack of wild dog-like animals. They used their staffs and weakened elemental powers to fight as the ugly beasts attacked, snarling, and gnashing their teeth with saliva dribbling from their mouths. She could smell the stench of something awful, worse than all the rotting fish guts back home by the sea. It was quite a while before the vicious animals gave up and ran back into the night, and only after one of them had clawed at a Nuff and left a nasty gash in its side.

Wisey continued; *Don't worry, those surface wounds are all healed; it's the deeper ones that we need your help with.*

His voice was clear; *As our supplies ran down, we began to lose heart. We felt like life had lost its meaning. Very little could grow in the purple half-light, left behind after the StoneKeepers vanished. We just drifted around aimlessly. Many of us suffered from terrible feelings of dread and despair and almost gave up hope.*

We didn't believe in ourselves anymore. We tried to pretend things were okay, but it didn't last for very long. We knew things weren't right. We'd lost our sense of enoughness and we cannot have balance on our planet because we are incomplete. Finding the four missing StoneKeepers; BaddyNuff, SaddyNuff, MaddyNuff and DarkyNuff, became our reason for being and our quest has been ongoing for deca-decazytags. Only when we have all of them amongst us again and have retrieved the InfiniKey, will we regain our full power. The return of BaddyNuff is an awesome first step.

"Oh, now I think I understand," Zara said out loud, breaking her own trance and bringing herself back to the present moment. She started wondering to herself why she had been so aggressive and sat there a little embarrassed.

They all stared at her; none of them knew what was about to happen next. Suddenly, everything seemed to get more tense and heavy but it wasn't because of the conversation.

The Commander Cratt approached StrongyNuff.

"Vostos soon, soon Vostos."

The buff Nuff looked up at him. "After this, it will be a relief."

"Relief no…not for Zak. Biiiigggg problem for him."

"There's no problem for me. I can handle it."

"You heard him, Commander, full speed ahead."

Outside the ship, the stars disappeared and swirling gases surrounded them; they were back in the Vostos. Zak had talked to the Cratt in the tunnels under Vivo to try to convince him to go the long way around, but they had to get back to Quomos, *fast*.

The X-ITs were sitting next to each other as Zak's eyelids suddenly closed and he was back in the same experience he had the first time around. Like before, he saw Yorazz and the others crack open revealing the reptilian monsters inside them. And, like before they chased him down the aisle until he came face to face with the cloaked skeleton at the end. Only this time Zak reared back and took a swing at it, shattering all of its bones that then scattered everywhere.

Zak was surprised, at first but then he started to smirk, turning around to face the lizard-like form of Yorazz that was coming towards him. As it got closer, Zak repeatedly punched at him with his right arm that was now like a piston. He was punching the lizard at an impossible rate until Yorazz collapsed. Zak looked down to see that his arm had actually become metallic.

At first, he was shocked but only for a nanosecond before the rest of the reptilians started jumping all over him. The more he fought the faster the transformation from boy to fighting machine took place. Finally, his new spring-loaded metal legs were kicking the life out of everything. His left arm had become a giant claw, and the monsters were now at the mercy of this young metallic master. Zak had become a different kind of monster and was making mincemeat out of anything that came towards him, hurling them across the cabin.

It was only once they were all defeated he realized, to his horror, that his entire body had become a machine. He started to scream, but as he did the soft flesh around his mouth hardened into metal and the scream stopped right in the middle.

Zara had no awareness of what was happening to Zak even his half scream did not penetrate her own process. Her appearance remained placid, at least to begin with as her eyes closed involuntarily. She was *seeing* everyone gathered around the Wellspring in the diamond-shaped area where there was now a ceremony in progress. She watched, along with Zak and Grandma Elizabeth, as BaddyNuff placed the huge green stone on top of his staff, and then secured it at the eastern point of the diamond.

Then WiseyNuff approached her.

"Zara, give me the Key."

"But it's only half of it."

"Half will be enough."

"To do what?"

"To get us into daylight and free us from this purple haze."

Zara looked across at Elizabeth who nodded her approval. So, she handed Wisey the Key.

He took it and placed it in the stone in the centre of the diamond-shaped area. The Key began to glow, and its light formed a beam that illuminated the emerald, which also started to radiate. But as the glow grew brighter, the ground started to shudder and shake and everyone was terrified.

Crevices started to open beneath their feet and to Zara's horror; Elizabeth fell into one of them, her screams echoing in the chasm below. Everything around them was collapsing again, crushing several Nuffs as more big stones fell. Then a huge fissure opened right between Zak and Zara splitting them further and further apart. They reached out to each other but the distance was too great for them to touch. Flames suddenly burst out of the giant rip in the ground and a massive figure appeared, blocking Zara from seeing Zak. There, standing in front of her, looking straight into her eyes was Shavolac.

"Zara! Some of my rage for some of your innocence."

She was mesmerized and started walking towards him into the flames. She could feel the intense heat surrounding her, drawing her in like a magnet towards the young man calling her name. Feelings she hadn't known before rose from deep within her, causing her to lose herself completely in the experience. Her skin began to burn and blister, until a few moments later, Zara herself became fire.

She woke up distraught.

"Zara." It was Zak. "Are you okay?"

She shook her head, still sweating from the heat unable or maybe unwilling to talk with him. He stayed by her side.

141

No one had completely *lost it* in the Vostos this time although some of the Nuffs looked shaken up. Smarty was comforting Weeze, who still hadn't really found himself again after the Dangroid invasion. Overall, there was an atmosphere of relief that they'd made it through, coupled with a feeling of exhaustion after all that had happened.

The silence was a welcome change for all the passengers, but the thought of what might lie ahead was keeping their minds from really turning off. Perhaps had they known the truth it would have been worse. The most important thing for all of them to do was to conserve their energy. After all, they were going to need every bit of it the moment they landed on Quomos.

Chapter Thirty-Two

In the meantime, somewhere in Sedah's Belt, the transmorphed Commander Pudrib had come out from behind the debris that was protecting the team from any prying eyes that might be on Scartuss. It hadn't been too hard to locate and they were pleased not to have lost time in the search. BiggyNuff had decided to land from the North after finding an area for their landing that had little sign of activity.

Just as they were on final approach, they saw several large craft take off from the West and head out into deep space.

All of them on board felt a twinge of fear and knew this was a bad sign. Through his blue enervisor, Biggy was able to catch a glimpse of the cargo on board the spaceships. He shuddered as he saw battalions of Terrortribes fully loaded with their fancy weapons disappear into the darkness. He was torn between trying to warn Wisey and the agreement he had made not to make contact unless it was a critical situation. He shared his thinking with the others.

"I don't know where they're headed but at least we know where Yezzadar lives."

"Yes, we sure do!" another Nuff replied. "And we still have to get what we came for. Unless we can find the antidote to the guppa that their guns fire, there are going to be a lot of casualties, somewhere."

Whoever the spy was on Quomos, it was clear they had been in touch with the Nuffs' four-eyed enemy. Yezzadar knew that the Warriors of the Purple Planet might be getting close to recovering one of the lost family members, and maybe even have found him. The Terrortribes were travelling at lightning speed to carry out their master's orders, and they wouldn't stop until they were done, or destroyed.

Commander Pudrib set the team down on Scartuss. All three Nuffs on board knew how hostile the inhabitants were and didn't want to stay very long. What they needed, were a few ampoules of guppa venom fresh from its source, so that the Yobuns could create an antidote. At this point, they were not sure exactly how they were going to get it.

Biggy had brought along a couple of Cratts and a new compact model of a robot known as a Pixsea. It was shaped like a clam, on short stubby legs, and opened up to display some classy equipment, all in miniature. He was looking forward to testing it and thought it would prove invaluable with the Tussites. Unknown to him, the Pixsea had been programmed with an attitude, so it was going to be harder to handle than the Cratts. They'd also brought one of the slick but rugged, all-terrain vehicles which they now climbed aboard. Pudrib stayed where they landed until she was needed somewhere else.

The darkness of the planet was intense. The air was very heavy and thick and it wasn't easy to breathe. It was important to stay hyper alert as the Scartusians had the reputation of coming out of nowhere, consuming strangers, without asking questions. They never took prisoners. Looking up, the small team could see very little as a thick gaseous substance, that Pudrib had penetrated earlier, surrounded the planet.

After driving for some time, they saw a large hangar and headed closer. The search party climbed down from the vehicle and moved towards it, unseen. The Pixsea was sent ahead and entered through a small hole in the metal door, which the Tussites used. It was a bit like a cat flap.

Once inside, the little robot sent out pictures that Biggy received on a band around his wrist. He could see about ten of the little spike-covered creatures busying themselves, in amongst a mass of large feet. It wasn't until the Pixsea turned off the zoom that the watching Nuff realized the feet belonged to about a thousand Terrortribes. They were hanging immobilized on racks.

He was stunned as he showed the picture to the others. "Our mission is to collect the guppa, not to destroy Yezzadar's army. It just seems like too good an opportunity to miss. I wonder if there's a way we can do it that makes it look like an accident."

They watched for a while to see if there was any pattern to the comings and goings of the Tussites. Inside, the Pixsea robot had discovered a supply of guppa in a drum and had signalled the others. It looked like it would be easy to get the substance, and they wouldn't have to disturb the little porcupine-like creatures. Better still, they wouldn't have to risk being spiked with the stuff. But would it be high quality enough?

After assessing the situation more fully, Biggy became concerned that the guppa may have been mixed with something, and that it might not be pure. He knew they wouldn't have time to come back to Scartuss to save the lives of those already wounded. He broke the news to the others.

"I hate to say this, and I know it will be very dangerous but, I think we need to capture one of these little creatures alive, so we can get the stuff from the source."

The others knew he was right but didn't like the idea at all.

"Okay, so we will grab the last small one before it leaves. Let's use the Pixsea to distract it so it separates from the others." It sounded so easy but they had never seen a Tussite wriggle and, they'd never heard a Tussite squeal.

As the creatures started heading out of the hangar, right on cue, the Pixsea made a noise that caught the attention of the last three Tussites, before they stepped through the door. They turned around to see what it was and split up to make a search. After a few moments, one of them came face to face with the Pixsea and squealed, alerting the other two. The little robot suddenly started twirling and dancing, much to BiggyNuff's surprise. He was thinking they were well and truly busted, but they were in for something even more amazing. One of the Tussites started to copy the Pixsea's dance moves thinking that this was Yezzadar's latest creation. The other two were amused but didn't want to join in, so left their fellow Tussite to be entertained, and headed out the hangar door.

The only thing the team needed to do now was to enter the hangar and capture it. As the Pixsea continued to distract the twirling Tussite, they approached and removed their outer cloaks. Two would not give them the protection from the quills but all three layered on top of each other might just work. They could also use the strap off the backpack to wrap around the Tussite to hold the cloaks in place. Whatever happened, they had to keep the little creature alive and not get spiked in the process.

144

The Pixsea knew exactly what it had to do, so started to teach the Tussite some new dance steps causing it to look down at its feet as the

Nuffs threw their cloaks over the Pixsea's toe-tapping pupil. The noise of its squeals shocked everyone and echoed throughout the hangar. Luckily, it was soundproof and no noise penetrated the shell of the building. They just had to make sure it stopped wriggling and squealing on its way back to Pudrib.

The team was now hatching a plan to destroy as many mechanical monsters as they could without leaving any trace of their presence. It wouldn't be easy, but they had to try. Together with the Cratts, they started messing with things in such a way that would cause the hangar to mysteriously collapse. They had removed the screws from some supporting structures ensuring that when the Tussites came back and opened the hangar doors—there would be an almighty crash and the Terrortribes would be crushed. Hopefully, by the time it all happened, the team from Quomos would be safely on their way back home.

They bundled the Tussite onto the vehicle, and to their relief, it was silent and still. BiggyNuff hoped it was also alive. Even as the small party made its way back to where Commander Pudrib was waiting, they had no idea how vital their trip would be.

At exactly the same moment that they saw the waiting SuperDodon, one of the Cratts spotted some wisp-like creatures coming their way. They didn't need to ask what they were. It was clear to them all that these were Scartusians looking for fast food.

"We have to move at lightning speed or we'll never get out of here alive. These folks hate visitors. Let alone kidnappers." The big Nuff was urging the others to climb aboard the SpaceJet as if they were turbocharged. "Hurry, they're coming closer, and they won't ask questions first."

The Tussite started squealing and wriggling as they tossed it into the craft. It was touch and go as to whether they were going to make it. The speed of the Scartusians was extraordinary; but then again, so too was Pudrib's.

Another moment and they would have been dinner. She lifted off in the nick of time. As the hostile residents gazed into the dark sky, it was clear it was not going to be their lucky night for a special feast. Fortunately, for the Nuffs, Yezzadar and the Scartusians never spoke to each other, so their visit would remain a secret.

As the SuperDodon flew high above the surface of the planet, the Nuffs couldn't help noticing that there were many more hangars; two, three, maybe four or more.

"Well, at least we've reduced our enemy's force, even if we haven't destroyed it completely."

Just before they headed out into deep space, they saw one bright light on the far horizon of this dark and dangerous planet. None of them knew that it contained something more precious to Yezzadar than all of his Terrortribes put together. This was the only thing that gave his life meaning, other than his obsession to defeat the Nuffs and claim dominion over Quomos. Even that was of less value to him than this treasure.

Chapter Thirty-Three

WiseyNuff's intuition was as sharp as ever. He had done well to dispatch Biggy to Sedah's Belt to find some guppa; they were going to need every drop of the antidote once it had been prepared. He knew that the instant Yezzadar heard of the StoneKeeper's rescue, he would not be able to stay away from Quomos. Wisey was acutely aware it would be a fierce battle that the mechanistic magician would not want to lose.

The top-secret nature of Biggy's mission prevented him from warning the residents of Quomos that there was a fleet of ships heading their way. Fortunately, Wisey's enervisor had regained its full power and he was able to see way beyond the purple veil. He had readied all the clans for the invasion. It would be the first battle of any consequence for zytags on Quomos, and the inhabitants were naturally apprehensive. Their powers were not as strong as they used to be and they had forgotten some of their fighting protocols.

Several squadrons of Dodons, with their red and yellow feathers, were clustered in the Dodons' den waiting for permission to transmorph. They were the same as the one that Zak and Zara had flown on when they first landed on Quomos. Pre-fight checks would soon be complete so there was nothing else to do but wait.

The smaller version of these four-winged birds was impressive and when transmorphed turned into a sleek but extremely fast flying machine. The SuperDodons on the other hand, although also fast, were excellent at providing cover for their smaller counterparts. Two SpySupers had already warned the Nuffs that there were 16 crafts approaching.

Captain Bushawoo had made good time, but the fighting had already begun by the time the Vivo team returned home. On the approach, they could see that some of the city domads had been struck, and smoke and flames were pouring from them. It looked like both the MetaDome and the Universal Hall were still intact, but StrongyNuff wondered for how much longer.

"Okay, so we have to go straight into battle mode, not ideal but let's do it?"

A chorus of "YoHa" echoed through the craft when Bushawoo touched down. The situation was far from perfect, as these Nuffs were weary from all they had been through since leaving on their mission to the other side of the Galaxy. Those amongst them who were Clan Chiefs knew only too well the importance of their role to keep spirits up and motivate their clan members. They had all done a great job of making sure that others shared the leadership in case such a day as this arrived when they were not there to guide them.

Nuffs were pretty empowered as long as they worked together and mixed their elemental sets; cooperation across the clans always brought the best results. They had learnt in the past that an overdependence on one element made them vulnerable to their enemies. Unless, it was a unique situation, like in the tunnels of

Vivo that demanded the special elemental force of one or other of the clans, either FireHerders, WaterWhisperers, AirSpinners or EarthTamers.

Moments after landing, an aperture opened in the side of the SpaceJet, and Strongy put his head out to check that it was safe for the others to disembark. He was able to get a look at the damage that had already taken place, and with an angry cry, he reached out with his paw and summoned the fire from a burning domad. Swirling it like bands of ribbons in the wind he wrapped it around one Terrortribe then another and another. He was going to make them pay dearly for their intrusion onto his planet, and he had the power of fire to do so.

More ships were landing in the distance as the robotic beetles were disgorged onto Quomos revealing the latest upgrades of their fancy weapons. Yezzadar had landed shortly after the first ships, which had caused many Nuffs to run for their lives. The squadrons of Dodons had sent one of the enemy ships plummeting to the surface. They were still doing their best to prevent some of the others getting too close to the centre of the residential area. It was a colorful and effective display.

Earlier, two AirSpinners had tried hard to create a tornado to envelop the mother ship. With their weakened power, it just caused some minor turbulence and the Terrortribes aboard clanged against each other. Yezzadar laughed out loud at the futile gesture.

"Ha, you don't have what it takes to even make me twitch, let alone get nervous." He had steered his ship to move low across the land until he found his way into a huge dark cavern where he knew he would not be troubled by any Nuffs. Once inside, and with the help of some other smaller robots, he set up a series of monitors and made himself comfortable, so he could watch the *show* from the safety of his cave.

Zara and Zak waited for the Nuffs to leave and moved to the front of the ship to get a view of what was happening on Quomos. Zak pulled back a membrane that lay across a hemispherical protuberance and, through the viewing port, they were able to see what was going on outside. There were touch controls to allow them to zoom in and out, as well as rotate.

"This is pretty cool, Zara, we get a birds-eye view from here."

"Ugh, Zak, you can do better than that—this is really serious. Yezzadar is destroying Quomos."

He paused for a moment and suddenly his whole demeanor changed.

"I know, but what does he want? Why is he here really? What's driving him?"

Zara was surprised at his questions. He asked them in such a strange way, almost as if he was robotic.

The two of them watched as SmartyNuff reached out and channeled a pillar of smoke into the face of one of the Terrortribes, causing it to stumble around while it tried to get its bearings. She then directed a much thicker second smoke pillar, causing the confused robot to stagger right into another of Yezzadar's creations, before losing its balance completely. Unable to regain any kind of equilibrium it fell. It landed on its back and shattered an arm, as it hit the ground, spewing out colorful sparks as the limb fell away. The crippled creature struggled to turn over but, like a real beetle, once on its back, it's all over.

It tried so hard to get to its feet and Zara felt a bit sorry for it, but CoolyNuff had called to the water in a nearby canal. The liquid rose up in a torrent and surged over the ground like a snake-stream covering the fallen Terrortribe and causing a short circuit of its system. The whole thing exploded in a massive shower of electrical fireworks. Then the charged water continued slithering along the ground. It carried the electric current with it and flowed beneath the feet of some more unsuspecting robots that spectacularly erupted into a bright-colored display of purple, green, and yellow sparks, before collapsing to the ground in a heap.

"Wow!" It was Zara. "The Nuffs powers are amazing."

"Yeah, and they're only running at 20 percent…"

"Zak, imagine what they are like when they are full on. Awesome! Let's hope we can help make it happen."

"Huh? Oh yeah." Zak was feeling a bit weird like something or someone was pulling on him. He kept remembering his Vostos experience and suddenly shuddered.

"Zak, are you sure you're okay?"

He grunted and nodded as they watched their friends continually assess the situation and savor their successes so far. Zara giggled as the Nuffs did the equivalent of a high five. *Hmm? I wonder if it's really a high four as they only have three fingers and a thumb.*

Their moment of victory was short-lived as the small band of Nuffs turned around just in time to see a phalanx of Terrortribes coming towards them. The two right limbs were made up of an assortment of menacing attachments, each as threatening as the other. But on every single machine, one of the two left arms was simply a GuppaGun and they were all spewing out the vile acid. Only one drop on fur or flesh would result in a living death, paralyzing the central nervous system so the victim could never move again. Fortunately, unknown to all present, BiggyNuff would soon be landing with the pure stuff so they could make the antidote. For many, however, it may be too late.

The X-ITs watched from inside Bushawoo wondering what they could do, as the situation grew more threatening.

"I've got an idea," Zara said, running to the back of the bird to where the StoneKeeper for the EarthTamers was still lying. Zak followed close behind her.

She moved to lean over him. "I have to talk with you."

She'd forgotten Yorazz was still there when he emerged from a dark corner of the craft.

"Leave him alone…" The Yobun stepped in between the humans and the exhausted Nuff. "…He needs to rest."

"But this is important, they're outnumbered." She could feel the anger at Yorazz rising inside her, and turned to BaddyNuff saying softly but urgently. "They need you out there."

"Look at him, he can't…"

She wasn't quitting. "He has to. There's no one else."

"It would kill him and there's no renewal anymore."

The Nuff looked straight at Zara. "How bad is it?"

Zak answered, "Really bad."

The StoneKeeper started to sit up only to be pushed back down by Yorazz.

"No!" He pulled the blanket back over him. "He stays here."

A loud explosion could be heard a little off in the distance, but the sound of metallic clattering was coming closer.

Baddy knew what he had to do. "Yorazz, either way, I'm dead. One way it's all of us, the other way it might just be me."

148

The StoneKeeper sat up again, only this time Yorazz pulled out a really fancy pistol-like weapon that none of them had ever seen before.

"You're staying here."

Zara was shocked and jumped back bumping into Zak and whispering, "He's the spy."

Zak suddenly realized she was right and stepped forward to confront the armed Yorazz.

He was now angry too. "So you're the one who put that thing in my ear?"

"Just keep quiet and get out of my way. You have no idea of the forces you are dealing with here." He aimed the gun at Zak.

"No, he doesn't yet, but I do." It was WiseyNuff.

They all whirled around as he entered the ship. Zak and Zara were relieved as Wisey continued, "Why is it that the most loyal friends sometimes turn out to be the worst traitors?"

Yorazz had the answer.

"Why? Because we welcomed you here with open arms and look what you gave us...no day and no night just an eternal purple dawn...all because you were afraid of something our children grow out of by the time they can walk. Our planet is dying because of you Nuffs."

Yorazz raised his weapon to fire at Wisey but Zara stepped in between them.

She started to speak, "Don't you even..."

The Yobun pushed her aside infuriating Zak. He dived and grabbed hold of the aggressor's weapon-arm and, using his momentum against him, flipped Yorazz over in such a way that he hit his head hard on one of Bushawoo's ribs, falling to the floor unconscious.

Zak turned around and, with a smug smile, reached down with his hand to help an opened mouth Zara up from the floor. She stared first at Zak and then at the fallen spy.

"Stop grinning, Zak. There's a war outside. We need to do something."

He didn't say anything; he just brushed his hands together as if he'd done the same thing a hundred times before.

Chapter Thirty-Four

WiseyNuff was clearly pleased with the way both Zara and Zak had shown courage.

"You have come far and learnt some of the ways of energy play. It will be of great value to you in your roles as X-ITs."

The two of them were proud to receive praise and acknowledgement from such a respected Nuff and watched him stoop down to take the weapon from Yorazz. He then went over to where the StoneKeeper was now sitting upright and gave him a hug.

"It has been a long time and much has happened since we were last together. We have never stopped searching for you, to bring you home."

Zak and Zara watched as the two estranged Nuffs looked into each other's eyes and a current of light connected their enervisors. It was a way of exchanging energy and information that only a few Nuffs possessed. This was a gift of power, and it took a lot of discipline to achieve.

Wisey broke the silence. "Now I see all that happened. No need for words." He turned and smiled at the two of them. "You will learn more about these powers. You already have them we just have to help you to develop them further."

A loud bang sounded not far from the ship and the spritely old Nuff turned around and walked down to the aperture.

"There is much to be done and we don't have too long."

"But Wisey I have so many questions. What about…"

Zara didn't finish her sentence before he was gone. She was starting to get quite irritated, as this was happening too often. Then, she suddenly got it. *No need for words.* She remembered how her grandma had taught her to tune-in. It was just a question of getting grounded and then focusing inwards; that was how to find the answers.

She quickly closed her eyes and imagined a long pipe-like cord running from the base of her spine right into the centre of the planet. She knew she could choose it to be any color she wanted, so this time she picked purple. *I think that fits this place.* She smiled to herself and quickly dumped all her questions and her fear thoughts down the pipe-cord so that she could be free of them. Zara then imagined a shaft of golden light coming out of the top of her head all the way up, as far as she could envision. Then she brought the pure energy back through the top of her head, into and around her body to complete the circuit. It filled the spaces that the fear had left behind. *Remember to do this often, dear one; it brings you back to yourself and closer to me.* In her mind's eye, she saw Elizabeth surrounded by Terrortribes. She gasped loudly.

"Zara, are you okay?" Zak was concerned.

"Yes, yes, just wait a minute…" She went back inside herself and saw that the sky surrounding her grandmother was not black this time, but purple. Zak stood staring at his best friend with her closed eyes.

"She's here, Grandma Elizabeth is here on Quomos. She stowed away on one of their ships and she's free. We must go and find her."

"Whaaaat? Are you serious?"

"Yesss."

Zara turned to BaddyNuff and helped him to stand up. He was a bit wobbly at first but soon got his balance.

"You have work to do." Zara had found a new source of energy and was buzzing.

The two of them helped him out of the ship and walked over to a pile of broken Terrortribes that their friends had dealt with earlier. They ducked down behind them just in time to see Captain Bushawoo find a noisy but effective way to eject the comatose Yorazz. After relieving himself of the last passenger, he transmorphed into his more natural shape and took off in the direction of the Dodons' den.

The X-ITs looked at each other and laughed, but the StoneKeeper was in another world. His left paw grasped the beautiful emerald-colored crystal staff, as he concentrated hard. His right paw was outstretched as if he was trying to manipulate the ground, but nothing was happening. He felt frustrated and exhausted as Zara and Zak held him up and encouraged him.

Zara was whispering gently, "You can do it, we know you can."

"I can't, I don't have the strength anymore…"

"So how do you get it?" Zak asked.

"There's no way, not without the InfiniKey."

"Well, will half the Key do?" Zara pulled out the pendant.

The Nuff couldn't hide his astonishment. "Where did you get it?"

"My grandmother gave it to me. Now do what you need to do?"

"We have to go to the Wellspring."

Zak's face fell. "But that's all the way over there…"

They could see it in the distance. It was in the mountainous area across the other side of the plain, which was now a battlefield. There were a lot of the Terrortribes between them and the pathway up to the sacred site, and that meant a lot of guppa. They were wondering how they could defend themselves and carry the shattered Nuff. It didn't look good at all. Zara's face fell too, as a couple of the poison quills shot past them. The two X-ITs knew that the heap of metal they were hiding behind wouldn't give them protection for much longer. Then suddenly, as one of the fallen robots sent out a spark, it gave Zak a brilliant idea.

"Zara, you take Baddy and head for the Wellspring. I'll do what I can to distract them." With that, he dived into a large hole in the belly of one of the fallen Terrortribes.

"What are you doing, Zak?"

He didn't answer, as another barrage of quills flew by and Zara ducked down again.

Once inside the carcass, Zak wriggled around and started to reconnect the wires and manipulate the controls. Zara watched as she thought she saw one of the arms move. Then the thing twitched more violently.

"Zak, that better be you…"

"It is. Now turn me over."

"What?"

Zak was well and truly inside the skin of the robot and eager to get it vertical.

"Zara, I must get this thing on its feet."

She got the message.

"Baddy, can you help me?"

"I'll do what I can."

The two of them grabbed under the shoulders of the X-IT possessed machine, and strained as hard as they could to leverage it upwards. Eventually, it flipped up as an almighty groan, followed by a cheer, emerged from the metal casing.

It was just in the nick of time, as several of the Terrortribes were a short distance away, and ready to attack. But before they could, Zak blasted them with the flame-thrower arm and roasted them as they exploded in a mass of sparks. Clumsily he turned around and gave a victorious grin through a small hole in the chest of the robot. Zara didn't smile back; instead, he could see from her expression that he better turn his machine fast.

"Zak!"

He whirled around and started throwing flames again.

"Zara, get Baddy to the Wellspring. Hurry!"

She grabbed a hold of the StoneKeeper and helped him up, willing him to find the strength he needed to get where they had to go.

Zak, in the meantime, had found a way to manipulate the guppa arm and had sprayed the acid in such a way that it sliced one of the Terrortribes into two sparking, and smoking halves.

"This is so cool," he said out loud to no one there.

Zara and her companion were dodging quills and robots and making some progress when the tired Nuff stumbled over the metal leg of one of the fallen Terrortribes. Zara tried to pick him up but he looked up at her, appealingly.

"I don't think I can go any further..."

She tried to lift him again.

"You have to...pleeease."

Then, from nowhere another paw appeared to help her; it was SmartyNuff. "Together, we can do it. I may not have helped you in the tunnels of Vivo but..."

Zara smiled at the Nuff, she was very glad to see her. But then she winced when she saw that her fur was burnt in a couple of places and she looked badly beaten up.

"We have to go to the Wellspring."

"Okay." She looked at Zara. "We'll make it!"

They each took hold of an arm and lifted the StoneKeeper to his feet, travelling as fast as they could towards the mountains. Behind them in the distance, near to where they had landed, Zak was annihilating robot after robot. He was much agiler than they were and was using some of the martial arts moves he'd learnt back on Earth.

The party of three had been making good time when they rounded a corner and were confronted by one of the robots, with guns blazing. They quickly backtracked and took cover behind a rocky outcrop.

"You stay with him and let me see what I can do," Smarty told Zara as she stealthily disappeared again around the corner.

She then stepped out confronting the oncoming Terrortribe that immediately fired its guppa quills. The AirSpinner focused her elemental powers to redirect the poison arrows, with the force of a cyclone, causing them to zoom into the mountainside piercing it like darts on a dartboard. Next, she created a mini dust storm by swirling some surface sand into a small cloud of soft powder around the robot's antenna, causing it to stumble away disorientated.

Smarty quickly turned and went back to where she'd left Zara. She smiled, and the two of them lifted the StoneKeeper, moving at rapid speed along the steep path to where he could work his magic.

The higher they climbed the more Zara could see the extent of the invasion; it was massive. She was worried about Zak and wanted desperately to look for her grandmother, but she knew intuitively that if they got him to the Wellspring it would help the Nuffs to embrace their fear and, defeat their enemy. She wasn't sure what he could do, but every part of her was convinced they had to get him there and fast.

Far below, Zak continued to smash the robots. He was actually enjoying himself and felt like he was mastering the art of mechanical combat. Practicing new and more intricate moves until…another battalion was offloaded from a nearby spacecraft and they started to smash him back.

Chapter Thirty-Five

Zara had lost all track of time when they arrived at the Wellspring. As was always the case on Quomos, the constant purple sky did not discriminate between night and day. It just stayed the same. She glanced around and remembered the first time she'd stood here; so much had happened since then, that she felt like a different person. Her thoughts went to Shavolac and she wondered if he was still walking the tunnels under Vivo, or maybe he'd returned to Rettosto to face his family.

Her mind was wandering all over the place. *Stay in the here and now and no harm will come to you.* The voice brought her right back to the present moment as BaddyNuff started to issue instructions.

"Place the InfiniKey in the centre stone and I will stand over there in my rightful place."

He moved very slowly across the diamond and stood where the StoneKeeper of the EarthTamer clan had been standing at the time when the long night fell. He held the large green stoned staff high above his head and began chanting. Smarty and Zara could do nothing but wait. They were anxious.

The chanting became more rhythmic, and the InfiniKey started to glow. A beam of light shot from it connecting to the stone on the staff Baddy was holding. This too started to glow becoming a deeper and richer green. He continued making the sounds with a smile on his face. The stone was restoring his power and he could feel it filling him up again.

"It's working. Did you feel that?" Zara felt a jolt. She was excited but scared at the same time. She was remembering her experience in the Vostos.

Neither of them answered him; they were watching the color of the stone deepen as it grew brighter and brighter. But soon Smarty felt the jolt too as the ground beneath their feet began to crack open.

Scared, Zara bent down to remove the InfiniKey but the StoneKeeper called out to her, "Not quite yet."

"But…" She waited.

The shaking was getting worse and then one of the remaining stone pillars crashed to the ground, just like it had in the Vostos. It was too much for Zara so she lifted her pendant out of the stone and placed it back on the chain around her neck. The ground stopped shaking immediately and everything quieted down.

Smarty went over to where the X-IT was standing to check she was alright, and the two of them looked across at Baddy. He was stooped with his shoulders rounded and his head down, holding the green crystal staff. Both of them were worried.

"Are you okay?"

Slowly, he lifted his head and to their surprise, his enervisor was glowing greener than they had ever seen it. He stood in front of them, healed.

"Yes, never better. Now let's see what we can do."

They watched as he held out both his arms. He moved them in a wave-like motion and the ground started to roll. Zara was watching in awe. The waves across the terrain matched the rhythm of the movement of his arms.

Zak, meanwhile, was up to his ears in robots and outnumbered by the Terrortribes that had surrounded him. He had no idea what to do next, when suddenly he felt the ground begin to shake. Quickly, he dived onto his stomach while all those around him began to stumble and fall, mostly onto their backs.

"Wipeout," he said loudly as he hit the ground.

The EarthTamer continued to motion with his arms as the rolling got more profound and deeper furrows formed. Zara could see across the plain. It looked like the ground had become liquid. The Terrortribes began to fall all over the place.

Baddy wasn't doing it alone anymore. Once the StoneKeeper had regained his full elemental force, so too did every other EarthTamer on Quomos. They were all using their power to dislodge the teetering robots.

As they continued, his breathing got heavier.

Zara was now really concerned. "Are you sure, you're okay?"

"I am more than okay."

Suddenly, Zara sensed something off to the side.

"Look out, behind you."

He turned to see a robot coming towards him with GuppaGun raised high. Before it could fire the poisoned quills, the Nuff brought his paws together and then parted them slowly but intentionally, opening a crack in the ground right under the machine. It fell into the crevice and as he drew them together again, the crack closed, crushing the robot in the vise and causing its arms to break off in a mass of sparks. He looked at Zara and smiled. She was now eager to leave and find her grandmother. Her work at the Wellspring was done for now. She grabbed Smarty's paw and they headed to the path down the mountain, leaving the StoneKeeper to continue making his furrows.

Strongy and Cooly smiled at each other, they knew what had just happened. Their powers hadn't changed but the stumbling robots gave them an opportunity to test out new moves. The FireHerder was repelling the flames shaping them into burning arrows and sending them back to where they came from, whilst the WaterWhisperer created a mini-tsunami that knocked over some swaying robots. Being an EarthTamer, WeirdyNuff was back on full power creating little molehill-like mounds in front of each of the robots for them to trip over. He felt alive again for the first time since the Dangroid left him.

Back in his dark cave, Yezzadar had been watching the whole thing on his viewing screen and had had enough. He shook his head and hit a switch causing all the remaining Terrortribes, mainly those with the upgraded stabilizers, to head towards his temporary headquarters.

Zak watched as they started to retreat and, still inside his robotic disguise, he followed them. As they lumbered into the cavern, he fired the GuppaGun on the one in front of him splitting it open so all of its electronic guts spewed out. It collapsed on the ground right at his feet. He targeted the second one and it fell victim to the acid blast. A third robot turned on Zak and pounded him with a sound vibrational weapon similar to the VibaZappa. The X-IT collapsed hard onto his back and was dragged into the cavern. Yezzadar had been watching it all from his ship and wanted revenge.

SmartyNuff and Zara made it down the mountain and after finding the others told them what had happened up at the Wellspring. Strongy and Cooly shared the story about a rogue robot and realized too late, that it was Zak. Concerned for his safety they all headed towards the cavern.

Yezzadar chose well, it was probably one of the darkest and deepest on the planet. They all gathered outside not wanting to go into the blackened interior when suddenly a mechanical voice echoed out of the opening.

"You can have the boy back if you give me the Key."

Zara didn't hesitate. "And you can have the Key if I can have my grandmother back." It was Zara.

"I don't have her."

"Liar."

Yezzadar was surprised at her fighting spirit. Zak was a little concerned too.

"Zara, it's me. Uh…don't push too hard."

"He's bluffing, Zak. I'm sure of it."

"I wish I were," Yezzadar said with regret in his voice.

Zara had heard enough and headed into the cave just as WiseyNuff joined the others outside.

Concerned, the older Nuff looked around. "What is happening here? Where are our visitors?"

Smarty answered first, "Zara has half of the InfiniKey. And Zak has been captured by Yezzadar."

Wisey pulled on his left ear and tugged at the fur on his chin.

"And they are both in there?"

Strongy nodded, as all the Nuffs stood and looked into the blackness. They could hear Yezzadar's voice.

"How many times do I have to tell you I don't have your…"

"Grandma!"

Zara was standing right in front of him when Grandma Elizabeth stepped out of the mother ship. He turned around, shocked to see her coming out of the doorway.

"She must have stowed away."

She came down the steps dressed in what she was wearing on Scartuss, but with the addition of her fancy blue sunglasses. Zara ran excitedly towards her but stopped a few paces away.

"What's the matter, dear?"

"You…you have your sunglasses on."

"Of course, you know they are my favorites."

"Yes, but you left them on the beach the night you disappeared. We found them."

"I had two pairs made because I liked them so much. Now be a good girl and give him the pendant. Then we can all go home."

"I want it to be you so much, but you have to take off your sunglasses."

"Why? What are you so worried about?"

"Remember you told me that Sylvameena, the shape-shifter, had one thing she couldn't change? The color of her eyes."

"Of course, but you don't think I'm…"

"Take them off now!" Zara was sure she was right.

Her grandma was shocked she'd never seen Zara this way. What had happened to her? Zak too was surprised but had noticed a big difference ever since the tunnels of Vivo and the encounter with Shavolac. Elizabeth walked towards her slowly. Zara didn't move.

As she got closer, her breathing started to change until it was a deep and sustained feline growl. The sunglasses fell to the ground revealing her dark amber eyes. As she morphed into her own silver humanoid form, Sylvameena lunged at Zara grabbing the pendant from around her throat, and breaking the chain.

It fell to the floor and the Agapanterran tried to catch it, but it gave her a gigantic electric shock that sent her reeling backwards onto the ground. Before falling unconscious, she yelled to Yezzadar. "Get it or…"

Zara quickly bent over and reclaimed her grandmother's treasure only to realize that Terrortribes surrounded her. They were coming from all directions. She tried running, but it was futile, they were everywhere and they were getting closer. Trapped and afraid she stared out at them when they suddenly began to stagger as if they were drunk. Then they started to fall as the ground underneath began to shift. Zara wondered what was happening. She turned around to see BaddyNuff standing in the dark waving his arms very gently, but enough to do what was needed.

Zara was very relieved, but then she was horrified as one of the falling robots let off a stream of guppa in Zak's direction. Luckily, because of the angle it fired off, the acid ended up pooling around the Terrortribe itself, which then dissolved into a puddle of molten metal.

A moment later, Zak and Zara both lit up with renewed hope. Three more Nuffs, Strongy, Cooly, and Smarty were standing alongside the newly retrieved EarthTamer, just as another of the robots lurched out of the darkness and threw fire at the StoneKeeper. Strongy raised his upper paws and deflected the flames sending them deeper into the cave, lighting it up to show all the fallen robots, and a few more still standing.

Protected by Strongy, Cooly churned up the guppa puddle released by the earlier robot and created a small wave of acid. He focused it on the flame-throwing attacker, dissolving its feet and sending it crashing to the ground. The three Nuffs then headed further into the cavern to eliminate the rest.

Yezzadar was angry and sensed defeat. He decided to abandon his hold on Zak and head to his ship, only to find another Nuff blocking his way. He was shocked.

"WiseyNuff, don't tell me you're not afraid of the dark anymore."

"Maybe a little…"

"You should be, all sorts of things can happen when there is no light."

He pulled out a laser-like pistol, the same as the one that Yorazz had used.

"Now stand aside. You know I'm the only one with the courage and superior skills to fix the mess your planet is in."

"Fix it or make it worse…all you want is the power."

"Ah, but it was you who allowed me to take it."

Yezzadar lifted the gun but a loud growl rose from the ground as Sylvameena came around from her electric shock. She roared again only louder this time, as she saw a fluttering shadow hovering above her.

Chapter Thirty-Six

Zara turned to Zak, they were happy to see each other again after all that had happened.

"Look, Zak, it's Aigledor. He's in his humanoid form but with wings."

Zak strained hard but all he could see were two gelatinous shapes, one on the ground and the other in the air.

"Huh?"

"Zak, don't tell me you still can't see them."

Zara watched as Sylvameena's amber eyes glowed in the dark. The feline queen transformed into her most comfortable shape—a large silver panther. At the same time, Aigledor became a giant golden bird.

He dived at her from above as she batted him with her outstretched paw so hard that he hit the roof of the cave with enormous force. The ceiling cracked open sending debris crashing to the floor and letting in a stream of purple light. Aigledor recovered quickly and dived again as they engaged in a ferocious battle, clawing at each other; their growling and screeching echoed throughout the cavern.

Near the opening, no one noticed a figure appear clutching a crystal staff. They were all transfixed, watching the enormous creatures rip and tear at each other. Zara was captivated, she'd never seen them fighting this close up before; for Zak, it was the first time he'd seen them at all!

A few moments later, Zara sensed a familiar presence. She turned around to see her grandma standing behind them, framed in the entrance to the cavern. She was overjoyed and moved towards her, stopping only for a brief moment to be sure that Sylvameena wasn't playing tricks on her. Now certain, she ran into Elizabeth's outstretched arms as her grandmother wrapped her up in a big hug.

"Grandma, you're alive and you're safe. I knew it!"

"Yes dear one, I am. It's good to see you. Hmm? I take it you found my secret space?"

"Grandma, I'm so sorry…"

"You don't need to be, I was about to tell you anyway. Are you both okay?" She smiled as she looked across at Zak, who was busy watching the fight.

"Yes, sort of…in some ways…but a lot has happened and I have so much to tell you."

"I'm sure. After this, you will become the storyteller. It will be good to…"

Elizabeth was interrupted by Sylvameena's roar as she continued her life and death struggle with Aigledor.

"Oh, dear. Excuse me, I must do something."

She let go of Zara gently and moved to where Zak was standing, and closer to where the massive creatures were fighting.

He was busy shouting. "Come on, Aigledor, you can do it—get her."

"Zak!"

He turned, his eyes bulging with surprise. "Grandma Elizabeth. But I..."

"Tsss, tsss, you're not helping the situation here."

"But..."

Elizabeth called to Zara, "You still have the pendant I gave you?"

Zara proudly handed it to her Grandma. "The chain broke."

"No worries, it can be mended."

With that, Elizabeth moved to the other side of the cavern. Zak turned to Zara.

"I thought we wanted Aigledor to win and that Sylvameena was the bad guy."

Zara looked at him, smiled, and shook her head. Elizabeth was getting closer to the fight and had fixed the pendant into a slot on top of her beautiful amethyst staff.

"Elizabeth. I'm happy to see you, I knew you were safe and we would find you." WiseyNuff was delighted she was there.

"Thank you, my friend, I am here and well. But there is important work still to be done."

"What are you doing?" he asked with concern.

"Breaking their trance," she said, focusing all of her energy on the InfiniKey

"Perhaps it is best to let them continue to settle it once and for all."

Elizabeth was firm. "No, it cannot happen yet. Not here, not now."

She held the staff up high above her head and repeated a phrase over and over again. The pendant started to glow and the whole cave lit up as if it was a sunny day. Everyone present was frozen in time, except for Yezzadar, Sylvameena, Zara and Zak.

The Agapanterran rolled away from the now immobilized Aigledor angry with Elizabeth for stopping the battle. Yezzadar stepped forward covering his eyes.

"Elizabeth..."

She was clear about what she wanted. "Go, both of you."

Yezzadar's four eyes stared out and he raged at her. "You can't leave it like this. Give me the Key now! I need it."

Zara's grandmother was fully in her power as Sylvameena joined Yezzadar in an attempt to intimidate her. Elizabeth thrust her glowing amethyst staff forward in the big cat's direction creating a flash of light that caused the feline to back off.

The Agapanterran knew she wasn't going to win and so to escape the light, she moved further into a corner of the cave snarling, with her tail between her legs. Yezzadar shook his head ruefully.

"You're making a VERY BIG mistake...you have no idea what I am capable of with my machines. I will right this wrong." He was seething.

"Go! There is no wrong to be righted, only a legend to unfold."

He climbed into his ship and in seconds the engines sounded, and he was gone. The glow from the pendant faded and those who were frozen came back to life. Aigledor saw Sylvameena disappearing into the darkness and turned into his winged humanoid form to face Elizabeth.

"Why did you do this? After all I've done for you."

"Lift yourself higher, Aigledor, and you will know perfectly well why this had to be done."

"Perhaps. But just as you do what you need to do, so too must I...it is the way it is."

He rose into the air and after transforming fully into an Auriandron flew after Sylvameena. She was close to the back of the cave, heading towards what seemed to be a dead end, with her coat glistening silver.

Just before she got there, she stopped abruptly having found what she was looking for. Roaring loudly, she leapt into a rift in the space-time continuum and disappeared, immediately followed by Aigledor. Their battle would continue somewhere else…for now.

Zara turned to her grandmother. "That was Aigledor, wasn't it?"

"Yes, it was." She sighed.

"Please, please tell me he's not my grandpa."

Elizabeth gave her an enigmatic smile and winked.

Zak was curious. "Why did you…er…let them go?"

Elizabeth smiled again. "You know, Zak, you really should have listened to my stories!"

Suddenly, BaddyNuff called out, just as the other Nuffs returned from decommissioning the rest of the Terrortribes. "Can you feel it? It's moving…It's moving…It's moving." He was leaning against the wall of the cavern and was almost ecstatic.

They all rushed over to him and then ran outside, where many more Nuffs were waiting. Everyone started cheering believing that the time of the purple dawn would soon be over, and the sun would rise again.

The sense of celebration for StrongyNuff was diminished by the news that BrightyNuff had been hit with guppa and was lying immobile in the medical domad. He wanted to go to her but he knew he had to stay, at least for now. There were many others, who had fallen victim to the poisonous acid. They hadn't yet heard about Biggy's secret mission. He had returned from Scartuss with a live Tussite and with the Zybuff's superior intellect, the Yobuns were preparing an antidote.

All would be well.

The celebration continued with a lot of hugging and cheering. CoolyNuff picked up SmartyNuff and spun her around, but quickly the expression on her face dropped and her smile of jubilation was gone.

"Look." She pointed to the sky. It's not getting lighter, it's getting darker and there are stars."

Everyone was horrified they knew what it meant, as the wild animals started howling in the distance.

Strongy was shocked as panic set in and Nuffs started running in different directions. "The planet's rotation didn't stop at dawn all those zytags ago, it was stuck at dusk."

In the meantime, NottyNuff, who had been wounded by guppa at the fight in the Dodons' den, had been chosen as the test case for the antidote. Although still a little weak, he was walking around and had made his way to the cavern.

With all the noise and confusion, no one had noticed him enter. Eager to meet his StoneKeeper, he found BaddyNuff still leaning against the wall and went over to him. He tried to help him stand up but the older Nuff shook his head, as others gathered around him.

He looked at Notty, a fellow EarthTamer. "Ah, young Nuff, my energy for this life has gone. It is for you now to take my staff and the stone."

Notty was stunned. He shook his head. "I don't have the power to take on such responsibility, remember I'm the one they call NottyNuff."

Baddy insisted, "You are more than enough, it is your destiny to be a great Nuff and you will live it well."

He handed him the large green crystal staff and the new StoneKeeper felt its potency run through him. He gazed with respect at his predecessor.

Baddy smiled at those around him and took a deep breath. "My part is played. Thank you for bringing me home."

He closed his eyes and slipped down to the ground as all remaining color drained from his enervisor. He had found the strength to do what he had to do, and he was ready to let go of this life.

For a moment, Notty just knelt there with the green light from his enervisor glowing a deeper color, as he cradled his mentor's head in his arms. Then, after a polite moment of silence, Strongy, hearing the confusion outside, reached out to the new StoneKeeper of the EarthTamers.

"Hey, it will all be okay, it's time for you to address the clans."

"Yes. I...er...know." NottyNuff was hesitant at first, as he was not used to showing up and speaking in public.

He stepped outside the cave.

"Er...um...I want you all to listen. The planet will...er...keep moving and the sun will come back again."

"Yes but what about this?" CoolyNuff was pointing to the night sky. "We're right back where we started."

"No, we're not."

It was a slightly disheveled Wisey. "We have come a long way. Yes, night has fallen on Quomos for the first time in deca-decazytags but we can take comfort in knowing that the sun will rise in the morning. This is the gift that BaddyNuff brought to us, it is time to face up to what we're afraid of."

"But it will be dark..."

"...Yes, it will be, but I have learnt today that fear is a wonderful servant and a terrible master. We cannot let fear run our lives or control our choices. We must embrace our darkness as well as the light, then it will lose its power over us."

A cheer went up as Wisey looked across at the X-ITs.

"Besides night time isn't all bad." He glanced upwards at the three moons of Quomos rising in the sky, and the galaxy's swirling star systems now visible for the first time in ages. Some of the younger Nuffs had never seen the sky this way, and a very small one jumped up to try to touch it.

Elizabeth turned to her granddaughter. "You and Zak will need to leave soon."

"But aren't you coming with us?"

"They need me here, more than they need an *old lady* back home."

Zara and Zak traded guilty looks as Elizabeth continued, "There are still some missing StoneKeepers to bring home; we only have half of the InfiniKey, and the souls on Quomos can't leave because the gateway remains sealed." She sighed. "The air is still polluted, the water is toxic, and the hot springs are cold. Quomos may be rotating but it is still out of balance. There is much to be done."

Zara was concerned. "When will I see you again?"

"Whenever you want to."

"So could I stay and help?"

"Yes, dear one, you can if you like."

Zara thought for a moment about her mother and father, and about Jake; she looked across at Zak. "Maybe not now, I think I'll go back. But Dad said we might move to London soon and...well, maybe then. This has been really intense."

Elizabeth was impressed with her granddaughter's thoughtfulness. She smiled and hugged Zara offering her words of love and encouragement. The youngster pulled away slowly, as her grandma gave her back the pendant.

"But Grandma, won't you be needing this."

"No, my dear, you hold onto it, for now, it's better that way. Just look after it and you will be protected."

Zara was happy to keep it and promised she would get the chain mended as soon as she was back in Devon.

Elizabeth looked lovingly at her granddaughter. "Remember this...time and distance are an illusion. Separation is the way we make sense of the physical universe, but it's not real."

"Oh, okay." She thought she understood what her grandma was trying to tell her, but she wasn't sure.

Elizabeth was content to have planted the seed.

The Vivo team, including an excited Chuttnee, was now surrounding the X-ITs saying their goodbyes. They had heard that Brighty had responded well to the antidote to all those present, especially Strongy, were relieved.

CoolyNuff gave them both a hug and told them it had been cool having them around. Strongy just pounded his chest and punched the air before putting his paws on Zak's shoulders.

"Stay strong, you've got it...believe..."

SmartyNuff still felt bad about not supporting them in the tunnels but Zara had long forgiven her. She gave her a big hug avoiding the areas where her fur had been burnt and told her with wisdom beyond her years. "Remember everything heals."

WiseyNuff was the last to speak.

"You have done well and we are grateful. Your power as X-ITs has increased. We will welcome you again before too long. Together, we have taken these first steps, but there is still a lot to do before Quomos is restored and the InfiniKey returned to its rightful place."

Zara looked at him. "Thank you for everything, it's been a real adventure, hasn't it, Zak?"

Her friend was back in his head replaying all the moves he'd made, and still annoyed that he'd fallen over just outside the cavern. "Er...yes, it has, really..."

They both knew that what Wisey had said was true and wondered what kind of new challenges lay ahead. Zara took one last look at her beloved grandmother and gave her another very long hug, so happy to have found her alive.

Then Elizabeth began speaking in an ancient tongue while waving her crystal staff in the form of the figure eight.

Before they knew it, the two friends were sucked into a vortex in the InfiGrid and were stretched into unbelievable shapes. They twisted and turned as they were shaken and tossed around. The second time wasn't quite such a shock, and it was nothing compared to the Vostos. Nevertheless, they still screamed.

Soon Zak and Zara were back in the cottage, lying on Elizabeth's king-size bed.

Zara sat up and spoke first, "Zak, was any of it real?"

"Huh? What are you talking about, Zar? You mean the game?" He jumped off the bed onto the floor a little embarrassed. Then looking at her, he asked, "Are you okay, you look a bit pale?"

Zara suddenly thought it was all her imagination. "Well, I...er...don't know, like I'm not sure, it's just that..."

"Zar, of course, it was real," he turned his head. "Look at the shaved patch where they took out the brain bug."

She was furious at first but soon softened. "You made me think that I dreamt it!" Then she put her hand in the pocket of her hoodie and pulled out the missing hair.

"I kept this safe in case your mum started asking questions. I'll tell her we were experimenting or something."

"Cool."

"I guess we'd better go down and see what's happened."

The tape was still there at the bottom of the stairs and so was everyone else.

Zak looked back at Zara. "It's just like WiseyNuff said, nothing's changed."

Jake ran over and barked at them, causing some people to stare...but only for a second, before they turned away and carried on with their conversations.

Zara glanced around quickly. "Let's get out of here, we can take Jake for a walk."

The two of them found his lead and headed straight for the front door of Grandma Elizabeth's cottage eager to get to the beach. They didn't notice the form of a feline curled up by the fireplace. They didn't see the silver cat with intense amber eyes that had been watching them as they came down the stairs and walked across the room. If they had, their mood might have been very different.

The Nuff Dictionary of Common Terms

Book One in the Trilogy
The Legend of the InfiniKey

Agapod	A hairy maggot
Aigledor	Sovereign ruler of the Auriandrons
AirSpinners	One of four Nuff clans
Aurabooster	Gadget for strengthening auras
Brain Bug	Organic spying device
Bubble Builder	Protective bubble for the EDZ
Captain Bushawoo	A SuperDodon
Chief Mystics	Wise-beings of the Smoothy Way
Choffles	A great Nuff delicacy
Chuttnee	The Nuffs' mascot
Coleoptera-Technology	Programme for the Terrortribes
Commander Pudrib	Another SuperDodon
Commecator	Communication device
Confidometer	Gadget for measuring confidence
Cratts	Long, tall robots
Crevice Crawlers	Lizard-like creatures
Dangroid	A reptilian parasite
DebrisDodger	Bushawoo's reputation
Deca-deca Zytags	A very long time in Nuff speak
Dodon	A big bird found on Quomos
Domad	Dome-shaped building
Dreadzog	A giant hairless Agapod
EarthTamers	One of four Nuff clans
Ellbe-L	A Vivoan
Enervisor	The Nuffs' third-eye
EDZ	The Energy Drain Zone
FireHerders	One of four Nuff clans
Flying Fluff Balls	Dusters found in the Universal Hall
FrightGeist	A spectre on Vivo
Grooglies	Green fruit base for Stealth Juice
Gumbats	Chuttnee's distant cousins
GuppaGun	Terrortribes' poison pistol
Hoverstools	Found in the Universal Hall
Jay-P	A Vivoan
MetaDome	The largest Domad
Nonagon Table	Nine-sided table
NuffNosh	Special food for the warriors

'O'	The Galactic Oracle
P44Ti	Prototype name for the VibaZappa
Pirsitta Pinto	A Vivoan
Pixsea	A clam-shaped robot
Purple Palace	The Nuffs' headquarters
Purple Planet	Another name for Quomos
Quomos	The Nuffs' home planet
Rotunda	A building on the Purple Palace
Safe-suit	Nuff wear
Scartusians	Inhabitants of Scartuss
Scartuss	A planet in Sedah's Belt
Sedah's Belt	The dark side of the Galaxy
Smoothy Way	A sister Galaxy to the Milky Way
Stealth Juice	Green liquid that turns you invisible
StoneKeepers	Custodians of a clan's power stone
SuperDodon	An interplanetary Dodon
SUSAs	Super Sensory Abilities
Sylvameena	Queen of the Agapanterrans
Tartokis	Vivoan horses
Terrortribes	Yezzadar's army
The InfiniKey	The Key to Infinity—a sacred amulet
Transmorphational	SuperDodon morphing process
Tussites	Inhabitants of Scartuss
Universal Hall	Meeting place of the Galactic Coalition
VibaZappa	Nuffs' weapon to annihilate the Terrortribes
Vivo	A planet in The Smoothy Way
Vivoans	Beings who live on Vivo
WaftWhiffer	Creature found on Quomos
WaterWhisperers	One of four Nuff clans
Wellspring of Everlasting Energy	A spiritual place and the source of Nuff renewal
Weeze	Another name for WeirdyNuff
X-IT	Extraordinary Interdimensional Travelers
Yezzadar	The Nuffs' archenemy
Yobuns	Tribe found on Quomos
Yoraz	Leader of the Yobuns
Zybuffs	Tribe found on Quomos
Zytag	A measure of time in Nuff speak

Printed by BoD in Norderstedt, Germany

Printed by BoD™in Norderstedt, Germany